THE PARCEL

ANOSH IRANI

SCRIBE

Melbourne • London

Scribe Publications
18–20 Edward St, Brunswick, Victoria 3056, Australia
2 John St, Clerkenwell, London, WC1N 2ES, United Kingdom

Published by Scribe 2017

Published by arrangement with Alfred A. Knopf Canada, a division of Penguin
Random House Canada Limited.

Text design by Terri Nimmo
Interior image: © Shahria Sharmin

Printed and bound in China by 1010 Printing Co Ltd

Scribe Publications is committed to the sustainable use of natural resources
and the use of paper products made responsibly from those resources.

9781925322262 (Australian edition)
9781911344452 (UK edition)
9781925548297 (e-book)

CiP data records for this title are available from the National Library of Australia
and the British Library.

scribepublications.com.au
scribepublications.co.uk

ALSO BY ANOSH IRANI

NOVELS

The Cripple and His Talismans (2004)

The Song of Kahunsha (2006)

Dahanu Road (2010)

PLAYS

The Bombay Plays: The Matka King & Bombay Black

Prologue

I go by many names, none of my own choosing.

I am called Ali, Aravani, Nau Number, Sixer, Mamu, Gandu, Napunsak, Kinnar, Kojja—the list goes on and on like a politician's promise. There is a term for me in almost every Indian language. I am reviled and revered, deemed to have been blessed, and cursed, with sacred powers. Parents think of me as a kidnapper, shopkeepers as a lucky charm, and married couples as a fertility expert. To passengers in taxis, I am but a nuisance. I am shooed away like a crow.

Everyone has their version of what I am. Or what they want me to be.

My least favourite is what they call my kind in Tamil: Thirunangai.

"Mister Woman."

Oddly, the only ones to get it right were my parents. They named their boy Madhu. A name so gloriously unisex, I slipped in and out of its skin until I was fourteen. But then, in one fine stroke, that thing between my legs was relieved of its duties. With the very knife that I hold in my hand right now, I became a eunuch.

Perhaps my parents had smelled the strangeness in the air when I was born, the stench of the pain and humiliation to follow. At the least, they must have felt a deep stirring in the marrow of their bones to prepare them for the fact that their child was different.

Neither here nor there, neither desert nor forest, neither earth nor sky, neither man nor woman.

The calling of names I made my peace with years ago.

The one I am most comfortable with, the most accurate of them, is also the most common: hijra. It means "migration," and we hijras have made it our own because its meaning makes sense to us.

I am indeed a migrant, a wanderer. For almost three decades, I have floated through the city's red-light district like a ghost. But this home of mine, this garden of rejects—fourteen lanes that for the rest of the city do not exist—I want it to remember me. I want it to remember even though the district is dissolving, just like I am, like the hot vapour of chai.

Come on. Who am I fooling? I don't taste like chai. I am anything but delectable. I have been born and brewed to mortify. At forty, all I have left is a knife dipped in the moon and a five-rupee coin given to me by my mother.

But mark my words: I will make myself a household name. I will spread my name like butter on these battered streets.

Underwear Tree had its name thanks to the array of underclothes that were left to hang and dry in its loving care. It was one giant hanger for clothes, a dhobi's delight. At any time of day, underwear in all shapes and sizes were caught in its branches like kites. Over the years, Underwear Tree served as a barometer for economic growth. If the elastic of the underwear was tight, it signified that the people living in the hutments below the tree were doing well. If the elastic was loose, it meant overuse for the underwear and hard days for the owners.

As Madhu looked up, she could see that the underwear that lay stiff in the morning sun was somewhere in between. Things could go either way from here. She, on the other hand, had only one place to go: Bombay Central for her daily bread and butter, and an array of abuses. But before going to work, she, as always, called upon that brave Maratha warrior Shivaji to kick-start her day as she inhaled his majestic beedis.

She sent the smoke skyward, toward the pride of her neighbourhood, until she tasted the last bitter hit. That final trace of tobacco surging through her brain was what she enjoyed the most. Before flicking the beedi away, she burned a hole in the fabric of her sari with the lit end.

It was a habit to rid her of anxiety; she also did it for luck.

She smiled as the beedi disappeared into a gutter. Even dead cigarettes wanted to get away from her as soon as possible.

No shirt, no pants, no tie, but she was an office-goer like any other Mumbaikar. Her working space was in the most prime location. Bombay Central was her terrain, and she had worked it more than any other hijra in the city. It was her designated area. Only a few hijras, from her clan, had the right to beg here. Any infringement from an outside hijra and Madhu would push a bamboo up her arse so deep, if she were to lift the bamboo to the sky it would become a flag—a trespassing hijra in a flowing sari hoisted among the clouds, singing in pain.

How she wished she had the strength to do that.

At forty, she was weak, her muscles looser than they had ever been, her belly resembling a hot-water bag, bulgy and changing shape without warning. The only thing she was capable of lifting was her middle finger. She showed it to passengers, in cabs every single day.

Only in her mind.

She had to respect the passengers. They were allowed to abuse her, but she could not abuse back. That was a hijra rule.

If someone abuses you verbally, take it. Do not react. Maintain your dignity.

This was one of the guidelines that had been passed on to her by gurumai when Madhu became a hijra. Gurumai had almost thirty hijras under her, loyal disciples. She was everything to them: leader, protector, and spiritual mother. But only seven disciples were permitted to live with her, and Madhu was one of these.

Gurumai was in her eightieth year now, and though her sagging chin was floor-bound, her head was still held high. She had instructed Madhu to conduct herself with dignity at all times.

But to maintain dignity, one needed to have it to begin with, thought Madhu.

To lose face, one needed a face. Not what Madhu owned: a visage confused beyond measure, man and woman fighting it out to see who gained possession. Female energy had existed within her since she was a child. It had been subtle at first, showing itself slowly, a thigh here, a shy look there, a giggle in the dark. But then the woman started taking over, mocking the man, eventually leaving him limp. Now the man of the past was seeking revenge, punishing her for getting rid of him, pushing his way to the forefront again. If the unrest did not stop, she would not have a face left. Only a skull would remain.

Madhu now realized that this was a pointless battle. She could never pass herself off as a woman. When others heard her speak, their eardrums curdled within seconds. Her voice was the first thing people heard—a brittle bray. Still, like a conch in battle, it was useful in Bombay Central, one of the city's noisiest areas. When she spoke, you had to pay attention.

Ready at last to open her account for the day, Madhu approached a taxi waiting at the signal. She reflected that, with the amount of time she spent at signals, she could be a traffic cop. But no—even that was too exalted a position for her. She was not fit to be a bribe-taking cur.

The man in the back seat was about the same age as her, his hand leaning out of the window, his silver watch too big for his wrist. There was a red thread around his wrist as well, probably given to him by his pundit.

"Give me some money," said Madhu. "In God's name."

She had said these words so many times it would come as no surprise if her tongue continued to roll them out hours after she was dead. She sometimes considered starting with something else, just once, but God had proven to be the most amicable mediator.

"May God keep you safe," she continued. "May your family and loved ones forever be blessed."

The passenger's ears were not affronted this time, but his eyes clearly were. He gave her a quick glance then looked away, straight ahead, at the back of the taxi driver's oil-covered head. It would take another three minutes for the light to turn green. Not a second more or less. Enough time for Madhu to make her presence felt.

So she bent lower and let her face do the talking.

Her skin was dark, but only in places, as though some mischievous spirit in his boredom had splattered tar all over it one night but failed to do a uniform job.

She moved a long strand of hair out of the way, one that had escaped the clutch of her hair band. Each time her fingers grazed her forehead, she could tell that her wrinkles were getting deeper, the skin harder. So she tied her hair back tight, real tight, stretching the skin on her forehead as much as possible. Nothing worked. Each day she woke up rougher, her body in some sort of race to look fifty. It wanted to be ahead of its time.

She knew what the man saw when he looked at her. She didn't need a mirror. She saw herself every single day in the eyes of others, and this man told her nothing new. She was an irritant getting in the way. If the man had insecticide, he'd spray it on her and watch her wriggle to the ground in squeaky spasms until she stopped moving.

He looked at her a second time. That was when the repulsion began to set in. Good.

"May God fulfil all your dreams," she said, raising her right hand, her palm facing the man, sending healing rays his way, from her palm to his forehead, to provide him with instant calm. It was a reminder that she was no common beggar. She was a mangti hijra—a mendicant who provided blessings in exchange for a meagre sustenance. Indian mythology had afforded her a special set of skills, but this man seemed to have forgotten that.

All he saw was a *thing* in a green sari. A sari that made her resemble a parrot, a gaudy creature that sat croaking on one's windowsill. She had a beak for a nose, and she had often thought of herself as a crow—her dark skin made her feel so—but today the green sari gave her a parrot's sheen, made her two birds at once.

If only she could fly.

But she had, in her mind. She had travelled all the way to the Himalayas and back without ever leaving the city. She was, without doubt, a wanderer. She had no choice but to traverse the territory—from pain to more pain, the Kangchenjunga of pain, she had experienced it all.

She had only one minute left before the light turned green.

She clapped her hands, twice. A loud, shrill *phat!*

It was the trademark clap of a hijra, open palms closing upon each other to produce the sound of a firecracker popping. It was the opposite of applause, a singular burst sent into the air, not in appreciation of anything, but a warning disguised as a plea; then two more in quick succession. She had been tutored for grace and authenticity by gurumai.

It startled the fool, made him angry.

"Move on, I have nothing to give," he said, gesturing her away with his hand.

Ah! He had made the mistake of engaging with her. The smart ones did not speak, ignored her with cold precision. This one was testy; his wife must be a nag, and this current encounter a reminder of her voracious appetite for brain-chewing.

"You're the first customer of the day," said Madhu. "Special blessings for you."

She gave him a crooked smile. It was in earnest, but over the years her lips too had decided to take a course of their own. She could not control anything anymore. Or perhaps her smile had turned on her because of all the false promises she had made. In truth, there were no special blessings she could confer upon this man. The most she could do for him was say a genuine prayer so that he might have a haemorrhoid-free day. That was the extent of her influence.

She moved closer to him and breathed into his face. All that TB, which she did not have, but could. It was a calculated move, to enter the universe of his taxi and dare cough inside it. But the man was tough. Not the slightest movement of hand toward hip, toward back pocket. Only thirty seconds to go; she was determined not to lose.

But then the unexpected: the taxi driver took pity on her. He reached into his shirt pocket and handed her ten rupees.

Ten. That was big for a taxiwala.

The passenger scratched his neck, but Madhu knew it was not his neck that was bothering him; it was his humanity. The taxi driver, a man of lower stratum, of lesser earning capacity than him, had given a hijra alms. What would the man's pundit say? How would this man peacefully eat his prasad when he went to temple the next day to pray that his dumb son might pass his exams?

Madhu had managed to disturb his sweet equilibrium.

"Just give the wretch something," said the taxiwala, without turning to look at his passenger.

Reluctantly, the man shelled out ten rupees. Of course he could not give less—his compassion had to match the taxi driver's. It landed on Madhu's palm, the first note of the day, the way rain brought relief to parched earth.

Before the taxi took off, she quickly threw ten rupees back into the driver's lap. The passenger failed to see this. Now that his ego was satisfied, he had leaned back into the seat of his taxi and closed his eyes.

The driver and Madhu had practised this routine for years. The taxiwala did not take a cut. He too mistakenly believed that if she uttered a few useless words, the hammer of misfortune would not strike him.

She slipped the first earnings of the day into a small pouch sewn inside her sari. There had been a time when she could wear a garland of money around her neck if she wanted to, but that was long ago. That was when she was silk, and men would slide up her legs like snakes, then disappear inside her valley for months, and come out fucked themselves, ravaged and shattered. Those were the days.

May they never return, she thought.

Hours later, the day's work done, she trundled back from the intersection.

Not home, not yet. At 4:00 p.m. she had called it quits, and now she was at Dr Kyani's dispensary, sitting on the wooden bench in the waiting area. The two prostitutes on the bench opposite her were trying to muffle their coughs. She might as well live in a TB factory. Everyone had a knack for developing it. At least it could be treated now, unlike before, when people had no other option but to sit and watch their loved ones being eaten up.

The compounder, Faruk, was at his station preparing his concoctions, his eyes squinting in concentration, his unwavering attention on mixing the right amounts. That's what made the difference between patients experiencing pain that was tolerable and pain that was gunshot piercing. If Faruk missed something, someone would spend the night screaming in agony or coughing their lungs out until they were ready to hang on Underwear Tree.

Dr Kyani was one of the last remaining doctors in the city who still created his own potions. It was an abandoned art, but Dr Kyani was a magician who refused to forsake old secrets. Everyone in the red-light district respected him, even the pimps, who would not know respect if it slid down their very balls. Even they, in Dr Kyani's presence, suddenly tried to become human by saying please and thank you. For they knew that when the sickness came—any sickness—only Dr Kyani could keep them from slitting their throats.

It was thanks to Dr Kyani that gurumai could sleep at night.

For years the cough had laid silent, deep inside gurumai, a rat in a corner, deathly still, until a few months ago, when she'd started coughing so much it was hard for her to speak. Even though gurumai's disciples knew what it was, no one dared voice it, until Madhu noticed blood in gurumai's spittoon and begged her to see Dr Kyani.

"I don't believe in doctors," gurumai had replied. "You know that."

For some time gurumai braved the fevers, the night sweats, the war in her lungs so tight she wanted to reach in deep and rip them out herself, until she was robbed of sleep five nights in a row and could not think anymore. Even then, her pride did not allow her to seek help. It was only when Madhu beseeched her, as a child would its mother, not in words but through the sheer helplessness on her face, that gurumai allowed Madhu to ask Dr Kyani for medicine.

It was very kind of Dr Kyani to treat gurumai. She was perhaps the only patient to whom he had ever given medicine without having checked her first. Gurumai said they were like lovers who had never seen each other and were having a long-distance relationship. When Madhu told Dr Kyani this, he allowed himself a faint smile. He instructed Faruk not to take money from Madhu that day. Gurumai was thrilled with her free medicine. It was as though Dr Kyani had sent her a rose.

Madhu thought of that first meeting with Dr Kyani as she collected the medication from Faruk. They had a routine now. No words were exchanged. She slipped him the money and he gave her twenty small pouches. Affordable and effective, they were an anomaly in the medical system: medication that worked. And for that reason alone, even though there was a jeweller's shop right next to his dispensary, Dr Kyani was the only real jewel around.

Madhu held on tight to the powders. Over the years, money and medicine had passed through her hands with alacrity. And she knew that money might come and go, but health loved to travel far, and once it left it would send a polite telegram: *I may never return.*

Just ask gurumai.

Madhu approached gurumai's home, which was also her own home, her little chamber of commerce, her refuge, her womb. As she climbed the wooden stairs that creaked a different tune every single time, she thanked whatever divinity was left in this world, the one that still had the guts to hover above the red-light area, for sparing her from any major sickness. Just as Dr Kyani had his doubts about pharmaceutical companies and their capsuled offspring, the hijras had a joke about God. Whenever he came to the red-light area and tried to heal anyone who was dying, or answer their prayers, he failed. It was too much for him to handle. So he outsourced his work to a woman. The goddess Bahuchara Mata.

Only the Mata, striding a rooster through the heavens, heard their cries. A sword in one hand and a trident in the other, she was the Divine Mother to the nation's hijras, and they went in droves to her temple in Gujarat to seek her blessing, alongside men who wanted a cure for impotence, and women who longed for a male child.

But the Mata did not heal anyone.

Healing was for the weak. Instead she gave the hijras the power to endure. She knew their life better than anyone else; there was no way out. One had to endure.

Before Madhu entered gurumai's room, she could hear muffled moans.

Gurumai was a successful hijra. She was enduring. On some days she was strong and loud and boisterous, and on others, she dissolved into the mattress quietly, ashamed of her body's current state.

Eighty was a ripe age for anyone living in E Ward. That is what the area was called by the municipality. Gurumai's home was in Part IV of E Ward. It was the most appropriate name for where they were located: *E* for Emergency. *IV* was not a number; it was short for intravenous.

For all those sick from the inside, gurumai offered hope. That's what she had done for Madhu. When gurumai had rescued Madhu from her family, Madhu was a shivering, jittery soul trapped in the wrong body. She still was. That was something no one could cure. But at least gurumai had steadied her hands.

In a strange way, watching gurumai struggle now with her body gave Madhu strength. It was preparing her for the storm to come, unlike some other hijras who looked into mirrors all day and cherished them, as though when they grew old the mirrors would give them their youth back, as though by looking into the mirror for an hour a day they were storing some life which they could later retrieve.

Gurumai was leading by example. She was breaking before Madhu's very eyes.

"Madhu . . . ," said gurumai.

"I'm here," said Madhu.

"Why is your mobile not on?"

"My mobile?" asked Madhu. "I was at work . . ."

It was embarrassing when Madhu got a call in the middle of her patter just when a passenger was about to fork out some cash. It interrupted her performance and took away from her appearance of destitution.

"Don't worry," said Madhu. "I got the medicine."

Gurumai shook her head. "You will get a call tonight," she said. "From Padma . . ."

"What does Padma Madam want with me?"

"Whatever she asks, you will do."

If gurumai had wanted to tell Madhu more, she would have. So Madhu asked nothing more. She opened one of the small white pouches and slowly placed it to gurumai's lips. When gurumai opened her mouth, Madhu tapped one end of the tiny envelope until the powder rested on gurumai's tongue. Gurumai swallowed it down like a prayer.

"My feet," said gurumai. "My feet . . ."

It was rare for gurumai to plead in such a manner; she was a commander, not a person who politely asked for a massage, but such were the workings of old age. It softened you up, made pulp out of your bravery, made you kinder than you actually were.

Madhu sat at the edge of the bed and began to massage gurumai's feet.

She could see that gurumai's eyes were open and she was tracing the movements of a lizard on the wall. Someone had gifted her wallpaper, a white background with orange flowers on it, but now the flowers had faded, and the wallpaper had peeled off, making the orange flowers look like they had been torn out and were hanging on for dear life, and the ceiling fan made those torn edges flutter, and suddenly Madhu felt an unbearable urge to tell gurumai something, but she did not know what.

Madhu sat in silence in the small chai house adjoining the defunct Alexandra Cinema. Even though she was with Gajja—the only man she could really talk to—her mind was racing.

Madhu did not like waiting for calls, especially from people like Padma.

It gave her the same tingling in the stomach that she got when awaiting test results. When she was younger, mathematics did that to her. She had simply failed to understand all those plus and minus signs, those triangles and multiplications, all that $x + y$ laudagiri. Then, when she became a hijra, the mathematics stopped and the medical tests began. She gave her blood only once to get it tested, and the waiting shook her up so badly it was mathematics all over again: $x\,(\text{Madhu}) + y\,(\text{disease}) = \text{suffering}$.

She had refused to go collect the results. She preferred not to know.

For that same reason, she did not probe into why Padma wanted to see her. She preferred to be kept in the dark, because once the light shone, it could be blinding.

The dark was where she was right now, with Gajja.

Gajja and Madhu went back a long way. He worked as a ward boy at the JJ Hospital on Nagpada, but he was hardly a boy. He was fifty, a short, stout Punjabi with thick forearms, a balding head, and ribs that had broken so many times he found it hard to sit still for too long. At least once every six months he ran his motorcycle into something, and when Madhu had once mentioned to him that it was perhaps time to retire the contraption, he had given her a lecture on how a woman does not know a thing about machines. She should shut her mouth, he'd said, and reserve her opinion for womanly things. He apologized later, but Madhu did not feel offended because Gajja had paid her the biggest compliment of all: he had called her a woman.

Now the two of them were quiet, inhaling the smell of cooking oil and onions that had seeped into the walls of the chai house. At one point it had served as the canteen to one of the oldest movie theatres in the country. Alexandra Cinema had provided comfort to many a British soldier during World War II, and had later introduced Indians to John Wayne and Tarzan. But over time, the English releases started to dwindle, and Tarzan swung away into oblivion, making way for two of Madhu's favourite actors—Mithun and Sanjay Dutt—until even they faded, and the B and C-grade Hindi movie posters that made the theatre blaze with flesh and blood and guns and rape were sent into retirement as well, either by the dwindling reputation of the theatre itself, its decrepit walls, or by the students of the Maharashtra College opposite the theatre, who tore the posters down, declaring war on cleavage both foreign and Indian. Now, there was just one sign that said "Dara-e-Deeniyat." The theatre had been converted into a place of worship. Where crowds once cheered and jeered and whistled at the screen five shows a day, the faithful now gathered in white and prayed five times. The building was a hollow version of its former self, its eyes carved out, its walls blackened by the soot of a small fire quelled in time, but the black and white floor tiles were somehow still intact, either in defiance of the worshippers or in deference to them.

It had been an unusually slow day for Gajja at the hospital. JJ was where the murder cases came, the hit and runs, the knife wounds, the bullet holes, the heads smashed in with hockey sticks. But today, Gajja had gone an hour or two without any work at all, and this had made him nervous, so he had guzzled down two large pegs of whisky and was now on his third. To support his drinking, he sometimes stole medicine from the hospital and sold it to prostitutes, who were willing to try anything to make the mind float and the body disappear. But he was not proud of this; if he were paid a proper salary befitting the work he did, he would not have to steal.

Gajja tried to cajole Madhu into drinking, but she refused. She needed to be clear-headed for Padma. A small lantern rested on the table between them, lighting up the roasted peanuts and Gajja's watery eyes.

"Come on," he said. "Have one small, loving peg."

There was nothing small and loving about whisky, Madhu wanted to tell him, but that would ruin his mood. No man had induced tenderness from Madhu the way Gajja had. He may have become rougher over time, but who hadn't? Her own skin was like sandpaper now, so why begrudge a man some hard edges? Even when he drank, he showed sensitivity: Before putting a single drop of liquor to his lips, he always poured some into his cupped palm and scattered it on the floor. "The first drops always to Mother Earth," he would say.

"What's wrong?" asked Gajja, seeing Madhu shift in her chair. "Want a better seat?"

Madhu shook her head. She was suddenly aware of the lantern and its light on her face. She wondered if the glow made her look softer. Perhaps the jasmines that were tied to the bun in her hair did the trick. No, she realized, they were more than a day old and must be hanging like shrivelled skin.

"I can get you a cinema chair from inside if you want," he said.

The theatre was closed now and forever, and Gajja knew that, but if Madhu wanted him to, he would break the iron grille that separated the two of them from the seats where they had spent so many hours and bring one to her. The man was still locked in the passion of years ago and failed to see how time had worked on Madhu so meticulously, with holy devotion.

Not that Madhu would ever want to sit in one of those seats again. She had first been here with her father to see a film, an English one, years ago, when she was a boy. Madhu had left home early with his father that day, accompanied him to work at Maharashtra College, sat in his tiny room while he corrected history papers, and then the two of them crossed the road to see *Guns of . . .* something—it was a long, hard name at the end. It had been yet another failed father-son outing, their last. They had failed so badly that the stench of it was more overpowering than all the dead bodies in that film.

She had returned to the theatre only a few years later, as a hijra, to do oral in the back seat. By then the theatre's reputation had gone down the drain like a super-fast cockroach. One time, she did oral during a morning show while an English picture was playing, and even though her mouth was full, her ears were turned toward the screen because the language sounded so odd. It was assaulting her, punishing her for abandoning it and turning to Hindi. Stubborn mule that she was, she made it a point not to be intimidated, and after that she watched whatever English movie appeared, to keep in touch with the language. She was only partly successful: when she tried to speak in English, the words rolled out differently than she intended, and she felt naked and mocked. She preferred to live in Hindi but became addicted to reading movie titles that were translated from English to Hindi. *Midnight Express* was *Aadhi Raat Mein Super-Fast,* and the public rushed to see it because they thought it was about a quick, loose woman. *The Godfather* was *Sabka Baap,* and some insisted it was about an old man who went about town fathering children with loose women. Every movie alluded to loose women; it was the manager's strategy, and it worked, and no one complained. When the man who translated the titles died—the same man who painted the billboards—Madhu took over. She begged for the job, offered to do it for free. She would supply the titles but of course could not paint any billboards.

Thinking about those days still afforded her a smile, sometimes. But each time she smiled, every time she relaxed, life tensed her up again.

Her mobile rang. She did not recognize the number, but when she answered, the voice at the other end was unmistakable.

"I believe gurumai has spoken with you."

"Yes, madam."

"Come to my kothi right now. I have some work for you."

By now, Gajja was in a trance of his own, trying to find the moon in the room. It was a game the two of them used to play when they were lovers, but that was eternities ago, in the land of youth and tight skin. Gajja was the only man who had been allowed to enter Madhu for free and had access to the parts of her that were not just physical. The first time he took her, he kissed her for what seemed like hours, but Madhu knew that Gajja was kissing someone else. That was why Madhu took Gajja's money during that first month. After that, when Madhu felt Gajja was kissing her—not the woman from his past—she put the money back into his shirt pocket while he was sleeping. After that, he never paid her again. Gajja was the only man she ever kissed. "My arsehole is public," she told him one day. "But my lips are private." It was her response to Gajja's "I love you, Madhu." She never used the word *love*. She thought it unlucky. For fourteen years, from the time Madhu was sixteen to when she turned thirty, he told her he loved her. And all he got in return was the line about her arsehole. Finally, when he left her for a woman, she told him she loved him, but it was at night when she was alone, and she said it to a cockroach on the wall.

Now they were just two people with a past. Physical touch was to Madhu what water was to rangoli—even a small drop could smudge the design, distort it beyond repair. But Gajja was drunk, and when he was drunk, he played their old game.

"Where's the moon?" he asked. "Can you see it?"

"No," she replied.

So Gajja looked this way and that, up and down, sideways, diagonally—he used every camera angle possible to look for the moon. Then he waited for Madhu to say her line, one she used to say with so much longing that Gajja would swear that the ghost of Ghalib had temporarily slid into her.

"It is a moonless night." She played along. "It is a moonless night."

When Madhu finally said those words, she knew that her flute was hollow and that her words had no music in them. But Gajja still clutched his heart. Three pegs down, he lay on the ground and looked up at her, helpless, lost, a man who had found the very surrender that Ghalib's ghazals had so drunkenly spoken of.

"There she is . . . ," said Gajja, pointing to Madhu. "There's my moon."

Madhu blessed her man. She asked her heart to scrounge together any goodness it could, and she directed it toward him because he was making a broken object feel human. He turned her rough to smooth, he turned the water inside her belly to sherbet; he was still the man she loved, except that love and touch were strangers now, travellers following different maps.

She tore the string of jasmines that were tied in her hair and slowly showered them on Gajja. He revelled in these drops of white, let them fall on his face, soft kisses from the love he once had. Then she left him on the floor. "I have to go," she said.

And just like that, the moon disappeared.

Outside, the red lights had come on.

Some were red, some were blue, and others green. It depended on the brothel owner's taste. When Madhu was young, it felt as though the whole area pulsated on its own, had a hunger to outlive and outshine anything or anyone. But now she saw the district as a collection of dead people that suddenly sprang to life only when the lights came on. It was resuscitated every night with an extra dose of doom, and it responded brilliantly, as though kissed by something holy. And indeed, something holy stood at its entrance, in the form of a small shrine, that of Sai Baba of Shirdi.

At the corner of Bellasis Road, just round the bend from the Alexandra Cinema, was a white-tiled wall with a hutch in the middle. There rested Sai, the bearded saint, guide, and solace-giver to both Hindus and Muslims. Madhu closed her eyes and passed her hand over the flame of the oil lamp that lay at Sai's feet, the only warmth most residents could hope to find on any given night. This was the unmarked beginning of the red-light district. It was here that taxi drivers dropped off the hungry, at a stand where pimps hovered over passengers, barely giving them time to exit the vehicles, showering upon them rates and body shapes, and the promise of orgasms so monstrous, they would make the high-rises looming against Mumbai's new skyline seem puny.

Opposite Sai, the convent school receded in the background, the white statue of Jesus perched high above, his arms outspread, looking down at the whores who stood by the school walls dressed in red and silver, shiny little ladies, as though they had swallowed all the firecrackers during Diwali and were now set-ting them off internally, in bits and sparks, night by night, for the rest of the year. Madhu knew most of them, some by name, almost all by face. It was best to keep track of faces, not names. Names stayed the same, but faces could change overnight. Sculpted by beatings in the dark, they assumed new forms. The loss of a tooth, or the rage of being raped by three, showed itself on the cheek like a hot flash. Yes, it was best to keep track of faces.

It was dhandha time, and one of the women on sale, a silver thing, was bargaining with a potential customer. This was Salma, a mainstay at Padma's brothel. She was out in the street snatching clients as birds do fish from water, right at the edge of the district.

"No, no, not two hundred," Salma said. "Three hundred is fixed rate, yaar. What a miserly prick you have. Kanjoos lauda!"

Salma was one of more than sixty women who worked for Padma, and even when she did not wear silver, she sparkled. Her skin was dark and there were small pimples on her cheeks, but she knew how to talk to a man. The bodies of the women were all more or less of equal mileage, but what set a woman apart, and Madhu knew this better than anyone else, was her ability to mind-fuck, to leave an invitation to bajao in the man's mind, so that if he hesitated about it for even a second more, the offer would expire and he would miss the earthquake of the century. Madhu had been a champion at this. Tonight she moved on, leaving Salma to her trade, ignoring a small surge of pride. It still came, on occasion, when she recalled the sense of power she had once felt. But it left her feeling stupid. Now she was a mere lemon peel lying on the road.

She walked past the numbered brothels: *Welcome 52, 63, 420.* The numbers had made sense in a government survey a long time ago, but now seemed completely random. She turned the corner, past Café Andaaz and the police booth, and entered a side alley toward the lair of Padma, one of the most powerful madams in the area. At one point, Padma had more cash flowing through her brothel than sewage through a gutter drain, but it was the power that came with the cash that was the greatest kutti of them all—the bitch could leave without warning and, when it did, deposit inside of you a stadium of emptiness.

Things had changed, reflected Madhu, since she had started living in this area years ago. The place had become more professional. Pimps now had business cards to provide an air of decency and professionalism to the rundown brothels. Nirmal, one of the pimps for Padma's brothel, was cajoling a couple of tourists—one could always spot the tourists; they smelled different, afraid but inquisitive—to try out the goods. He handed them his card, crumpled at the edges and damp from his own sweat, which announced with great pride that the brothel had A/C. The card had a sketch of a sandy beach on it, which had made Madhu laugh when she'd first seen it. There was even a phone number, for return buyers.

"Do you want to in-joy?" Nirmal asked. "Should I make your prog-raam?"

Nirmal was young, not more than twenty-five, with straight hair that fell just below his eyebrows, and unlike some of the other pimps in the area, who were tough and dirty and stank, Nirmal kept himself fresh and non-threatening so that tourists weren't intimidated and fell for his bait. Pimps with stubble and heavy, cold hands were allocated to the locals.

"You don't have to sex them," Nirmal said in English to the tourists. "If you want oral only, that also I give." Then he corrected himself quickly: "Not me, not me, I don't give oral."

The tourists smiled, charmed by his talk.

"Nepali, South Indian, all types I have. Christian also. Just come see," he said. "If you want, we show oreejnal report."

The report business was a sham. There was a new report each month, from some quack with a medical degree who had a deal with all the brothel owners in the area. Sick or not, the prostitutes got a clean bill of health, as spotless as the marble floor of a five-star hotel. Real tests were a waste of time, money, and blood. Even if the report was genuine in the morning, by the end of the day, five truck drivers had entered the woman. The "pojeetives," as they were called, were in the thousands.

They looked fine until they became sick and weak and fell like flies, only to be swept away the next morning with the lazy swish of a broom.

Madhu looked up at the three-storey building that was Padma's brothel.

Built during British rule, the structure was over a century old, and at one point had housed just as many women. Now the number was a mere fraction of the twenty thousand women who worked the district, but when the sex was on, the building rumbled. The dirty glass windows were a patchwork of purple and green, and some of the panes were broken, exposing the rusted iron grilles, while others were shuttered with wooden boards. Wires looped precariously from one window to the next, like garlands, then ran in a vertical mesh all the way down to the street level, ready to electrify those who touched them. But it wasn't the wires that made the place sizzle. It was the burning of skin, and Madhu could feel the moans of the customers just by standing underneath this tower of flesh.

A couple of fat, defeated women stood on the balcony, staring blankly into the space below, inhaling petrol fumes, their ears no longer sensitive to the car horns, the buzzing of scooters and motorcycles, or the sudden jamming of brakes, noise they had perhaps accepted years ago, the sound of their own lives coming to an abrupt halt. Their bodies, once butter, were now layered; these were women whose girth would certainly be noticed on any street corner outside the district, but inside this frenzied menagerie they were insects, insignificant yet capable of transmitting disease. Way above these women, on the rooftop, three men lay sprawled like panthers on a tree branch, scanning the labyrinth of streets below. These were the "watchers," the eyes of the brothel, who noticed the movement of the flora and fauna beneath. Even a slight deviation from any of their prostitutes, a single attempt to move beyond their allocated boundaries, and they were beaten with wooden sticks the way mattresses are thrashed until the dust comes out, then slowly settles back again.

There were scores of brothels such as this one, some smaller, some larger, and even though the district spread out over fourteen lanes, the majority of the brothels conglomerated between Lanes Fourteen to Ten, stuck together in desperation, conspiring to form one of Asia's largest red-light areas. When Madhu had been in school, when she'd worn a boy's uniform, she had learned about a triangle somewhere far away, and how people got sucked through it into another world. The red-light district was exactly like that. Most of the prostitutes had been tricked into landing here, some came on purpose, but everyone got lost in its black hole of existence. It slowly stripped away the past until you were reduced to a nameless, past-less creature unable to find a way out.

The world saw the prostitutes standing on display behind huge windows with bars and called these rooms "The Cages," but Madhu knew there was only one cage. It started at Alexandra Cinema and went all the way down to Underwear Tree. This was a cage without bars, and it had a name, and if Madhu were to come back to earth in another life, she would do so as a Mumbai tourist guide, and her mother-father would know this from the start because the minute she slid down the clouds and into her mother's womb and out again, she would begin speaking, and her first words would point to this open-air cage, to this wound in the city, and as more and more nurses and doctors and ward boys gathered around, she would announce with the pomp and splendour of a lion tamer, "Welcome to the Cage. Welcome to Kamathipura."

As Madhu climbed the stairs to Padma's brothel, her slipper got stuck in a nail. Perhaps it was a sign for her to stop and turn back. But no, that was not possible. It was thanks to Padma that gurumai was able to own her current abode. Here, in the district, favours stretched on for decades and had more value than currency. Padma had known that by helping gurumai, she would have access to all her hijras as well, and they would have no choice but to do her bidding, which was why Madhu was climbing her stairs now.

It was a long, steep walk to the first floor, thirty stairs in all, through passages sprayed with paan and urine, until Madhu reached the reception area. The first floor was where the more expensive, cleaner women were housed. A bearded guard sat on a stool, but did not flinch when he saw Madhu. A hijra was hardly a matter of concern or importance. The guard was more interested in making sure that the tourists Nirmal had brought up were feeling at home. They were seated on a sunken sofa in the "showroom," cold beers in their hands.

She moved on to the second floor, the clash of light and darkness jarring. It made no sense to a visitor, the way the showroom was bursting with light but the corridors and stairs were uneven, shadowy crevasses where one had to watch each step, eyes adjusting like an animal's. This set-up was for the police, in case of the obligatory raid. The wiring of the building was in such disarray that there wasn't a central fuse for the guards to snap shut. So it was prudent to keep the stairs in darkness so the insides of the brothel could go dead and quiet when needed, and just as quickly come back to rude life.

The second floor was where the second- and third-hand goods were stored. It was the haunt of truck drivers, labourers, servants, laundrymen, and watchmen. Too broke to visit the first floor, they fed on the cheapest women, who were paid as little as a hundred rupees. What these women lacked in looks, they made up for by tolerating beatings, the pulling of hair, and the burning of thighs and vaginas with matches. This was also the floor where Padma lived, so it was no surprise to Madhu that it was guarded by Hassan, loyal and robust, more concrete than man. Padma believed in battling it out in the trenches with her troops. After all, she had got her start as one of them.

"Wait here," Hassan said to Madhu.

She could see that he had been expecting her. He got up from his stool and pointed at it for her to sit on, but Madhu knew it wasn't out of courtesy. He wanted her to be the eyes for a moment, to take his place at the tower. Hassan was a feverish being, so used to not sleeping at night that his eyes had forgotten how to close. He drank as he neared the end of his shift, at 4:00 a.m., to knock himself out, the booze tranquilizing him into baby sleep, where he was no longer responsible for sensing danger.

As instructed, Madhu sat on the stool and lit a Shivaji. The climb had made her pant, and she was getting anxious. She needed some of the warrior's guts to soothe her. He, too, had instructed his Marathas to keep an eye out from the Pratapgad Fort for the invading Mughals under Afzal Khan. Long ago, Madhu had loved hearing from her father tales of Maratha bravery, of how Shivaji duped the Mughals, outsmarting them with guerrilla warfare. These had been the only times her father treated her like a son, so she never tired of listening to the stories. And she loved how Afzal Khan's head was buried under a tower after Shivaji's victory. There was no documented evidence for this, her father had told her, but he shared this story with his students at Maharashtra College anyway.

Now, Madhu reflected on how Padma had Shivaji's guile. It had helped Padma sustain her reputation as one of the most feared madams of Kamathipura, until the mantle had recently been taken over by another woman, Silver Chaya. Padma had no silver teeth like Silver Chaya, whose mouth shone in the dark when she spoke. Padma was simple and plain, and vocal in her disdain for men. Silver Chaya was a voracious lover, but Padma was now in her seventies and had long ago become an ascetic. She dealt in flesh but never partook of it. She was like gurumai, an overseer, an orchestrator of life and the destiny of human beings. But none of this was evident when Padma was a young girl. If anything, she had been a mere twig snapped off a branch and thrown to the side of the road for any traveller to trample upon. That was how gurumai always started Padma's story when she told it to her hijras, with the smoke from her beedi rising to the ceiling just like Padma's eventual rise to power.

After what had happened to Padma as a child, gurumai had said, she vowed to never be vulnerable again, to never leave things in the hands of a higher power. If that higher power was taking a nap, like in her case, things happened that one could never truly recover from. "But then I told myself that if God was sleeping while bad things happened to me, then I could use that same nap time to make good things happen as well," Padma had told gurumai.

She had always been a child of Kamathipura, back when Sukhlaji Street was known as "White Lane," on account of the British troops that came to anchor their cocks. And it was in "Safed Gulli" that her father's face started turning white too, and his lips, the coughing disease feeding on him right before her very eyes, as though it had bought her father's lungs at an auction and was now enjoying the merchandise with absolutely no regard for the twelve-year-old who sat praying in front of a small picture of Lakshmi, while her father kept assuring her between coughing fits that he would never leave her, trying to hide the blood at first, but failing so pathetically that they both knew he would soon be joining his wife, who had died giving birth to Padma.

When he did go, a neighbour took Padma in.

For one whole year, this neighbour treated Padma as her own, held her close to her chest even though her husband did not like it at all. Padma could give the cough to both their children, the husband said, and she was a sly devil, she hid the cough, she went outside and coughed, so it was gullible of the woman to think that Padma had been spared.

But Padma had been spared. She had been spared from the cough, but not from puberty. Not from becoming a woman. Nothing could stop that.

After one whole year of eating meals with her new family, she was sold. She was not even sent far away. She was sold into a brothel only a few feet away, on White Lane itself. It was a matter of convenience, and when she had been broken, several times, until she accepted who she had become, she went across the street, to the woman who had taken her in, and asked her point blank if she'd been in on it. But the woman just shook her head, and from the single tear that rolled down her cheek, Padma knew she hadn't known, or if she had, she was powerless. Then it dawned on her that her father had failed to look after her, even though the cough wasn't his fault, and now yet another man had failed her. One good, one not so. Either way, it did not matter.

From then on, even when she was spreading her legs ten times a day, sometimes fifteen, she never lost that burning desire for power, to never be at the knees of a man again, and she quickly shrugged off any tears and self-pity and focused on rising to the top, which in her world meant owning her own brothel. Her father's illness had pulled her out of school, it had torn her like a page from a book, and the wind had carried that small page to a small bed, which became her working space seven days a week for the next five years. It was her prison, and if she used her head, it could become her liberation too.

Her lack of resistance was misconstrued by the madam of the brothel as the sign of someone who was sex-mad, and that was perfect for Padma, because no one detected the cold reasoning under her heaving breasts; no one realized that she accepted prostitution as work, just as a man accepted going knee-deep in a sewer to clean up shit for the rest of the city. The man did not choose that job; it was given to him. It was the same with Padma, except that by the time she was eighteen, her owner, the same madam who had bought her from her neighbour, declared her a free agent. From a sex slave, she was now an adhiya prostitute.

"What I paid for you, you have earned out," said the madam. "From this day on, you will get paid. Half of what you fuck, you keep."

"Thank you" was all Padma said.

Then, about ten minutes later, she went back to her madam.

"How much did you pay?" she asked.

"For what?"

"For me," said Padma. "How much did you buy me for?"

"What difference?"

"I want to know how much I was worth."

"Three hundred rupees."

The sum made Padma reel, but she did not show it. Three hundred rupees could be considered a fair amount at the time, especially for a poor family, but it was also incredibly low. It made her realize that she had no place on this earth at all, that as a girl she had the same importance as a rubber tyre, or a clock, or a pair of shoes.

"I'll make you a deal," she told the madam. "I'll look after the books for you as well. I'll manage the place. That way you can rest."

"What do you know about accounts?" the madam asked.

"Nothing," said Padma. "But then again, I didn't know anything about cocks either."

She got the job. It was not the books Padma was after. It was the police. If she had access to the books, she would know which cop to grease, which dick to moisten with her own cunt, and she dove into her dual role with the passion of a woman putting herself through a business degree. When the time came, when the madam was on her deathbed, Padma was twenty-five, a veteran of the business, and had saved enough money to call it a small fortune—but it still wasn't enough. So she went to a moneylender, took a loan, kept her breasts as collateral, made him feel as tall as any building in the city, told him that the goons that worked for her madam could be at his disposal as well if they went into partnership together. She told him it was important for them to own the brothel, to buy it from the actual owner. The day she got ownership of the brothel was the last time she gave herself to a client. This was in the 1960s, when Madhu hadn't even been born and the opium dens on Sukhlaji Street gave everyone equal rights by sending them all to heaven. This was when Padma single-handedly caught the imagination of Kamathipura.

She hired two men—Hassan the watcher's father was one of them, a striking Pathan, and the other was a thin hero-type, with a knife tucked in his belt—and she walked across the street from her brothel to the home of the man who had sold her. She carried a steel thali in her hand, with a small bowl of sugar and a wad of cash tied with a brand new rubber band. Seeing Padma in her new incarnation made the man nervous, but she reassured him there was no need to be. Padma was there to pay her respects. She fed the man sugar with her own hands and gave him the money, thanked him for her success. If it hadn't been for him, she said, she would still be poor and helpless. She touched the feet of the woman who had looked after her for a year just like she had her own children, and then went back to her brothel.

Nothing more happened for an entire year.

And that was fine. Padma waited. She knew that once the man had tasted money, he would want more. The day he ran out, he came to her brothel. He came for a loan, he said. He was going through hard times, and she was like a daughter to him. Would she help him out?

Of course she would.

She asked him to wait while she went and fetched the money. She came back, like before, with sugar and cash. But this time, the hero-type held the man's hands from behind. The Pathan was about to give the man a thrashing, but Padma told him not to be immature about things.

Once again, she fed the man sugar with her own hands.

"Please," she said, "eat."

She even brushed away some of the sugar that was on the edge of his lips. Then she instructed her men to take him outside. They thrust him to the ground, bound his feet, and tied his hands to a telephone pole, so he lay prostrate on the ground facing the sky. It was ten in the morning and passersby tried to avoid the man, not wanting to get in the way of what they assumed was gang rivalry.

But there was no gang, just a lone woman smearing sugar all over a man's face.

Padma smeared the sugar with such deference she might have been a potter moulding clay into her own creation. His face, his eyebrows, his ears, and an extra dose in the centre of the forehead with her thumb as though she was putting a final bindi on him.

Soon, all the girls from her brothel came to see what was going on. The men from nearby shops came. The postman came. The milkman came.

So did the ants.

Hundreds of them, crawling their way to the man's body. So many hundreds of black ants, so many hundreds of red ants, soldiering their way to the sugar. The man begged for forgiveness and in his terror blurted out what he had done for all to hear, and in doing so negated the possibility of any intervention, which only suited Padma.

Then, when the first bites began, the man went quiet.

A few seconds later, he sent out a scream so high it brought his wife to the scene.

When she saw that Padma had not only tied up her husband, but was coolly sipping chai and watching, she was sure Padma had lost her mind.

Padma looked at her and said, "Forgive me."

Then she touched the woman's feet. "I hope you understand. Just remember, you will always be looked after."

Perhaps the woman did understand, for she turned away and left her husband screaming his heart out, as if that might be the only way for him to get in touch with it.

When the blood trickled, White Lane turned red. It became "Lal Bazaar."

In this fashion, Padma had added her own memorable hue to the place and, at the same time, sent a humble message to the prostitutes under her command, should they have any delusions of escaping or disobeying her. Her story spread through the fourteen lanes of Kamathipura faster than syphilis.

When the man's face was a gnarled caricature, a stray dog licked the sugar off it.

Hassan signalled to Madhu that Padma was ready for her.

"You know where to go?" he asked.

"Yes," said Madhu.

"Then go. I have to keep guard."

She passed five rooms to her left, and the doors were shut, which was a good sign for Padma. It meant business was brisk, except for the two women standing on the balcony outside their respective rooms. Both were in their late thirties. The makeup on their faces was too light, a garish contrast to the darker skin of their necks and arms. Their lips were so red they sent off the flashing alarm of a siren, a warning not to enter, rather than a seductive invite.

Madhu peeked into one of their rooms. The women rented them from Padma at the rate of twenty rupees per client. A small child slept on the ground, huddled in a corner, its head leaning against a stainless steel trunk that contained all of its mother's belongings: her clothes and combs, her makeup, her memories—all of it had to fit in one trunk. If it didn't, the woman had too much of a personal life and needed to be cut down to size. The blue walls of the room were so dreary they made the steel trunk stand out. If a client showed up, the child would be placed under the bed, and the bedsheet adjusted in such a way that it would fall over the edge like a waterfall, cutting the child off from mother and customer, until the next one came. Madhu could smell the sex in there: the sweat, the cigarette smoke, the chewed tobacco, the attar of prostitutes—water was added to the empty perfume bottle in a desperate attempt to gain more mileage—and the incense stick in a corner of the room trying in vain to counter all the other whiffs. She drew her head back. This was the collective scent of a cheap, violent fuck, the odour of enslavement.

More rooms, more closed doors.

In the corridor, a young boy was drawing something on a piece of paper. He had a small flashlight angled on the ground so that it lit the paper while he practised writing his name, but the way he made large loops on the page made Madhu think he was drawing. In another room, a prostitute was breastfeeding her child. With her mouth half open and her head against the wall, she looked comatose, and the baby was literally hanging off her breast. It was hard to tell if she had any nourishment to provide at all. Perhaps, thought Madhu, it was the other way round. The child was resuscitating her, urging her to find the will to carry on.

Padma's room was the same as it had always been, with its old four-poster bed that had belonged to the original madam of the place. Madhu had heard from gurumai that after Padma's husband died, it was the only thing she brought back into the brothel. "Who did I think I was, aiming for a normal life?" she had told gurumai about her marriage. She had two children, gave birth like some blessed factory in consecutive years at the age of forty, and her husband, a postman, gave Padma a new life. Or so it seemed. Less than three years after they got married, the postman's liver failed. And he was a teetotaller, which made Padma realize, once again, that a whore is a whore is a whore. How dare she move out of the brothel into a regular flat, where the vegetable vendor came right to her doorstep?

Even her children felt wrong. Without their father she knew she would fail them terribly. Each time she played with them, she had a foreboding that something would happen to them too, since they were both girls, so she gave them up to a couple who could never have children of their own, on the condition that they leave the city immediately, not tell her where they were going, and never return. The more untraceable they were, the longer the distance between her and them, the safer the children were.

The bed from the brothel was the only remnant of her old life. Even though she had shared it with her husband and children, it had remained her throne, the source of her power. She had felt a surge of accomplishment the first time she'd slept on it as the owner of the brothel. But taking it into her flat with her husband had been a grave mistake, and letting her children sleep on it an even graver one, and so it was returned to its original place.

Madhu looked for a moment at the legendary bed, which gave off an aura of power even in its owner's absence. Padma was not in her room. It meant she was in her office.

It had been years since Madhu was inside the brothel, and the passage of time made her feel lost and dizzy. Although she was on the second floor, she felt she was in the belly of this building, about to meet its architect, while the air got tighter and the light scarcer.

She knocked on Padma's office door and waited.

When there was no response, she pushed the door slowly, until she saw Padma seated at a small desk, a ledger in front of her, pencil in hand, her steel-rimmed glasses sitting low on the ridge of her nose.

"I have a job for you," said Padma.

Straight to the point. Time was electricity to Padma. She tried not to waste it.

She was thinner than Madhu remembered, more wiry. The skin on her forearms was scaly. Even though she was indoors, and alone, and in her own domain, she wore her white sari over her head like a hood. The embroidered lining on her sari was the only bit of fizz allowed in the room. There were no jingling bangles on her wrists, like she used to have. The hood of her sari slid down but she did not bother to pull it back up. Her hair was scant and silver, stiff and alert, not an ounce of life flowing through it.

"A parcel has come," she said.

Parcel. Madhu tensed. If tongues kept the shapes of the words they had used, she would carve out that word from anyone who had ever spoken it.

"I need you to look after it," said Padma.

"Me?"

The tip of Padma's tongue touched the corner of her lips. "Yes, you."

"But . . . but I no longer do this work."

"You like living on a beggar's salary?"

"No, it's . . ."

"A new cop has come. He's young and wants to prove himself. Maybe his sister was a whore and she died, who knows. But he doesn't believe in Gandhi. This is one case even the Father of the Nation cannot solve. So I need someone experienced."

In most situations, a bundle of five-hundred-rupee notes made the law bend and break. The Mahatma's face on the currency made the exchange all the more shameful, and hilarious, as he passed through the hands of the corrupt and ruthless. Whenever they counted money, their fingers grazed his cheeks, made them go red hot in embarrassment.

"Madam, I'm out of touch," said Madhu. "I'm not—"

Padma suddenly stood up and slapped the ledger shut, displaying a sprightliness that Madhu could only hope for if she lived to be Padma's age.

"You will come out of retirement," she said. She opened a drawer and threw a bundle of notes at Madhu. "Advance. Your gurumai will be proud of you. Now follow me."

Madhu froze. She was not prepared to meet the parcel. It was too soon. It had been too long since she had last dealt with one. But if she showed any more hesitation about accepting the job, Padma wouldn't take kindly to it, and neither would gurumai.

"From now on, you will use only this," said Padma, placing a mobile phone in Madhu's hand. It was an old instrument, no larger than the sweet biscuit Madhu dipped in her chai each morning, and judging from its dents, must have had its share of falls.

"The SIM card is new. No one else has this number. After the job is done, you will return the phone to me."

"Yes, madam."

"Do not make any calls from this phone, except to me."

"Yes, madam."

"Now come," she said. "You've been away for a while."

Nothing had changed. At least, nothing that mattered.

Unlike before, there was no guard on floor three. But the same padlocked grille that was found on floors one and two was here as well, just as Madhu remembered, and it slid so smoothly when Padma pushed it aside, it felt ominous.

The room behind the grille was full of ceiling fans, most with cracked wings. There were steel trunks covered with cobwebs, mounted on top of each other, some piles higher than Madhu herself, the topmost trunks perilously balanced and ready to fall upon the slightest provocation. The windows were closed, barricaded with wooden panels hammered one on top of another. Music crept in from the outside, from the taxis and video game parlours below, muffled drumbeats and tinny female voices that sounded far, far away.

"Don't clean anything, don't move anything, don't dust anything," said Padma.

As her eyes adjusted, Madhu could make out an old bicycle leaning against the wall, its torn rubber tyres glued to the metal rim in bits and pieces like wet tar, and behind the cycle, a familiar small wooden ladder. Padma stood near the cycle and looked above it, up at the ceiling. Madhu's gaze followed, and she too stared at the ceiling. Madhu could detect a heavy silence emanating from that corner. Her ears picked up a single rustle, the movement of someone's leg, a toe scraping the edge of something. Padma took a key that was tied around her neck with a black shoelace and gave it to Madhu.

"Her name's Kinjal. She got here this evening," she said, and left.

The minute Padma mentioned the parcel's name, Madhu knew the process had begun. Starting now, the parcel would have to be emptied of her past, and it did not matter what it was. Kinjal was a fine name, but so was Ritu or Lekha or Aarti—a parcel's name had no power, because no matter what, all names added up to one thing: zero.

Whoever Kinjal was, wherever she was from, Madhu prayed that she had a natural tendency toward stillness, for it would make her life easier. One had to be still; one had to forget movement. The mind had to be taught how *not* to travel, because if the parcel decided to catch some ticket to the past or to a station called Hope, her skin would peel. First, it was the skin, then the deeper layers of flesh dissolved in fear, then the bones crumbled as though they were never sturdy to begin with but made of some sad powder, until the soul was finally visible, so it could be wiped clean and a counterfeit could take its place, fresh from Padma's mint.

Madhu readied herself for the parcel's face, because she knew that in it she would observe the same cycle of confusion and fear and prayer that moved round and round, just like the giant wheel in Lane Fourteen opposite Suleiman's Restaurant. The children would laugh and urge the man in charge to turn it faster, failing to realize that the man wasn't turning the wheel at all—he wasn't even touching it. It was the wheel of fate, or the wheel of destiny—you could call it anything you wanted, call it the laugh-a-minute wheel of life, who cared, it ran on its own, powered by some invisible source. If that felt like a lie, you took the first left from Alexandra Cinema and then turned right, and there it was, for all to see, a pathetic giant wheel, moving on its own, the children screaming in delight as it kept them gobbled up in its seats, all safe and barred, while the operator chewed paan and for the sake of appearances kept it spinning, knowing full-well that he was doing this just to earn his bread, because even if he decided not to play along and stopped putting his weight on the wheel, it would continue to turn, and the last thing it required was his damn consent.

2

In the arena of sex trafficking, the players were always the same: a member or trusted aide of the parcel's family; the agent who dealt in parcels, commonly known as the "dalal"; and finally the brothel owner. These were the constants, the trio that worked in perfect harmony like stars aligned in the heavens, constellations producing the same effect: a brilliant explosion of pain.

For the parcel, that pain was now just a bud, a promise of days to come, and no one knew this better than Madhu. She placed the ladder against the wall. The ceiling wasn't that high; five rungs were all that was required to get her there. She pushed the wooden panel up with her palm and slid it across. She had definitely gained some weight since she'd last been here. Her waist barely fit through the opening now, and a couple of rough edges scraped her belly.

She had entered the hollow space that would become her operating chamber for the next while. It was still dark in here, but she could already detect the parcel's movements—those hurried, useless movements. As always, there was a small flashlight near the right-hand corner of the loft. She groped for it but did not switch it on.

Madhu knew that the moment she pushed that switch, she would be in charge of the face she saw. Those eyes would be hers, that brain hers, even the smallest flitter of fear that darted across the parcel's face like a bird in the sky.

But it wasn't time yet. First, Madhu ran her hands along the cage bars. The ring that she wore rattled against them slowly: *rat . . . tat . . . tat . . .* The gaps in time were deliberate, so slow as to make the parcel wonder if they were even real. The dust in the loft made Madhu sniffle, but she did not sound like a person taking in breaths; it was more a reptilian crackle, like the way light bulbs sometimes hissed when hot. Her grip on the flashlight grew harder. For a brief moment, she closed her eyes, almost in prayer, because she knew that the next time she opened them, she would be using light, that most beautiful of things, to destroy.

Most of the young girls Madhu had seen were from Nepal, and a majority of them had not even heard of Bombay. There was one girl, years ago, who had not known what India was. Her village had been so tiny, so remote, she had no clue that there was anything beyond it. She lost her mind in only a few days.

When it came to the opening of a parcel, Madhu did not believe in the conventional approach wherein the madam and a couple of prostitutes pinned the parcel down to a bed while the customer broke her in. The parcels momentarily turned into eels, the terror electric, until their muscles went limp. There was no doubt that this was the quickest method, and it required minimal effort on the brothel owner's part, but Madhu surmised that in the long run it was counterproductive. The sudden breaking in dislodged the parcels so badly that they teetered on the edge of madness for years, and some clients had a problem with sleeping with what they thought were mental patients.

Madhu's approach was subtle. She knew that the instilling of fear in a parcel was a moot point, since the girl had been catapulted thousands of kilometres away from family and landed in a cage. Fear was essential, but it had to be built upon. It had to be layered, over time, like wet cement, until it solidified and ended up as the very foundation of the parcel's being. Then Madhu would be the only one who could help ease it. The conventional method was not only barbaric, it also damaged the goods to the point where mending was impossible.

Madhu took a breath, then blasted the parcel with light. The parcel huddled, her back against the cage bars, trying to find space where there was none. She was exerting pressure against the cage bars, but Madhu knew that the more you pushed, the more things closed in on you—and this was one of the rules the parcel would have to understand, one of several rules that the cages taught its newborns.

The girl seemed to be about ten years old.

Her hair, parted in the centre, ponytailed on either side, was pressed to her head with a healthy dose of oil. Tiny earrings dotted each lobe. Her eyebrows were long, but her lashes normal. Healthy cheeks, typical of Nepali girls, but not too puffy. Skin the colour of brown rice. Madhu could not discern the tint of her eyes because her gaze was fixed to the floor. Her nostrils flared; the tightness in her lungs would be doing that.

The parcel, Madhu decided, was at that stage where she could grow into anything.

Her looks were ordinary enough not to promise any celestial blooming, but at the same time, she was . . . not pretty, but calm. No, perhaps calm wasn't it.

She was clean. Yes, clean. Not in a soap-scrubbed way, but her skin, her shins. No scars left by childhood games or boils, no chicken pox marks on her face. The place under her eyes was sunken, but that was to be expected. One hour in this cage was enough to do that. There were no signs of beating on her. The way she sat, crouched, suggested that there were no internal wounds either. No bruised ribs or swollen kidneys. Madhu was no doctor, but this much she could tell. Internal damage had a way of pouring out: suddenly the eyes would flinch or the feet would twitch. This one sat reasonably still. Not too still, though, because that part hadn't come yet.

Madhu had always resented these virgin girls. These yet-to-flower kalis were the reason eunuchs had been sculpted in the first place—that and God gifting hermaphrodites to mothers. The Almighty, caught in the throes of some divine nasha, occasionally did the job only half right by giving a boy child a penis the size of a seed or, in a moment of misplaced generosity, bestowing both a penis and vagina. Who knows what he smoked up there; if that formula could somehow be obtained, Kamathipura's opium dens would rise from the ashes again.

In being asked to be this parcel's caretaker, Madhu felt the weight of history repeating itself. Throughout the ages, eunuchs had served as protectors of harems, rakhwalas of precious vaginas that meant the world to the men in power. If other men had been left in charge when kings went to war, by the time they came back, chooth-walls would have been ruptured beyond repair by guards, cooks, gardeners, court jesters. So the eunuch had a place. Some even rose to the position of high-ranking government officials, or served as confidantes to members of royalty. The severing of their penises meant that they were severed from their families as well, rendered unfit for society, which made them subservient to just one master—as Madhu was to gurumai—loyal to a fault, out of helplessness. However, that same loyalty afforded them a level of prestige. Eunuch slaves were status symbols, exchanged as gifts between noblemen, or demanded as part of the war-spoils when a kingdom was lost. To this day, hijras were exchanged between hijra leaders. When Madhu was at her sexual zenith, such was her demand that she had almost been bartered away to another guru, but she had begged and pleaded with gurumai not to trade her. Gurumai would have made a fat profit from the trade, but she gave in to her star hijra's histrionics. It was an act of generosity gurumai never allowed Madhu to forget.

But now, Madhu reflected, history had been perverted. In this cramped loft, there were no kings, only the kingdom of Kamathipura, and this parcel might be worth protecting, but Madhu's function was to protect her and keep her safe until it was time to *not* protect her—history made topsy-turvy.

Moreover, the moment at which Madhu would have to let go of this parcel was not in her hands. Unlike a fruit that tasted hard and bitter if eaten before it was ready, a parcel's ripeness depended not on the state of the parcel, but on the one who tasted her.

Madhu knew that Padma already had a buyer for this parcel, someone who was eager to pay a bomb for a virgin child—which made this parcel different from the others who arrived in Kamathipura. This parcel had been commissioned. Padma had been very clear that this one was true maal, a real virgin. Normally, when clients were told that a girl was seal-pack, it wasn't the case. The girl had already been broken, but because she had not yet been sold on the market, she was still considered virginal and was presented as such to clients. In reality, she had been raped repeatedly by the agent during transport, on the train itself. How fitting, thought Madhu, that this was done in the cargo compartment, because the word *maal* literally meant "cargo" or "commodity." The girl had been bought for a price and was no longer human. She was being converted into cheez—a thing to be consumed.

A parcel that had been opened on the way was sold at a higher price because it had already been tamed. The brothel madam would not have to go through the trouble of disciplining it, of having it opened. That was a headache.

This parcel's case was different. She would not be taken in the brothel itself; something more rare would occur. She would be transported to someone's home or to a hotel room nearby. That was why Madhu was being employed. She would act as the carrier. The parcel needed to be packaged in such a way that it looked like it belonged in Kamathipura. And who better than a hijra to undertake the task of transformation?

The parcel raised her head toward Madhu and then looked down again. Madhu turned the flashlight off, but she was not ready to make herself visible. Not yet. The parcel was murmuring something, mumbling away, her jaws hardly able to open. Words had no weight; they were as weightless as the motes of dust that stood in silvery columns under dangling light bulbs. Madhu's aim in this first meeting between herself and the parcel was simple: to share the same physical space. There was no need for talk. When two bodies met, raw truth was exchanged.

And the truth was that a ten-year-old girl had been sold into slavery.

Madhu took one last look at the parcel and went down the trap door. That was enough for now. As she placed the ladder back next to the bicycle, she pondered the meaning of magic. Magic wasn't about making things appear out of nowhere. Any amateur could do that. Magic was to make what was real disappear. To wipe out from existence. To turn against God.

He creates, thought Madhu. I erase.

Madhu walked through the lanes of Kamathipura: Lane Fourteen, Lane Thirteen, Lane Twelve . . . She descended deeper and deeper into the core of her settlement. The streets were rough cement, eaten and dug out, but the foundation of their hardness had been laid years ago, in the 1800s, when the first prostitutes wafted through them, danced and spun around, and eventually collapsed, only to be replaced by other bodies. Next, the criminals came. Once the working girls had made the place unacceptable to society, it became the perfect hideout for thieves, goons, small-time smugglers, and young men with moons in their eyes looking to make their mark in the criminal underworld. While they hid in the shadows, there was always the fold of a woman's underwear to play with. If a thief's hand got too restless, itched for a lock to break, he could slide it up a thigh or two during his hiatus. Slowly, the respectable families started moving out of the area and only the prostitutes and "kamathis" remained, the artisans and labourers from whom the place got its name. The families that had respect but no means to move out had to stuff handkerchiefs in their mouths whenever someone asked where they lived, because the assumption was that if you lived in Kamathipura, you were cheap, you were easy, you had flies coming out of your mouth when you yawned.

But gurumai had taught Madhu that this place did have one saving grace. What Kamathipura offered its babies, no other locale in the city could. To any new entrant, gurumai always gave a brief history of the place, and then the moral: "A child of Foras Road does not have ambitions. It does not seek love. It does not want. It does not beg for happiness like normal human beings do. That is our strength."

When Madhu was a young hijra, thread by thread gurumai had woven a tapestry so fine that Madhu was mesmerized by her gall, the sheer glory of a reject rejecting the rest of the city. But Madhu had not realized that gurumai was talking about the children of female prostitutes; she was not referring to hijras. Hijras were never born in Kamathipura. They were always from somewhere else. They were immigrants, and, as such, they were morons with dreams. And although hijras may have been adopted by Kamathipura, they were confined to a two-storey building known as the House of the Hijra. It was the unofficial womb for members of the third gender, and it was Madhu's home. For bodies like Madhu's that were neither here nor there, Hijra House offered a fixed address for the soul.

Before India's independence, a lot of white memsahibs who stayed in the area employed hijras to do the daily cooking and cleaning. Over time, the hijras became more than just servants—they were confidantes, trusted aides, not just to the white women, but to the rich Indian women as well. When India finally broke free of the British and the white women went back to England—and some of the Indian women moved elsewhere—they gifted their homes to the hijras. That was how Ramabai Chawl and the area surrounding it had become a hijra haven. All this Madhu had been fed by gurumai—stories sequestered into the very fabric of her being to keep her proud and loyal, and fearful.

By now, Madhu had reached her asylum. The moment she turned right from the laundry, the darkness took on a different scent. There were no street lights in this lane; it lived in the dark. At the beginning of the lane, the carrom players, mainly steelworkers from the adjoining mill, sat on wooden stools, making shots at impossible angles, while their cigarette smoke created a hazy cloud that climbed the walls of the public urinal and disappeared toward the roof, where Devyani, six foot three inches of human draped in black, straggly hair falling to the waist, stood in a sari. Every single night, Devyani smoked ganja and planted herself on the roof of the public urinal. Unlike a lighthouse, which emits a blinking signal, Devyani merged into the sky, appearing only when there was trouble. Then her teeth would flash as she descended onto the ground with alarming speed to prevent some macho lund from ill-treating Roomali—Roomali, who at this moment was leaning against the wall of the public urinal, wooing her next client. With its layers of makeup, her face was a sudden shot of white in the dark, and the red lips made her look clown-ish until she began to sweet talk. Then there was no mistaking her wiles. She wore shorts, which was a violation of the hijra code, but as long as she brought in some coin it didn't matter to gurumai.

Madhu took the stairs and was greeted by dour-faced Sona. Gurumai always teased Sona that she must have been a wrinkle in her past life, specifically a wrinkle on someone's arse, which is why she always made that stinky face. But it was not a past life that Sona could not shake off; she was trying to forget her brothers in this life and how they had treated her when she was Suresh. She had run away from a small town in Gujarat when she was sixteen. Her brothers had followed Suresh to drag him back home, but when gurumai told them that he had already been castrated, they spat on the ground and left without even meeting with him. Suresh hadn't been castrated. It was guru-mai's way of showing Suresh that family ties meant nothing. "See how quickly they turned," she told him. To this day, Sona could not get over it; she was always replaying some stupid reconciliation scene in her movie-projector mind.

In the hall, the TV was on but no one was watching. Tarana and Anjali were stuck together as usual, glued to each other by a common bitchiness. They whispered all day and night, bring-ing bits of gossip from all corners of the city and churning them out after adding their own giddy bile. Tarana and Anjali were among the lucky. Their progression from man to hijra had served them well. Their lips were full, their lashes long, and there was hardly a trace of hardness in their faces. As well, their breasts had grown, and for this more than anything, Madhu wished them slow, painful deaths. Anjali had taken hormone injections and was now reaping the benefits. Tarana didn't need injections. Her breasts just grew with the randomness and unreasonableness of tumours. Madhu too had experienced growth. After her castration, it had surged through her like a beautiful promise and had enervated her. But somewhere down the line her breasts had failed to fulfill her as she had thought they would. Madhu believed that the reason they had never fully come into their own was her own disappointment. It had stopped them from flowering.

The others had just finished eating dinner. Madhu had already eaten with Gajja, but she did not want to tell them that. Her sisters were jealous of her friendship with Gajja. It was rare for a man to devote himself to a hijra even after their relationship had ceased to be sexual.

Besides gurumai, the only fellow hijra whom Madhu could confide in, the only one she had real feelings for, was Bulbul. She had been Madhu's friend since the day they met, but she never listened to a single piece of advice that Madhu gave her. Tonight Bulbul was seated solemnly on a chair in front of a mirror, combing her hair. Madhu had told her not to do that in front of the others, because they sniggered at her. As if to prove her point, when the comb stuck in the frizz of Bulbul's locks, Anjali pounced on her.

"Traffic jam in your hair?" she asked.

Bulbul was getting old—nearing sixty now—and the more she combed her hair and put makeup on, the easier it was for her to look like a mistake. Madhu had tried explaining this—subtly at first, then with the audacity of a truck horn—but Bulbul just didn't get it. Her name itself, Bulbul, now seemed cruel. She loved to sing, but the voice that had once been passable was now hoarse, no longer fit for singing at weddings and childbirths. It was more for selling pots and pans at cheap prices. "Comb your hair when it's wet," Madhu had told Bulbul a hundred times, but Bulbul was so afraid of catching a cold, she continued to make her hair desert dry. It always looked as though it had taken the wind as prisoner. She had become fragile and paranoid, but vanity had not left her. She was obsessed with her looks and loved to pose for tourists. She never took money for a photograph. "I will lose my looks if I take money for this face," she said in earnest, another admission made aloud that had become a catchphrase for the others in her absence.

Bulbul lifted her chin in an attempt to tighten her skin, but the only result was the tautness of another jibe from Anjali. Madhu shot a glare in Anjali's direction and she cooled down, but it was too late: Bulbul was hurt and made a dash to the toilet. She would urinate, no doubt, but she urinated tears—that's how sensitive she was.

Tarana and Anjali went over to where Bulbul had been sitting. They smiled naughtily at Madhu, as if to say, "Allow us at least this much." When Madhu nodded, they quickly grabbed Bulbul's mobile phone and started going through her photo gallery. These were photos Bulbul had taken of herself, and she thought no one else knew about them. Now even Sona rushed to the phone to join in, and the giggles began.

The mobile phone's flash had made Bulbul look grotesque at times, with the dip of her lip trying to twist into a smile, one eye slightly smaller than the other, wrinkle upon wrinkle showing itself through layers of pancake makeup. Each image was that of a human being deluding herself, and it made Madhu feel wrinkled as well, shrunken and spurned. Then Anjali flicked to a new photo, one Madhu had never seen before, of Bulbul with a fake cockatoo on her shoulder. Sona was the first to burst. She tried not to be so shameless in her laughter, but all of them, including Madhu, began to break like eggshells. Anjali barely had the strength to put the phone back in its place before Bulbul returned from the toilet. They tried to control themselves but instead collapsed to the floor in a cackling heap, and Madhu knew then that Bulbul would give her an earful that night. She'd know that they were laughing at her and would want to know why, and Madhu would have to make something up. But for now the photographs had served their purpose: they gave Bulbul the illusion of beauty and the rest of them a chance to be children again—brash and hurtful, in love with laughter.

There were two types of moans in Kamathipura.

First, the obvious ones, from customers shivering above bodies on rent, letting go for a few seconds with one *aaah*. Second, the *aaah*s of suffering: voices rising in pain, softer than the ecstasy of customers but more fevered. Because Madhu slept on the floor at the foot of gurumai's bed, it was the second type of moan she had to contend with. Tonight, gurumai was trying to clear her throat of phlegm and was calling out Madhu's name. But she was not awake. Gurumai clutched a small pillow, gripped it in her sleep. Madhu rubbed gurumai's feet. The warmth of her palms on the soles had always soothed gurumai, and now the contortions on her face eased slowly, until it was time for another dream to own her.

On the floor, Madhu's phone blinked and vibrated. It was Gajja.

"Where are you?" he asked.

"Home," she whispered.

"Come to Lund Ki Dukaan."

"I can't . . ."

"You have to. The Mary's here and Salma's in top form."

The mention of the Mary lifted Madhu. Every so often, a female Samaritan came from the calm meadows of the middle class with free condoms and advice. These were well-meaning women, but it was hard for them to understand that when you have lived in Kamathipura for as long as Madhu had, there were things more fearful than becoming a pojeetive. Still, along with a minor dose of empathy, they offered major entertainment. They had good Christian hearts and their attempts at helping allowed them to sleep well at night. This was consoling to Madhu: most of the time the existence of people like her tended to disturb others; at least she managed to help these Marys get some sleep.

She gave gurumai's feet a final rub.

It was well past midnight now, and Madhu thought of Tarana and Anjali, the two young stars of the brothel, on duty right now in another section of Hijra House, sucking and cooing like ravenous doves. They were always the last to sleep, at four in the morning, after they had been taken "royally," as they liked to say. But the less lucrative hijras, the ones gurumai thought of as charity cases, had already called it a night and were sleeping around gurumai's bed as though she were a planet pulling them toward her. Sona was snuggled up to the corner of a wall, mistaking it for the nook of a lover's underarm. Sona did not take clients or lovers. She only performed at weddings and knew in her heart that with her bushy eyebrows and guttural voice, she was too unattractive for sex work. Bulbul was facing heavenward, her hair split on either side of the pillow in uneven streams. She'd gladly snuggle up to anyone who would have her, but takers were few. The bodies of Devyani and Roomali lay contorted on the floor, as on most nights. They thought so much about the past that it took them a long time to fall asleep, only to wake up exhausted, singed by their own recollections. These were the seven chelas of gurumai, who were allowed to serve their mistress by staying in Hijra House. They were lonely disciples whose destinies were stitched together by the thread of being born different—and what a life they had made, all runaways landing in each other's arms. Madhu left them to their sleep, grateful to her sisters and gurumai for providing some familiarity, some cement, in a life that would have otherwise been a mudslide.

Down the stairs she went with the excitement of a child, and before she knew it, she was stepping in the potholes and dog shit of her locality with abandon, toward the Dick Shop. The name was Gajja's invention. He had wanted to paint a sign that said "Lund Ki Dukaan," but the management preferred a low profile. Still, they appreciated the gesture. The Dick Shop was an old Irani restaurant that had been converted into a small cinema. It was no substitute for the Alexandra, but at least it lived. It was illegal during the day and grew even more illegal at night. Starting at noon, for fifteen rupees only, the shop screened the latest blockbusters on a large TV. Most of Kamathipura had seen *Don 2* before most of Mumbai, and when *Don 2* was released, *Don 2* was all that played—from noon to three, three to six, six to nine, and from nine to midnight. The afternoons and evenings might have belonged to King

Khan, but the nights went to the porn stars. At the stroke of midnight, flies opened and cocks emerged, on screen and off. Sometimes it was foreign porn, white men and women glowing like aliens, so clean, so hairless, so pink. Sometimes the South Indians took over, the dusky bodies and hairy vaginas having their own draw. Madhu had never understood porn. It was like watching the same news item over and over.

The owner of Porno Parlour—its other, English, name—had an understanding with the NGOs and cops. Once in a while, they would allow the Marys—in Kamathipura they were all called Marys—to hold workshops and address the audience, because the crowd that came here would ordinarily never attend an NGO gathering. At the moment, some poor Mary, a new recruit, would be getting the fright of her life, because Salma was in gear. A new Mary, with her broken Hindi, hiding behind her cross, was always a sight to behold.

"Come on!" said Gajja. "You're missing everything."

He dragged Madhu inside so forcefully that Madhu almost missed a step in the dark. The room stank of sweat and Dettol. The sermon was on. Gajja had saved a seat for Madhu on the wooden bench closest to the entrance, one of many that had been stolen from the convent school nearby. The benches were perfect for Porno Parlour because they had desks attached to them, which served as a cover for masturbating men and prevented them from squirting the person in front. When the school complained about the theft, the owner of Porno Parlour offered to return them, but not before casually mentioning to the cop on duty that the desks had been "spoiled due to excite-ment." The school suggested that the owner consider the benches a donation.

Thankfully, the new Mary was not demonstrating the proper way for a woman to make a client wear a condom. Everyone in the audience had been taught that a hundred times, but still someone from the crowd, a gent usually, would say, "Show me, show me!"

Madhu spotted Salma two rows ahead of her. She was ominously quiet.

The Mary was showing a short video, and with every frame, Madhu could tell Salma's fuse was getting shorter. Gajja had already filled Madhu in: Salma had been asked to calm down by the Mary and her male colleague, and had been on the verge of being thrown out, but Salma had apologized, which she always did, especially when she didn't mean it.

As statistics poured onto the screen, a man's voice emphasized the numbers in a cheap, theatrical tone: *A decade ago, there were one lakh prostitutes in Kamathipura alone. Now there are only twenty thousand.*

Even though the numbers had dwindled, Salma clapped. It was still her moment, after all. The Mary glared at her.

On average, each sex worker services ten men in one night.

Salma nodded her head vehemently. "Corr-ect," she said, in English, to the Mary. "This phillum is showing the reality."

Madhu did not understand why they were being forced to watch the statistics. Such things were a showcase for outsiders to induce pity and donations. Maybe she had missed something earlier.

Kamathipura is the second largest red-light area in Asia.

"What?" said Salma. "We are not first?"

As the facts continued to parade across the screen, the audience grew bored—cows chewing on grass. Madhu felt

further and further removed from the video the Mary was playing for them. Thankfully, the voice soon faded away into the
even more humiliating sound of a sitar wailing.

"Any questions?" asked the Mary. "Any questions about precautions? It's your life. It's worth fighting for."

Salma put her hand up like a good schoolgirl. "If a client hates
to use condoms and starts slapping me around when I insist,
what should I do? Do you have any precautions against that?"

"Well . . . ," said the Mary. "You can come and speak to us
privately about that."

"But I'm asking you now. If my cunt is public, why should
my questions be private?"

"We can counsel you accordingly," said the Mary. "We can—"

But the man in the first row interrupted her. "Put on the
triple X, yaar!"

Fed up with the sermonic turn the night had taken, he wanted
to skip the previews and go straight to the hard-core porn.
Madhu was not surprised. In single- and double-X movies, there
was a storyline and no intercourse. That was for amateurs. Even
Gajja found single- and double-X films redundant. "What's
the use of a story?" he had asked Madhu. "We know where the
cock ends up!"

"Yes, yes," echoed another man. "Put on the triple! Stop this
AIDS phillum! You are trying to scare us! AIDS is not real!"

Ah, there it is, thought Madhu. There was always that rare
coconut, always male, who believed that AIDS was a phantom,
something religious people and the government had concocted to
restrict the enjoyment of sex. Even if a pojeetive worm existed,
the thinking went, if one drank a soda or anything fizzy immediately after intercourse, it would flush out the worm through the

urine. Madhu had heard men speak this way time and again. She thought it best to let them believe in the power of soda.

She could sense Salma getting hot again, burning with the desire to speak. Two other people had disrupted the proceedings, so there was no danger she would be singled out. She turned around, faced the audience, and took off: "These bhenchoth randis come here to teach me—*me*—about sex? I have swallowed more sperm than they have drunk water!"

Gajja laughed. He loved Salma's tirades. He called her the greatest orator in the city. If only some political party would recruit her. No one else could speak with such candour.

Salma's truth had landed flush on the Mary's face.

"Chudayl, take your condoms, blow some air into them, and fly away from here," Salma added with a flourish of her hand.

The Mary ignored her and waved a packet of condoms. "These are chocolate flavoured, so they will taste good," she said.

"I hate chocolates," said Salma softly, without anger.

The Mary ignored her.

"You're not listening to me," said Salma. "The last thing my father gave me before he sold me here was a chocolate."

Madhu saw the way Salma suddenly quietened, going into a shell as though her head had become soft, as though the skull had turned to pulp at the mention of chocolate.

Madhu understood. Even Madhu had her chocolates—the things that reminded her of home, of people she had loved or had made the mistake of trusting. No matter where people were or what they were doing, their chocolates had a way of taking them back.

Madhu was ten. He lived with his parents and younger brother in a one-bedroom flat in a building called Shakti. It was 1984— an important year in his life. It was the year he made his first real friend, a boy named Taher, whose father owned a stationery shop just below the building. Taher and Madhu went to the same school, but until 1984 they rarely spoke. No one noticed Madhu except when he had to walk to the blackboard to spell out an English word. Mrs Bhaskar loved to give them spelling tests.

"Who would like to spell *obedient*?"

"Who would like to spell *continent*?"

"Who would like to spell *miracle*?"

No one would, so the pupils were chosen randomly by Mrs Bhaskar's crooked finger. Her forefinger was malformed, bent permanently, and when she looked at one student and said, "You," there was confusion because her finger was point-ing in another direction. The students learned to look in her eyes to gauge correctly.

"You," she said. "Yes, you, Madhu. Come here and spell *canal*."

Madhu knew how to spell the word. He was *sure* he knew. But when he was halfway to the board, someone said, "He walks like a *girl*!"

Madhu froze. He just stood there in his short pants and felt as naked as a gushing river.

"Is there a reason you are standing in the middle of the class?" Mrs Bhaskar asked.

Of course there was. He had been found out.

But Mrs Bhaskar was so concerned about *canal* that Madhu's feelings did not enter her mind. The minute Madhu resumed walking, the laughter became even louder because now he was trying *not* to walk like a girl. What resulted was a new kind of human being who tried not to sway, who became stiff and professorial. Madhu made it to the board, spelled the word, and fled to his seat. It was only when he sat down and read what he had written that he realized how scared he was. Instead of the word *canal*, he had written three others:

I am sorry.

His father had tried so hard to make him a boy. How could he fail at something he already was? Mrs Bhaskar must have seen the pain in his face because she never called him back to spell anything. But the damage had been done. After that incident, Madhu tried not to walk much when other people were around.

The only person who showed him kindness that day was Taher. He did not look at Madhu but he did not laugh either. He was quiet even though the boy next to him was grinning.

That was enough consolation for Madhu.

A couple of weeks later, Taher took Madhu by surprise once again.

It was a Sunday morning and a cricket game was on. Five a side, the boys from Madhu's building versus the richer ones from Navjeevan Society, the building opposite. For the past hour, Madhu had heard that wretched red rubber ball being thwacked around behind the building. The shouts of excitement only made Madhu feel more out of sync with life, and he sank to the floor. The hard tiles became an ocean in which he could drown. He imagined diving into the wet floor and resurfacing as an Apsara, a celestial being with whom he'd felt an immediate kinship when he'd encountered her in the Amar Chitra Katha comics. So he rose from his ocean bed to get some air, to show himself unabashedly to the fishermen and hunters and whoever else might be on shore at the time, without realizing that he was standing right by the kitchen window.

The minute Taher saw him, Madhu ducked out of sight.

Then he heard a boy's mother call him home. There was a protest from Taher and the others that this boy was the only one left to bat, but the mother didn't care and the son went home. Madhu heard the boys from Navjeevan shouting, "We won, we won, we won," and then, "No double batting, no!" And then Madhu heard his name.

What had he done?

Taher called out his name a second time. "Come down and bat," said Taher.

"What?"

"You're on our team. Come down and bat."

"But . . ."

"Come down, I said."

Taher was so firm, so tough. And he wanted Madhu. It was this fact that had Madhu running for the stairs. His mother did not mind. She was, as usual, praying before the picture of Shiva with deadened devotion, but she managed to send him off with a smile. If only his father were home, Madhu thought, he would have been proud.

Someone explained the match situation to Madhu, but he wasn't listening. The bat was too damn heavy and he had forgotten how to hold it even though his father had tried to teach him several times.

"We need four runs to win," said Taher. "I hate these

bastards. I want to win."

Bastards. Yes, the entire lot of them. Anything for Taher.

The bowler came in. Madhu closed his eyes and thought of Kapil Dev, that great all-rounder, because his father loved Kapil. But this was no time for inspiration. It was a time for miracles.

Something connected.

Madhu sent the ball flying into a second-floor window. Glass shattered. It was a six; they had won. Taher jumped in celebration as the opposition skulked away, but Madhu stood there frozen, terrified that his father would have to pay for the broken glass. They were the poorest family in the building.

"Never mind," said Taher. It was the window of his own flat, and he would never replace the glass because it was a symbol of victory.

Madhu's head was spinning. He was associated with victory. He was a symbol. Taher thumped him on the back. Madhu thumped him back.

Then Taher smiled at Madhu. A soft breeze hit Taher's cheeks and made him squint, and Madhu was overwhelmed with love. He tried to shake Taher's hand to thank him profusely. But he ended up holding it instead—only for a second or two, but it felt like forever.

It was Monday by the time Madhu landed on earth again.

When he entered his classroom, he was not ashamed to walk. He walked to his seat and took his time. During the first recess, he waited for Taher to come over and say hello. He would have gladly accepted even a sneeze from Taher, but no word or gesture came his way. During the lunch break, he went outside and sat on his favourite tree branch. He ate his lunch here, alone, five days a week. The tree's white branches were like tusks, and it was on this tree that he had started to like the feeling of something hard and solid between his legs.

"There's our champion," said Taher.

He had appeared suddenly, accompanied by Nitin and Sohail, neither of whom had ever before talked to Madhu.

"Hi," said Madhu eagerly. He jumped off his branch. "Hi . . ." He had no idea what to say. Most of his conversations were with himself.

"I heard you smashed a huge six," said Sohail.

"Yes, I broke his window," said Madhu proudly, looking at Taher. "We really showed them, those Navjeevan bastards . . ." He forced the words off his tongue, feeling like a charlatan.

"You want to play with us again?" asked Taher.

Every cell in Madhu's body wanted to refuse. Holding a bat again would only remind him of his disapproving father.

"Sure, I love cricket," he said.

"Come with us," said Taher. He put his arm around Madhu, and Madhu went electric. He could have given light to an entire slum.

"Where's the bat and ball?" he asked.

"We don't need one," said Taher, and he pushed Madhu to the ground. Madhu wanted so much to believe that he had stumbled and caused his own fall. But he could not convince himself that Taher's foot had landed on his stomach by accident. He squirmed in pain.

"Why did you hold my hand yesterday?" asked Taher.

Madhu wanted to answer, but he was drowning in two separate streams of tears coming down his cheeks. The drops from the right eye were because he was in physical pain; the ones from the left were because he had allowed himself to think that he had made a friend.

"Do you know that the boys from Navjeevan saw you hold my hand? I'm the bloody captain!"

"I'm sorry . . . I was only trying to shake it . . ."

Perhaps it was because he crawled away that Madhu was saved from being beaten further. But he understood something valuable as he hid under a bush for the next hour. He would not be allowed to walk tall, to make friends like normal boys did. He had been sent to this earth to grovel, to make his acquaintance with the worms and the weeds, and when he longed for company or support from the outside world, only a stray dog would show up, the way it had that day, raising its hind leg, showering upon that bush something pungent and acidic, preparing Madhu for the taste that his life would have in the years to come.

Gajja had passed out with his head on the desk at Porno Parlour. Madhu left him there and walked to Padma's brothel with Salma. On the rare occasion that Padma was unwell, Salma ran the day-to-day activities of the place and was hoping to someday occupy a full-time managerial position. But until then, she continued to take whoever paid her.

Madhu understood the detachment that a prostitute required. After so many years of service, Salma had learned how to disassociate herself from her body. It was the same for Madhu. She remembered how once, when a man was inside her, she had seen both him and herself from a distance. She had been so outside herself she thought she had died. But she had come back into her body the minute he was done, and once again felt its agonies and petty complaints.

"This new parcel . . . when should I meet her?" asked Salma.

"Not yet. But we both have to be prepared. If she is to be transported, I am her adoptive mother. But once she's opened, you will be in charge of her. That's what madam said."

"Things are so complicated now. Before, there was no mother. I was just left in the dark. If the cops found me, they fucked me or took a bribe. It was so simple. Why is madam doing all this?"

"The cops are turning honest."

"And I'm a virgin," said Salma, "who has never even *seen* a cock."

At 3:00 a.m., most of the sex workers were wrapping things up for the night. They sat on the brothel steps, lifting their hair to wipe the sweat off their necks. They looked like factory workers with aching muscles. Young men in tight jeans and spiky haircuts stood around motorcycles and spoke about their exploits, boasting about which prostitute they had slept with, or how many. Salma went up the stairs to join the snoring of several others. The women's dreams would criss-cross in the dark, and they would all wake up at around noon, when the designated chai maker would prepare the morning brew.

Madhu climbed the stairs to the third floor, wondering if she should feed the parcel. She decided against it. It was too soon for her to provide any comfort. The first night was all about submission.

The parcel was crouched into a ball in the cage, more in a collapsed state of exhaustion than sleep. Even when Madhu aimed the flashlight at her, she did not move. Madhu felt disoriented as she studied the parcel. She would have to tread carefully with this one. Sometimes the parcels lost their minds sooner than expected. Sometimes they never came back. Some clients were okay with sleeping with a drugged doll; others were not.

The smell was very strong. The parcel had urinated in the cage. Madhu hated this part, the stripping away of all human dignity. But it had to be done. It was for the parcel's own good. The more useless she felt, the more she would listen, and that would enable Madhu to get through to her. It would help Madhu save her from greater pains and indignities.

It was time for Madhu and the parcel to meet. Madhu rattled the cage bars with the flashlight. The parcel snapped awake, as though injected with adrenaline. She tried to sit up but her elbow gave way. Slowly, Madhu turned the flashlight away from the parcel and detected the stream of urine that had trickled toward a corner.

Most of these Nepali girls had never seen a hijra. Madhu had a flower in her hair, but she knew it did not make her softer. Through the cage bars, her face would look even more contorted—the blood-red lips, the jasmine in her hair failing to offset the manly face, the dark circles under her eyes only proving that she did not deserve sleep. Madhu knew that she did not need to act threatening. Her natural face was enough. She wished she could adjust the amount of light, make it softer, the way candles made even evil things glow and allowed one to find a glimmer of hope in them.

She quelled her shame and lit her own face in the flashlight's beam. It had been years since she had done this. Years ago, her face had been pretty. It was different now but not meant to scare. She hated the line that she would speak next. She had to run the line in her head for a few seconds because her Nepali was very rusty. She knew it in bits and pieces, had picked it up from Roomali, her hijra sister from Nepal, and from the parcels of the past as well. But she was worrying needlessly. The moment she opened her mouth, the words just flowed.

"Now think about what you've done," she told the parcel.

———

As she walked down the street a half-hour later, Madhu's stomach growled. While the rest of Mumbai slept, Sukhlaji Street was awake. Some called 3:30 a.m. the wee hours of the morning, but for Madhu it was still night. A kind of pulse came from behind closed doors—the heartbeats of prostitutes thinking of their families, their faint, tiny breaths seeping through the cracks of windows, making the air staler with the same old sighs and longings. The slurred speech of an alcoholic tried to cross the street to reach the ears of another drunkard, and stray dogs covered with sores limped like handicapped angels, wondering why no one was bandaging their blisters. The city never slept—that is what people said time and again. It never slept, thought Madhu, because wounds were wide awake.

The opium dens of Sukhlaji Street had shut down ages ago, and the semi-transparent skeletons of the addicts who had once drifted through this area were long gone. Madhu had learned that no one died on opium; they became lighter. But then opium gave way to heroin, and suddenly men and women were turning white in the darkness, their veins freezing toward death. The new drug had proven to be too much happiness streaming through bodies not trained for it. Heroin had started to catch on when a man walked into the opium dens with a VCR and videocassette. His employers had filmed for the den owners how to use this drug, how to prepare it, how to inject it, how to push it into the body like a child going in, an abortion in reverse, hot and fresh, cooked to enter and die.

Now only one skeleton remained, but he was no addict.

He was called Maachis because he was matchstick thin, and he sold sweetmeats: warm, sticky gulab jamuns that melted in the mouth so fast, the tongue desperately tried to savour every bite, only to sing for more. For Madhu, they were a habit as addictive as heroin, and they were the last sweet thing left in her life. They had once been gurumai's addiction as well. For years Madhu could hear gurumai slurping over gulab jamuns like some gluttonous thing in the dark. But since her health had started to wane, gurumai ate them only a couple of times a year, as a treat for surviving.

If it were not for the gulab jamun, Madhu might not have become a hijra, for she would never have met gurumai. And if it were not for her father, she would not have gone in the middle of the afternoon, in the scorching heat, to Geeta Bhavan to buy gulab jamuns. Madhu remembered the day well. "Sir," as Madhu's father was called by the students at Maharashtra College, had been correcting history papers all morning, occasionally mumbling to his wife that his intelligence had not been rewarded, because his brother, less educated than him, had become a successful businessman, and here he was, in a flat bought from his younger brother's charity, a humiliation he would never recover from. He took his glasses off his nose and said to Madhu, "Get me some gulab jamuns."

Madhu's mother gave him the money. His father was never to be bothered with matters as trivial as money, although Madhu knew that was all he cared about. His mother would never buy anything for herself; she would save every rupee like it was a human life, and thank God she did, because it helped in times such as these, when her husband's salary was a slow train, approaching at an agonizing pace. As Madhu went down the stairs, he imagined he was following an escape route or pathway to another land. He tried so hard not to think of himself as defective, but now, in his tenth year on earth, the heavens were speaking to him, saying, "You're right to think that way. You leaked out of God's palm; you slipped through the cracks." To make things right, the gods in heaven had given his parents another child, a *real* son, who was now almost a year old. They doted on him obsessively, as though he was a combination of movie star and spiritual guru, when all he did was shriek and shit through the night. So in addition to his own imperfection, Madhu had been carrying his brother's magnificence for the past year, and it was becoming too much to bear. The weight of his thoughts was so heavy it took him ages to cross the road to Geeta Bhavan.

He paid the man at the counter, wondering if he should stick his hand in the plastic bag and eat one there and then. The thought of going back to his father made him swallow two. He wiped his sticky hand on his shorts, and then he felt the urge to wipe his hand on his thigh. As he did, he felt a shadow fall over him—or maybe it was a breeze, or the promise of a breeze, only darker.

That mouth, those lips. That eternal pout.

The words that came out of that mouth flew toward Madhu with such purpose, they were unlike anything that had come his way until then.

"Kya, chickni."

Hello, smooth one.

The mouth belonged to a tall man-woman in a sari, with hair parted in the centre, large gold earrings dangling from either ear, a nose flattening itself out, trying to cover as much area as possible, and lips—Madhu could not get over those red swollen lips.

She grinned, and so did the two others beside her. Madhu took one look at them and dropped the bag of gulab jamuns and ran. He heard raucous laughter before it was drowned out by the horn of an Ambassador that almost ran over him. In his hurry to cross the road, he caused a chaotic tangle of cars and motorcycles and a string of abuses. By the time Madhu got to the other side, the apparition was already there, waiting for Madhu with the bag of gulab jamuns.

"Chickni," she said again, "don't be afraid."

She bent down to give Madhu the gulab jamuns, but not before she slid her hand in the bag, picked one, and popped it in her mouth. Madhu could smell her breath. Her lips were red from betel juice, ruder and flashier than any lipstick.

Madhu did not know it then, but this would be his gurumai. His mai-baap, his "mother-father," his shelter, his solace, his destruction.

For once, the street Madhu lived on had not been mundane. His whole body was throbbing wildly. He had seen these apparitions before, but never up close.

By the time he rang his own doorbell, he felt pleased to see his father.

But from that moment on, gurumai never left him. Her words hummed in his head with the authority of an anthem, as though Madhu were a country and the song had been composed just for him.

Chickni. She had referred to Madhu as female. It made Madhu feel strangely empowered. His ten-year-old body felt long and powerful and free, and this so scared him that he wanted to sleep between his mother and father but his request fell upon deaf ears because the baby had that spot. He felt a beautiful rage against his brother and stayed up all night begging Shiva to make his mother's nipples poisonous.

It had now been thirty years since that day when Madhu first met gurumai. In that time, the shopkeepers from his childhood, who had sold smuggled Rado watches and playing cards with naked women on them, had died; police commissioners had come and gone; and the children of Kamathipura had grown up to become drivers and watchmen. In that time, Madhu had stopped wearing men's underwear and started wearing panties, and the very buildings that housed the brothels were in danger of being reduced to rubble, made into large vacant spaces ready to be plundered by real estate developers. Bulldozers would soon be showing up on doorsteps like metal gangsters, like great conquerors, but one thing remained constant: the fear and exhilaration and confusion that Madhu had felt that day. There was no single word to describe what he had felt when he and gurumai met, just as there is no one word you could say to a mother whose child has just died. There were many words and they were all useless. And when Madhu felt useless, as she did right now, she put her hand into the plastic packet and slipped a gulab into her mouth.

3

No matter how late Madhu went to sleep, she was always the first to wake up. The slightest hint of light was enough to get her boiling water for chai. Years ago, when she was the pick of the brothel, she was allowed to sleep until noon—those thighs and eyes needed pampering. Now it was Tarana and Anjali who were accorded special status.

"Boil one of those crows in that chai," said Sona. "They never let me sleep . . ."

Roomali was already awake. She had put on her reading glasses and was practising the English alphabet in a notebook. Devyani's first action of the day was to iron her black sari. By the time Bulbul had emerged from the toilet, gurumai was circling an incense stick around the framed picture of the poet that adorned her wall, a sign for her disciples to stand in line with the night's earnings in hand.

Most hijra gurus had a photograph of *their* gurus, whom they paid obeisance to, but gurumai's source of strength was no hijra; she revered a poet who had lived with his wife in Delhi, and who had taken gurumai under his wing when gurumai was just ten.

When gurumai was born, it was clear that nature had given her both male and female organs, but in such minuscule doses that she could claim to be neither. Her parents had to choose one sex, and so they decided gurumai was a boy and named him Lalu. Even though gurumai's family begged the midwife to be discreet, secrets, like pus, have a way of leaking out, and when the honour of the entire family was at stake, when gurumai's sisters and brothers were spoken of in hushed tones and even *their* gender was questioned, gurumai's parents had no option but to distance gurumai from the rest of the family. When word came that a poet from Delhi was looking to hire a boy servant from their village who spoke the same dialect as his wife, the opportunity was God sent.

When little Lalu was dropped off at the poet's home, he was terrified to see so much furniture, all the lights hanging near the poet's table, and all the pens, and the cold Delhi air went straight for his nostrils and tried to drill right through to his brain. The poet sensed how lost the boy was. He held his hand and told him not to worry.

"I will look after you," said the poet.

But Lalu was not sure what this meant. He thought the poet was teasing him and would send him back to the village because he looked so small and weak. And that would dishonour his family even more.

"I can cook well," said Lalu. "I'm strong also. In the village I used to . . ."

The poet's smile disarmed Lalu, made him stop.

"All you have to do is talk to my wife," said the poet. "Remind her who I am, remind her who she is. I will tell you things each day and you will tell my wife, again and again. I know it will prevent her brain from getting sicker."

The doctors had told the poet that he was mad to think that way—the illness was irreversible. The poet had replied that of course he was mad. He was a poet, after all.

The things that the poet told Lalu made him respect the man. He told Lalu how they had lost their only son in a car accident, after which his wife's condition started to deteriorate rapidly. But instead of searching for flames that could reach God and burn Him, the poet's wife told him to write even more, things about God, good things, mysterious things. The last thing she told the poet was that there was no answer to their pain, and there never would be. That was the first lesson young Lalu learned and accepted, that there was no answer to his question: Why was I born this way?

"*Why* itself is the illness," the poet told Lalu. "Why did my son die? There is no answer. None at all. You see?"

Later, when Lalu mustered enough courage to tell the poet's wife the truth about himself, that he was incomplete, he figured it was safe because she would not respond or tell anyone. But there was a flicker in her eye; it lit up, the way eyes do when they spot the truth. About a year later, when he told the poet as well, the man smiled his kind smile and said, "It's okay." It was the first time someone had accepted Lalu.

The next three years were the best of his life. But when the poet's wife died, something in him disintegrated too. After they burned her body, the poet patted Lalu's head and told him to go to bed; he needed to be alone. When Lalu woke up to urinate, he noticed that the table lamp was on. The poet's head was on the table and he had slit his wrists. When Lalu looked down at his own feet, he saw that he was standing in a pool of blood. Gurumai told Madhu and the others that for years she did not wear red nail polish because looking at her feet reminded her of that night.

There was an envelope on the table with Lalu's name on it. Lalu could not read or write, but he knew what his name looked like. The poet had shown him the letters several times. "It is your face on paper," he had said. "You must know." Lalu's face now contained a thick bundle of rupees. If Lalu woke up the other servants, he would never get to keep that money. They would accuse him of stabbing the poet, too. He had no choice but to run.

But where to run to?

He was now a muscular youth with nowhere to go. And for those with nowhere to go, there was only one city. "She is mother to all," the poet used to say. "The dreamers, the losers, the rejects, the ugly and the beautiful, the legless, the penniless, the runaways, the forgotten—she will take them all, but there is one thing she asks for, just one thing that you must possess for her to accept you."

"What?" Lalu had asked.

"Guts," the poet had said. "Bombay wants your intestines."

So he caught a train to this mother city and found his way to Kamathipura. He later liked to say that the hijra within had guided him here, to Hijra Gulli itself, but this was not so. Exhausted, he could not bear to walk another inch, so he snuck into the hutch of a horse carriage outside Bombay Central station and let it take him where it pleased. It turned out that the stables were on Bellasis Road, a street that ran parallel to Kamathipura. Bellasis Road was where the Arabian mares were kept, pets of the British women who sat on them and went for gentle strolls with parasols attached to the saddles to prevent their cheeks from getting red. Others, less adventurous, had horse carriages made for them, symbols of love from their lovers and husbands, each one more ornate than the next. After India got her independence the British sold their mares to the locals, who in turn used the carriages for commercial purposes. The first two faces that Lalu saw up close in Bombay were those of white horses which had just come in after a long ride along the coast of Marine Drive. Their slobbering tongues were the warmest things he had felt against his palm, and they comforted him as he spent that first night in the hay.

Even today, the stables were still around. So was the poet— on gurumai's wall. Not in a photograph, but in a sketch made from gurumai's memory of him. She had asked an artist to do it for her, one who sketched criminals for the police. This was long before Madhu's time, but it was said that gurumai had described the poet with such love that it brought tears to the artist's eyes and he refused to take even a paisa from her, and from that day on, he stopped drawing criminals for the police.

Today, the guts that Bombay required were still strong within gurumai although her body was waning. She tried to be in good spirits. Her back was erect, she seemed to be pain-free, and her silver hair was shining. This was something Madhu could not understand. Perhaps it was the advantage of refusing to see the doctor. It was best to be blind to the symptoms of your illness and weakness. That way, they had no power over you.

"Can you hurry up?" gurumai asked Sona. "Or are you waiting for your balls to grow back?"

"Sorry, I thought . . ."

"I can do puja with one hand and collect money with the
other," she chided as she continued circling the poet's picture
with the incense stick.

Sona, along with Bulbul and Devyani, was a badhai hijra. She
and her sisters showed up at weddings, uninvited mostly, sang
and danced—their performance generating the gift of fertility
for the newlyweds—and bowed before the family patriarch,
who gave them a cash gift that could run into high denomina-
tions, especially if Sona decided it wasn't enough. Sona's talent
on the drums was matched only by her ability to negotiate—
she did not hesitate to take a man into the corner and sweetly
threaten to lift her sari and expose her barrenness for all the
wedding guests to see. The inauspicious act did the trick at
weddings, and the trio would usually be offered food and sherbet as well as money.

If they were on a household visit to celebrate the birth of a
male child, which was the other duty of badhai hijras, any stin-
giness would result in Devyani putting her hand on the child's
forehead and uttering a vitriolic curse for this male to turn out
just like her: impotent and seedless. Once wallets opened, so
did Devyani's heart, and then Bulbul would take over and bless
the child, reverse the curse, and promise the father that the child
would do him proud by spawning a few macho mards himself.
She was the sponge that sucked away any feminine tendencies a
male child might have.

On some evenings, when the wedding party was large,
Tarana and Anjali tagged along as well to add glamour and

class to the proceedings, or so they themselves proclaimed. Otherwise they sat at home and looked pretty until 7:00 p.m., when they lay down on bunk beds and let the city's lunds enter them. Middle-class wives who refused to part with their precious arseholes did not know that Tarana and Anjali were providing that service to their husbands. At a thousand rupees per shot, they were a premium product, and they charged an even higher fixed rate for the whole night. It was always better to be bought for the whole night, because at the most, the man would take them twice, and so drunk was he by the second time, he would not be able to locate the arsehole. Tarana and Anjali would simply give him the illusion that he was penetrating them by letting him slide back and forth between their legs. It was a trick the hijras used and enjoyed; it was their little joke on the male species. Whenever the rest of the hijra community—the ones who only begged or blessed newlyweds for a living—looked down upon the dhandhewalis, the hijra prostitutes took solace in the fact that they were capable of tricking men, making them limp and powerless, even if for a few hours only.

According to the hijra code, those hijras who did sex work were prohibited from living under the same roof as the badhai hijras, but gurumai paid no heed to rules; in her mind, they reeked of hypocrisy. If the hijra community refused to acknowledge that prostitution was the chosen profession of some, what sense did the rule make? Plus, she had told Madhu, Hijra House was not a *roof*. It was an entire world, and she its central sun.

Right now, her burning glare fell upon the cash that Sona presented to her. "Not bad," said gurumai, counting the money.

"But there should be more."

"There's another hijra gang that has been making the rounds in our area. No one will give money twice to us. They say we have already collected."

"They have to be fakes," said gurumai. "No real hijras would dare to come in my area."

The fake hijras were also known as "berupias," cross-dressing men who still had their genitals. They had no business posing as hijras but had discovered that it was a lucrative side income. Even if men had been castrated and were eunuchs physically, it did not automatically mean that they were hijras. Castrated or not, the hijra was a state of being, a space that the members of the third gender navigated and that was mainly defined by the guru-disciple relationship. One had to be initiated into a particular gharana, one of seven hijra households, by a guru. To be a true hijra, one had to undergo a series of rituals and familiarize oneself with hijda-pan, the hijra way of being.

Madhu had caught one of these fake hijras about a year ago. The signs had been evident: She did not know the name of her guru or what hijra household she belonged to. And the charlatan had not known how to respond when Madhu spoke in Farsi, the secret language of the hijras, a strange mixture of Urdu and Hindi that had nothing to do with the Persian language. Also known as "Ulti Bhasha," it was an upside-down tongue that had been devised by the hijra gurus ages ago, similar to the code priests used in places of worship so that the average pilgrim could not decipher what they were saying. While the code had been developed by priests so they could ply their trade, the hijras went one step further: they used it for protection.

Madhu could see the frustration on gurumai's face. If she were even half the hijra she had been ten years ago, no imposter would have the courage to enter her domain. She was counting Sona's money again, ruminating. These fake hijras were making holes in her pockets.

"I have made business cards," said Bulbul.

"Hah?"

Bulbul handed gurumai a laminated card with her passport-sized photograph on it. It carried her name in Hindi, English, and Marathi, along with the name of her gurumai.

"All of us can have these made and hand them out . . . so if anyone comes to collect, they can match the face," said Bulbul.

Gurumai chortled, a piggish snort that made everyone else gather around the business card. On the back, Bulbul had printed, "BEWARE OF FAKE EUNUCHS."

"Maybe you should put a photograph of your arsehole instead of your face," gurumai said. "Because that's how most men would recognize you all."

But then gurumai could see that Bulbul had made a genuine effort, and perhaps it was not such a bad idea after all. So before Bulbul tragically retreated to the bathroom, gurumai turned to Roomali, who was next in line to hand over her earnings.

Roomali had her head down. Her days were reserved for learning English and how to read and write Hindi. She had already succeeded in writing words such as *pen* and *sun* by copying them down from her textbook. She wanted to adopt a child of her own someday, and in moments when she was feeling low, she would write the word *mummy* a hundred times. This was one of those moments. As lean as the very roomali rotis she was named after, she stood still, a forlorn silhouette, her previous night's mascara smudged with tears and the morning's deposit of mucus. She gave gurumai a couple of crumpled notes that she had crushed in her nervousness. Gurumai did not say a word, which was perhaps even more humiliating for Roomali than if she had been mocked. She had not lived up to her potential, the way gurumai thought she would, and that sentiment cut through the silence loud and clear.

Madhu quickly moved in to take Roomali's place. Madhu, once the jewel of the brothel, was now a mere beggar. The day her gurumai relegated her to the streets, five years ago, to compete with legless men, widows, and pickpockets, she knew she had reached a low point. Hijra gurus also made pojeetives do begging work. It was an unsaid rule: when hijras were too sick and ugly to fuck, too weak to sing and dance, begging was their only recourse. By demoting her to the streets, gurumai had made Madhu feel like a pojeetive even though she wasn't one.

Gurumai wasn't surprised when Madhu handed her the initial payment from Padma. It was far, far more than what the others had collected.

"Where's *that* from?" asked Bulbul.

"Kutti, tera kaam kar," said gurumai. "Stick to your task."

From each bundle of cash, gurumai kept half. The rest she handed over to the respective earners. That was how the tradition worked. Fifty per cent of the disciples' earnings went to the guru. It seemed steep to some chelas when they first entered the clan, but the payment included food and rent, and spiritual guidance from gurumai. More than anything, it was the semblance of a family they were paying for, and the comfort that when they fell ill and were old and infirm, they would never be alone. "And don't forget the police," gurumai always reminded her hijras when they—especially Tarana and Anjali—bitched about giving up half their money. "Who will protect you from them? Only I can oil them, line their pockets with hash and cash, so that they will leave you to your work."

Madhu went to the dressing table that she shared with Bulbul and put her money in there. Out of the corner of her eye she spotted Roomali stuffing a meagre amount into her English textbook. Madhu took a couple hundred rupees from her share and slid them into Roomali's hand while no one was looking. She winked at Roomali, whose tiny eyes widened in eternal thanks. Roomali did not know what to say, but even if she did, Madhu would not have heard her. She had already sped out the door to feed the parcel.

Downstairs, the morning's rhythms gave Madhu a sense of calm. The laundryman was hanging white shirts to dry, the scavengers were on a smoke break after scrounging through the night's garbage, and temple bells were sounding, their shrill rings jolting Madhu into walking faster. She had told the priest she would come meet him, so the bells were like the ring of a mobile phone, a where-are-you call. She entered the temple and collected a cloth bag from one of the devotees. The knot was secured tight, and the form of the thing inside the bag was long and coiled and it thrashed about from time to time to show its displeasure.

Her next stop was a toddy shop. She paid the man, removed the marigold that adorned the mouth of the bottle, and gulped the white ferment down. Breakfast done, she hurried past the Khubsurat Beauty Parlour, remembering that she needed to get her eyebrows done. The parlour had a new sign up: "Beauty

Class (only for ladies)." Outside Padma's brothel, a new DVD store had opened. Inside, boys were watching an action movie on the computer screen. Distracted by a car explosion, she stepped on a discarded blue shirt with blood stains on it before she rushed up the stairs.

This time when Madhu went through the trap door, the parcel was awake. Good. Madhu doubted whether the parcel had slept even a wink since she'd last seen her. That was the purpose of the statement Madhu had left her with: "Now think about what you've done." It disoriented the parcels completely, made them think they were here because they had done something wrong. They would recount the last few days that they had spent with their mothers and fathers and look for signs of anger or disappointment from either parent that would help them identify why they were being punished to such an extreme. But they had done nothing, and when they could not find a reason, it drove them crazy, and they could not hold down the smallest morsel of food because their bellies were so full of guilt.

The parcel was holding the cage bars, shaking them, and for a second she looked like a possessed little thing. Human beings were all the same, reflected Madhu, no matter where they came from. Under duress, all were animals, trying to flee with the same clumsiness. The begging and pleading had begun. Madhu did not look at the parcel's face; she didn't have one as far as Madhu was concerned. As the parcel's voice rose, Madhu stayed completely still. But in staying still, in trying to block out the parcel in front of her, the only place available to Madhu was the past. She remembered her first parcel, and the second, and how they had come to her, and why she agreed, rather *chose*, to do this work.

She thought of it as an act of compassion.

In her heyday, when she was put on display in Hijra Gulli on the veranda of the brothel, lit up like a bird in a cage, her skin smoother than anything in the vicinity, she'd had a young cop as a client. He was a junior constable who paid her on time, was respectful, and had a wife. Madhu took a liking to him because he never fucked her in anger. He did not treat her arsehole as a complaint box for his furies and failures, as most men did. But then one night he blew her apart, which was fine—once was okay—and she was getting paid, so who was she to talk about quality control? It was what he did after the sex that got to her. He sobbed.

He had been asked by his superior to conduct a raid on Padma's brothel. And so he had, swift and silent as a knife in the night. His superior told him he was not to harass Padma; the raid was simply a formality, for there was "pressure from above." But what he found there made him faint in rage: a girl, about nine years old, talking to herself, locked up in a cupboard. He took her back to his station, and his superior said, "Good work. I will handle it." So the girl was fed and the young cop was told to go home. The next day, he found the girl in the lock-up. She was in a cell by herself so no one could harm her. But why were they not trying to find out who she was?

The answer came in the form of Padma, who walked into the station as though she was the girl's grandmother and took her back to the brothel. No reports were filed, nothing. The young cop received his share of the bribe, which he had to take if he wanted to keep his job. "This girl, she has gone mad," said the young cop to Madhu. "They even know her name: Nilu. She used to be able to read and write. Now she has lost that.

The whole time in the lock-up, she kept scratching the wall. I have a daughter. She is only one year old, but I wish she had never been born."

For the first time, Madhu did something without gurumai's permission. She went up to Padma and introduced herself. She looked like she was on fire and her reasoning was just as searing. "We are all women," said Madhu. This made Padma sneer, but that was okay. "Each time a man rapes a girl, he is raping you, he is raping me," said Madhu. The facts were simple: Almost every brothel madam had been raped in the past. That is why they were able to do this work. It had happened to them, they had survived, so there was no reason the girls would not. Rape was like the common cold. You had to catch it at some point.

"What do you want?" Padma asked.

"I want to take the power away from the men."

"Without men, this game doesn't work," Padma replied.

"They are destroying the girls."

"Why do you care?"

"I used to be a boy once," said Madhu. "But in my heart, I was always a girl. And it is men who fuck us up. It is men who make us who we are. But you are not interested in my life."

"That's right," said Padma.

"Then I will say this: it is bad business. That girl, Nilu, has lost her mind."

The mention of Nilu's name made Padma take notice. She sat up a bit straighter. "How do you know her name?"

"It doesn't matter, Padma Madam," said Madhu, offering respect because it would be unwise to get too much of an edge. "All I'm saying is that the girl will be of no use to you now. No man wants a crazy, even if she is underage."

"I'm listening," said Padma.

"Madam, I will keep men in this game, but I will use them differently. I will use them in such a way that the girls won't lose their minds."

"Does your gurumai know you are here?" asked Padma.

"No, but I'm hoping you will speak with her," said Madhu. "And whatever I make from parcel work will go to gurumai."

Madhu knew that money would keep gurumai happy. The fact that Madhu was wanted by Padma might make gurumai appreciate Madhu even more.

"Fine," said Padma. "The next time a chhotti batti comes, I will send for you."

A girl was not called a "parcel" then. The code name was "chhotti batti." Madhu did not know who had coined the term, but "little light" did not sit well with her. It meant that the light in these girls was being snuffed out, and Madhu's aim was to somehow keep even a tiny spark alive. Not a spark of hope, not at all, because that was the deadliest of sparks, but something, a small, good-for-nothing spark that would prevent them from going completely mad. So she had replied to Padma, "Yes, call me when the next parcel arrives." It just came to her, that word, and perhaps there was a better one out there, but it was her first contribution to the game.

Madhu knew she needed to have a game plan, one that made business sense to Padma. The brothel pimps—not the clients—were the ones who inflicted the most damage, so Madhu had to keep them at bay. To train the girls, the pimps burned their soles with hot irons. Madhu explained to Padma that dainty parcel feet were a delicacy for men. They should be left untouched. When vaginas were burned with cigarette butts, marks were left there as well, and while drunken men did not care about aesthetics, the girls developed infections that would render them unfit for consumption. Thus, step by step, Madhu appealed to the common sense in Padma, and even though Padma knew what Madhu was doing, something within her thawed, and just an ant-sized piece of her allowed Madhu in.

"As long as the girls listen, I don't care what you do," Padma said.

Obedience was paramount. The pimps prepared the parcels for whoredom by plundering them beyond belief, turning them into vegetables. But if they were meat, meat they would remain, thought Madhu. She wanted their minds, not their bodies. It was only through their minds that she would be able to access them at a later point. If the mind was yours, the body could be made to withstand any indignity, she figured. Hope was taken away through the body, but it could be reinstalled through the mind at a later point, if required. But how to discipline them without raping them? How to scare them without thrashing them?

The pimps did not realize that because they tortured the parcels so much, the parcels began to prefer their cages. The only time they were let outside was when they had sex with a client, so the cage was home, the dark sanctuary where the parcels found relief. They adjusted themselves to their new domain quickly, the way tiny animals did, sensing the danger outside, realizing that the cage was their friend. The bars were trying to keep them in and safe, just like the arms of their own mothers and fathers who had tried to protect them but could not. At least, that is what some parcels believed.

When Madhu finally got the call from Padma that a new parcel would arrive in a day, she still had no answer as to how she would train them without physical violence. Yes, she could disturb them psychologically, but not too much because the mind was the very thing she was trying to save. She lay in the dark that night, listening to gurumai's snoring and thinking how much it reminded her of her father, that deep, disgruntled growl voicing itself against the world, even during sleep. When he was a boy, the young Madhu had imagined that his sleeping father was not human. His skin was so smooth and oily, completely hairless. By day he was a harmless, well-mannered history teacher, but by night he was a bald snake hissing away at the injustice in his own life, and just before he plunged into the deepest sleep, he let out a final hiss, the way a wick was extinguished, water over dreams. As Madhu lay awake beside gurumai's bed, her father's memory made her shiver. Then it made her shiver again, this time with excitement. Her father had shown her how to train the parcels without laying a finger on them.

When the parcel finally stopped howling, the silence brought Madhu back to the present. But as soon as the parcel saw that she had Madhu's attention, the countless questions began all over again, begging questions, cries for help that fell upon Madhu's skin one after another: "Who are you? Why am I here? There is a mistake. Where am I? Please, please, please." Most of these pleas slid off Madhu's sari on their own. The few that remained she brushed off with a flick of the wrist.

"There is no use screaming for help. No one will help you."

"Please . . . ," said the parcel. "Please . . . let me go . . . I want . . . to go home . . ."

"This is home," said Madhu. "If you want to be happy, you will listen to me. To listen to me, you have to be silent. Do you understand?"

But the parcel did not. She had a new burst of energy, fresh grief and fear, and she let out even sharper howls and sudden sobs that echoed in the loft.

Madhu took the cloth bag that she had picked up from the temple on her way to Padma's. What lay inside was still, but it was breathing. She did not want to alarm it: if it started thrashing about in the bag, it would be hard to contain. She needed to be calm. Madhu shone the flashlight on the cloth bag. The moment the parcel saw the bulge in it, like a long, slender stomach pressing against the cloth, she became quiet.

"I want you to remember this," said Madhu. "Remember this, because from now on, each time you scream, each time you disobey me, I will make you go through this again and again."

The parcel was fixated on the mouth of the bag. As Madhu opened it, she placed it between the cage bars and let its contents slide out, as though she was pouring oil into the cage. What slid out wasn't oil, but it was just as slippery, and when the parcel heard its voice, she let out a wild shriek and begged for mercy, as her skin was covered in something truly living. It was trying to tell her something; it was speaking into her ear, telling her to be quiet, but the parcel failed to understand, and she continued to scream. So it left her ear alone and slithered down her neck and back, and it touched so many parts of her that she thought there were three or four nightmares in the cage when all along there was but one.

4

Whenever Bulbul cooked, she tied her hair back in a bun and blasted the radio at full volume. Madhu was at the other corner of the brothel, pressing gurumai's feet, but the crackle through the speakers still irritated Madhu. She knew Bulbul believed that someone was sending her messages through the radio. Bulbul had a lover once, ages ago, and when his family members found out that he was seeing a hijra, he was prevented from doing so. Bulbul believed that each time a certain song was requested on the radio by a caller, it was on behalf of her ex-lover, who was telling her to hold on. She was the ultimate romantic: imbalanced and delusional.

If love was making Bulbul imbalanced, gurumai was caught in the grip of the latest disease to have captured Kamathipura. Madhu believed it would result in more casualties than anything the area had experienced thus far. It would be more lethal than the disease that made the pojeetives.

It was called real estate.

For years the people of the city had fought over space. Which had been fine all this while, thought Madhu, because the poor were used to sleeping within inches of each other. So what if someone's arm touched another's face or someone's knee poked someone's stomach? The poor needed warmth, didn't they? But then the country had opened up her legs to the world, and everyone and their father wanted to slide in. Now, the middle class and the rich were battling it out. Bombay had been stretched, forced to reach Malad and Mulund and Borivali. In the city itself, the slums needed to be cleared in the name of civic duty. The homes of all the people who worked as drivers and cooks and watchmen and servants in the houses of the rich and not so rich had to be broken; they had to relocate. *Send the Bangladeshis back. Why are the Biharis here? Maybe the government should issue visas for this city. Maybe the . . . wait a minute. What's this place?*

Madhu imagined a builder looking at Kamathipura and his mouth watering. Something was making him hard and it wasn't the prostitutes. Acres of land in the heart of the city? What had once been a phantom, barely recognized by government and civic authorities, a place where only crows and cats cleared the garbage each morning, was seen to occupy a prime position on the city map. The builders started hounding the landlords, who then began courting the tenants as though they were hot brides. Some fell for the bait and began to vacate. An agent was currently spinning a similar yarn for gurumai, except that gurumai was no tenant. She owned the damn place. Madhu massaged gurumai's feet and kept her ears open.

"Umesh, we are happy here," said gurumai. "I have told you that already."

"But I can make you happier," said Umesh.

"I'm old now. If my disciples are happy, I'm happy."

"Then do it for them. Sell it for them."

Gurumai indicated for Madhu to press her feet harder.

"You know how I bought this place?" she asked.

"You borrowed money from Padma," said Umesh.

"That's what everyone thinks," said gurumai. "But I did not borrow money. I borrowed her influence. Money I already had. A local gangster had his eye on it. I went to Padma and she sorted it out for me."

"Why are you telling me this? I'm not forcing you to leave. I'm making you an offer."

"If it wasn't for Padma, I wouldn't even meet you. But I understand that your grandfather was the one who lent her money when she was setting up. So in a way she is indebted to you, and I to her."

"That's how things work around here. We do favours for each other."

"Then let me do you a favour and show you around," said gurumai.

She adjusted the key around her neck, spat her paan into a spittoon, and got up.

"Come," she said, and gestured toward the stairs.

Was gurumai taking him upstairs? The rooms up there provided not even the remotest comfort.

Gurumai opened the door to the kothi, and Umesh was made to stare at twenty bunk beds, small dingy holes, some with caged fans, the kind found on local trains. The lower bunks had wooden footrests, and each one had a nylon string from which a curtain hung, a curtain that had once been white but was now puddle brown.

"This is where the sex happens," said gurumai. "Not just hijras, but female prostitutes also, those who are too haggard to be employed by any brothel. They rent a cubicle out for almost nothing."

The place had an overpowering odour, which Madhu noticed only because of the way Umesh stood. She could see he was trying not to let it show.

"They may have just one client for the night and earn enough to recover the rent money and perhaps eat one meal," continued gurumai. "I sometimes let them stay an extra day because otherwise they have to share the footpath with a dog or rat."

Madhu glanced at the far corner where she used to work. She'd had her own section with a bed and curtain to cordon off the star from the ordinaries. She'd even had a wash basin and clean towels, a small mirror, and a hook on the wall for men to hang their clothes.

Next, gurumai took Umesh to the sickroom. It was where the pojeetives were kept. Thankfully, there was only one in the sickroom right now. She was middle-aged but her body was crumbling at a rapid pace. When gurumai entered, the hijras who were looking after the pojeetive stood up in greeting. These were hijras who had been blacklisted by their gurus for misdemeanours ranging from abusing or assaulting a guru to quietly slipping money to the very families that had disowned them and left them in the gutter. The list reached all hijra leaders with alarming accuracy and speed. No longer affiliated to any guru or household, the outcastes were secretly taken in by gurumai on the condition that they nurse the pojeetives, or any hijra who was old and ill. They made their money by prostituting themselves in the bunk beds next door. It was the only way. If they begged on trains or asked shopkeepers for alms and were reported to their leaders, it would be the end for them. Until they had enough money to pay the fine to re-enter the community in front of a hijra committee, the bunk beds were all they had.

"Come," gurumai whispered to Umesh. "Meet her."

"No . . . ," said Umesh.

She took Umesh's hand and led him to where the pojeetive lay. The tired figures of eight hijras loomed around him. Madhu knew some of them well; others were just silhouettes she had seen over the past couple of months. A hacking cough broke the mood, and Umesh skittered away like a bird upon hearing a loud sound.

But the cough was not from the pojeetive. She was totally still, so thin that she might as well have been skinned; layers of life had been removed from her. Her body was wet from sweat and she was shivering. Even the slightest touch of a cloth upon her skin made her bawl—such was the burn she felt upon touch. Seeing her made Madhu wonder what the point was, why God would allow such a worm to develop. The only answer was that at least there was an end. The pojeetive worm was saying, *Come home. Suffer quickly, quietly, bravely, and come back fast.*

Gurumai made Umesh bend down. A white cake had formed around the hijra's lips, frothy bubbles, some of which had dried at the corners of her mouth. Gurumai took the dropper that lay beside the hijra's head, dipped it into a bowl of water, and pressed it until it was bulbous.

"Make her drink," she told Umesh.

She handed the dropper to him. Madhu could see that this was something he had never witnessed: a few square feet of intense suffering, the plundering of the human body and spirit, a few square feet of sheer courage, a hijra's refusal to expire, a tiny lamp in prime property. Drops of water fell into the hijra's mouth, but she did not know it. Her eyes were closed but her mouth was slightly open, the gap between her lips forced out of total exhaustion.

With the two of them kneeling side by side, gurumai turned to Umesh. "Do you see why I cannot sell this place?" she asked. "Where will my children go to die?"

Once Umesh had left, gurumai told Madhu, "After meeting a real estate agent, I'm beginning to like the local pimps more."

Madhu could sense that gurumai was about to go on a tirade. Thanks to Umesh, Madhu would now have to listen to how screwed up everything was from the government to onions, from religion to the peeling plaster on the walls of Hijra House.

"As though our lives are not hard enough!" said gurumai. "Then this lund comes along with his fake smile and offers to make it harder. He's a transparent bra trying to hide a nipple."

Madhu cringed upon hearing that word: not *bra* or *nipple*, but *transparent.*

Because she knew that she was no different than Umesh. At any moment, the secret she carried within her would spill out and be visible to all. She had not told anyone about it, and especially not gurumai. If her current work with the parcel was shameful, what she had been doing for the past few years, surreptitiously at night, was even more so.

Bridges. Her secret was her addiction to the city's bridges.

Many of the bridges in the centre of the city ran parallel to buildings, so close that Madhu could stand on one and see straight into people's homes. A few years after the JJ Bridge had been built, long after the tired motorists of the city had begun treating it like some sort of salvation, Madhu had begun using it too. After that, the Kennedy Bridge, Grant Road Bridge, and the Bombay Central flyover had made her habit spin out of control. Standing on bridges, staring at the people in the city's buildings, became her smack, her ganja.

When gurumai had exhausted herself with her outburst, Madhu stepped outside to clear her head. Her feet took her past Underwear Tree, toward the very bridge where her habit had begun. It was the bridge of her childhood, and from it she could see the building in which her parents still had their flat. Both were alive. Her father was in his seventies now, her mother was a few years younger, and the son that God had given them was breathing too. She had not seen her brother's face up close since leaving home long ago. The thought was terrifying. But she had seen his form. Now she stood where the shop Geeta Bhavan used to be, in the exact spot where she had been rubbing the sticky juice of gulab jamuns on her thigh when gurumai had first spotted her.

Madhu stooped under an old rusty tin roof. Geeta Bhavan had shut down years ago, and all that remained were cement bags strewn on the ground, old newspapers, pieces of wood, and a weak barricade to demarcate the property line. There was a new ATM just a few feet away, and a modern American-style hair salon, but Geeta Bhavan itself, once crowded with the happy hum of housewives and servants and taxiwalas, was now just a hollow frame, sharing its emptiness with the flats above it. Madhu imagined it was haunted now by the ghosts of men and women who'd died of diabetes. She felt the anger of the ghosts who had eaten too many sweets; all they could do now was rustle old newspapers like the wind. Once upon a time, Madhu had thought her father would join them, but it turned out that the man was so bitter, no amount of sugar could kill him. He would die of old age, she guessed, peacefully in his sleep, giving others around him the illusion that he had led a good life. As for Madhu's mother, when she met her maker, she would be charged with cowardice and choosing one child over another.

Tonight the lights were off in Madhu's childhood flat. She trudged toward the bridge that went up toward Diana Cinema and Tardeo Circle and started to cross. She knew exactly how many steps she needed to take before she had to stop: forty-seven.

She was on her fifteenth step now, the spot where the banana seller stood. She bought a banana for four rupees, and by the time she'd unpeeled and eaten it, she had reached the forty-seventh step. She stopped and looked over the side at the lane below the bridge, which was full of tailor shops. Not a soul was around. The signboard for Champak Tailors had not changed in years. Champak specialized in Punjabi suits and school uniforms. Madhu's father used to take him to Champak, and he would always tell the man to make Madhu's shorts long so that he could wear them for the next three years. The waist was to be kept loose too, for the same reason. Madhu's dream had been to have Champak stitch a dress for him, not some stupid school uniform, so he'd always eye the dress cloth in the shop window, the Punjabi suits on display, the glitter of stars caught on cloth.

On Madhu's twentieth birthday, she had fulfilled that dream. She went to Champak in all her hijra finery: new bangles, a nose ring, a sari blouse that showed off her midriff—her bosom was supple enough for her to know exactly how much to pull in and how much to jut out. She told the tailor that she wanted to have a Punjabi suit. She thought he might ask her to leave, which is why she went just before closing, when no customers were around. But no, he took her measurements with his tape just as he had when Madhu was a boy, made notes in his ledger with his half-chewed-up pencil, adjusted the glasses on his nose when he checked her bosom, and gave Madhu a furtive glance of approval. Then he asked for an advance.

Madhu paid in full. At the time, her arsehole was a cash crop. When Champak asked for a name to write down in his ledger, she said, "Madhu."

"Don't you remember me?" she asked.

Of course Champak did not.

"Madhu," she repeated. "Rathod Sir's son."

Champak was speechless. It did not matter. Madhu's idea was not to scandalize him; it was to humiliate her father. The next time her father came to Champak for Madhu's brother's uniform, Champak would tell him about Madhu's visit. That would be enough.

Before Madhu left, she told Champak, "Make sure you keep the length exact. Don't make it long, like my shorts."

Then she winked and walked away. It had been one of the great moments of her life—if she could call her days and months and years a life. It certainly didn't seem like one when she stood on a bridge alone, like she was doing now, and ate a banana for dinner because the mere sight of her childhood home and her brother's clothes hanging outside to dry were enough to cramp her belly. No, what she had could not be called a life. It was one long stretch of chutiyagiri. A highway full of roadside stalls where the only food served was rejection.

Madhu was not only a glutton for punishment; she was a fraud. One of the first things demanded of hijras when they were initiated into the community was that they sever old ties, physically and emotionally. They were trained to shut out their mothers and fathers, brothers and sisters. The old life was old skin, and only if they shed it would their true form reveal itself.

It was invigorating, in the beginning. It was what Madhu had wanted, and there had been fresh petrol in her legs and heart, churned out each day by the desire to never see her family again, to cause them pain, the way they had her. But the petrol had long ago run out and her tank was dry. All that remained was an exquisite self-loathing.

Now, instead of a human being, there was a soft, ungainly pulp standing on step forty-seven on the bridge whose name she knew and wanted to change. It had the worst view in all of Mumbai: the view of a building called Shakti. Madhu could still see herself walking out of that building, two years after she had first met gurumai and the two hijras. As she stood on the bridge, she saw her twelve-year-old self again.

Her twelve-year-old self stands at the circle just before Underwear Tree, staring at three irresistible figures. She knows what they are. By now, her father has called her a hijra several times—meaning everything from freak to coward to effeminate disgrace. The three hijras share a beedi. One mouth to the next, like close friends.

Madhu crosses the street and follows them. He has no idea why. He just knows he must.

They stop at a shop that sells motorcycle seat covers. A variety of seat covers hang on a wall: silver, blue, yellow. The one that catches Madhu's eye is a leopard skin seat. Gurumai strokes it while the shop owner hands her money. Gurumai closes her eyes and seems to be praying over the seat cover. Then she blesses the man and they move along the street to where women make cane baskets. One of them is chopping the cane with a small handsaw. Another sharpens the cane with a knife. Madhu knows this area is forbidden. He has been told by his father never to go there. "Don't even *look* there," he has told Madhu. But Madhu has seen his father take this route on his way to the college.

Madhu has never walked on his own this far away from home. He hears his father's words again, "Don't go this side," but he twists them, or lets one word drop, and hears, "Go this side." Madhu is enamoured with the way the three hijras walk; no one he knows can sway their hips that way. Like the pendulum of the clock in school, those hips never swing even an inch more or less on either side.

As he walks farther, everything comes rushing madly toward Madhu: goats covered in sawdust from the lumber mills; cats licking their way through tiny piles of garbage; a public urinal near a wafer shop, one smell destroying the other; a mosque bluer than any sea he has seen; fat women with thick eyeliner, brushing their teeth with black paste; doctors' dispensaries with open sitting rooms and sick women sleeping on benches. All of these things move toward him. No one cares that he is here. No one's eyes are on him. He is free to walk here. He is not being watched. But he has lost the people he was following. They are no longer visible, and he does not know where he is or for how long he has walked. He turns around but cannot see the way home. Then he bumps into someone. She looks at him. And he stares at those lips once again.

She looks at Madhu again, closely. Madhu has changed since she last saw him. He has grown taller. She stares at his legs; they are the best things he has.

"Chickni," she says. Then she turns to the others. "Do you remember this one?"

But the other two don't. Or maybe they don't care.

"What are you doing here?" she asks Madhu.

"I . . ."

"Tell," she says.

"I'm lost."

"Lost?" She grins. "Where were you trying to go—school?" The other two cackle.

"Come sit with us," she says.

"No, I have to go."

"But you don't know the way," she says. "Sit."

She points to an old wooden bench. It is one of three at a chai stall.

"Cutting," she tells the man who is brewing tea in a kettle with bruises all over it. She pats the wooden bench and Madhu sits next to her. She puts her arm around him. He shivers from her touch. When the chai arrives, he cups both his palms around it for warmth even though it is May. She asks where he lives. Madhu's father has told him never to tell strangers anything, but Madhu gives her his exact address. She asks if he has any brothers or sisters. Madhu tells her about his brother. She asks what his mother does. Madhu describes how his mother used to stare at the picture of Shiva all day and pray. Now she has stopped praying. She cooks and cleans and looks after his brother.

"And your father?" she asks. "Why do you hate him?"

"I . . . ," Madhu stutters, astonished.

"He's the only one you haven't spoken about. That's how I know."

His father thinks Madhu has failed him. Madhu is not the son he wanted. Madhu's walk is strange. He doesn't have friends. Once his father took Madhu to see a movie, just the two of them, upon the insistence of Madhu's mother, and when Madhu's arm touched his on the armrest, his father moved it away. When his father drinks, with every out-breath there are silent curses and questions to God about Madhu's . . .

"Go on," she says. "About your what?"

"Nothing."

"About the girl in you?"

Madhu gulps down the last of his chai and gets up.

"How old are you?" asks gurumai.

"Twelve."

"I can help you understand what you are feeling," she says. "No one else will be able to."

"How do I get home?" asks Madhu. "Please tell me."

He is scared and wants to go back. Even home will do.

"No matter where you go, you will never be home," she says.

For a brief moment, there is sadness in her eyes when she says this. Her gaze is somewhere else. But the fire in those slits returns, and she points to the bylane that Madhu must take to get out of here. As Madhu leaves, she says, "The only place you will ever be able to call your home is where we live. It is called Hijra Gulli. You will find me there in this life but not in the next."

Now gurumai's words rang in Madhu's ears all over again, on step forty-seven.

She had not moved an inch. Her brother had finally come out for his night smoke. He worked somewhere that required him to wake up in the wee hours of the morning. There he was. The sibling whom Madhu had not seen up close in decades. What had they told him about Madhu? What lies had Madhu's father made up? And when would Madhu's mother learn that silence is not golden?

Her brother had been four years old when she left. He was the first one to fuck Madhu up the arse. It was no truck driver or watchman. It was his own brother who took his long, invisible cock of perfection and slid it inside Madhu, inch by inch, each day. He did this when he received hugs warmer than fresh cooked food, he did it when he got fresh cooked food before Madhu did, as though Madhu's muscles were weeds that should not grow, and he did it when he looked in the mirror and their mother combed his hair and forgot Madhu's. He made the mirrors at home turn against Madhu, because every single time Madhu looked into the mirror, he realized it was lying. Those reflections—they were not Madhu. Madhu's brother was the truth, and he the lie.

The hijras who spoke English called it being taken "royally." It meant that everything was lost and plundered. Through that one opening, the entire kingdom was ravaged. It was also called "paani dhura lena," or "to make the water leak out." Madhu's brother, Vijju, dear Vijju, had been the first to make Madhu's water leak, because Madhu had cried day in and day out, realizing that he would never be worthy of his parents' affection.

In this way, Vijju had played an important role in Madhu's continuing affiliation with the hijras after the initial encounter. Madhu found he could not stay away from them, and a few months later, he went looking for Hijra Gulli. The simplest thing, he decided, was to go back to the chai stall. It took him a while to find it. When he asked the chaiwala where Hijra Gulli was, he was told, "I don't know." Madhu explained that he had been here with the hijras some months ago, but the chaiwala said he was busy—could Madhu not see that he was working? Whenever he inquired about Hijra Gulli, the person he was talking to would clamp up as though Madhu had mentioned something dangerous or spat out a contagious bug. So he waited at the corner of Foras Road and Sukhlaji Street. It was the middle of the afternoon. He waited until he saw a hijra. Then he followed her. She was Madhu's compass, and she led Madhu to the abode of the third gender, where the mistakes of the maker were hidden from public view.

Gurumai was outside on a cot, having her calves pressed. There was a chillum in her hand, and when she saw Madhu, she coughed in surprise. She was pleased. Gulab jamuns were served just for Madhu. Then Madhu was introduced to the clan. It was obvious that gurumai was someone powerful. She commanded respect, so when she fawned over Madhu, the others had to as well. At the time, she had more than thirty disciples living with her.

Gurumai told Madhu that she understood his pain, and she saw a good future for him. She would take care of things. Madhu had no idea what she meant. She said that Madhu was an adult now and capable of making his own decisions. But Madhu protested that he was no adult; he had just turned thirteen. So gurumai explained, while gulping down gulab jamuns, that being trapped in his current state meant Madhu had more life experience than most adults, and that he should add at least five years to his current age, which would make him eighteen.

Once again she said, "I will take care of things."

"How?" asked Madhu.

But gurumai did not answer. She explained instead that the Hijra Gulli building was for her family. She was the guru and the rest were her disciples. She thought of them as her daughters. She said that each of her disciples could have her own disciples as well. So each chela could be a guru as well. But she was the overlord of the household, without question.

Madhu asked what sort of work they did. Gurumai replied that they were in the theatre business, and the hijras roared with laughter, cackling and shrieking. It was the truest laughter Madhu had ever heard. It came from deep inside the belly. Madhu felt it was not directed at him, and he bathed in it. For once, he was part of an inside joke, even if he did not understand its meaning. Then gurumai said that her door was always open for Madhu. He was not poor or homeless, and yet gurumai's offer of shelter made sense. She could see that Madhu lacked a mother's warmth and a father's guidance.

"I will be your mai-baap," she said. "Your two-in-one. Both mother and father."

"What do I have to do in return?"

"You'll see," she said. "But don't worry. I will take care of things."

Then gurumai told another hijra to show Madhu around. This one was kind-hearted. Madhu could tell by the way she looked at him that the two of them were going to get along, even though the hijra was almost twenty years older. Looking back now, Madhu was struck by how strange it was that he had already been thinking about getting along, as though some higher part of his brain had known what was going to happen. This hijra took Madhu to a dressing table and made him sit on a stool.

"You're pretty," she said.

"No," Madhu said immediately.

"Just look at yourself," she said. "So fair, so smooth."

Madhu wasn't that fair, but compared to the others, maybe.

"Why aren't you looking in the mirror?" the hijra asked.

But she did not push Madhu to look. Instead, she removed some of the red bangles from her wrist and put them on Madhu, one by one. Madhu's wrists were too slender for them, but with each bangle, he felt as though a holy amulet was covering him, offering him the tenderness that he had been so callously denied. Then she held both his hands and covered his face with them, as though they were playing hide-and-seek and Madhu was being asked not to look. But what she was doing was helping him peel off the shame that he felt. She was unmasking it, and when she said, "Open your eyes," he looked straight into the mirror, into his own eyes. He noticed that his eyes were dark brown, and maybe it was the afternoon sun that was making them glint, but he had never seen them turn this particular shade. Then she looked at his neck and stroked it, as Madhu wanted his mother to do so badly, and he wondered how his mother could be so cold as to stop caressing him just because she had another, healthier son. Vijju's memory brought the ugliness back to Madhu's face, and it must have contorted, because the hijra had to hold Madhu's chin up again, steady him, make him look in the mirror once more. This time, Madhu straightened his back and his neck felt vast, as though a thousand tongues could lick it at once. He did not feel aroused, but joyous, and the hijra must have sensed it, because she kissed him on the cheek and took the bangles off his wrists one by one, looking straight into his eyes as she did so, and Madhu sank into hers. A deep friendship was born there and then, a friendship thousands of years old—they could have been sisters in the same harem or just old men who would have given up their lungs for each other.

The hijra put the bangles back on her wrists and told Madhu that he should go home, but he was to remember how beautiful he was, and that gurumai had great things in store for him.

"You have what it takes," she said.

When Madhu asked, "For what?" she said nothing. Then she told Madhu that she had to leave to meet her lover. Things were getting ugly because her lover's family had found out that he was in a relationship with a hijra. She was scared that it was going to be the end of things. Would Madhu pray for her? But she believed in love more than a prayer, she quickly said. More than anything else, love had the power to make anyone melt—anyone except politicians.

Madhu said, "Fathers too."

"Come by anytime," the hijra told Madhu. "Next time we will powder your face and try eyeliner, okay?" Madhu's spirit soared at the thought. As he got up from the stool, he asked her one last thing.

"What's your name?"

"Bulbul," she said.

Nine bangles on Madhu's wrist had made him feel more loved than nine months in his mother's womb. That evening at home, his father demanded to know where the hell he had been, and Madhu said, "For a walk." He had walked straight into his future.

Hijra Gulli became his haunt. He tried on makeup, learned how to shuffle cards like a shark, chewed paan, smoked beedis until his tongue burned then gargled like one possessed so that no smell lingered when he got home, made lewd jokes, learned about two types of cocks, cut and uncut, understood the differences between a hermaphrodite, a transvestite, and a transgender, and heard gurumai's famous line, "The Third World is not a place, it is a gender." Madhu visited Hijra Gulli in short bursts—a quick afternoon here, a short morning there—but never at night. He was given entry into the hearts and lives of its inhabitants with total generosity, and there was only one room he was never to step into: not the randikhana with its bunk beds, not the sickroom, but the room through which he would later be transported into the Third World—the operating chamber. It was there that he would become a "chhakka."

In cricket, a chhakka is a six; the ball clearing the boundary is the ultimate hit for a batsman. Hijras are also called chhakkas. It was something Madhu never understood, because a chhakka, unlike a hijra, is a *desired* result. So why assign an undesirable such as her that tag? But now from her place on the bridge, as Madhu watched her brother go back inside his flat, the term suddenly made sense. She imagined Vijju, who must be thirty-one years old, returning to a wife and child. Each morning, the five of them would wake up as a family and not even think of its sixth member. She was the sixer, the chhakka, the one they had forgotten.

5

In Kamathipura, a parcel died twice.

The first death was the breaking in. The second, more painful, death happened when the parcel realized that she had been discarded by her own family. That was when survival lost all meaning, and compliance became a sensible option. Anything that happened to the parcel from that point on was perfunctory, as boring as the words in an instruction manual. Of course, when physical death finally came, in the form of disease, old age, or suicide, it wasn't death anymore. It was what the parcel had secretly been working toward.

But no matter how hard the truth hit the parcel, hope had a strange way of creeping back in, and there was a fine line between hope and denial, a line that Madhu herself had walked skilfully. In a parcel's mind, there was always the pathetic notion that her parents would come looking for her. Madhu too still believed that if she stood on that bridge and spoke to her brother, told him her story, he would remember her. She was disgusted that some part of her still longed for her family.

"Do you want me to open the bag again?" she asked the parcel.

She turned the flashlight off. The conversation she was about to have worked better in the dark. The blackness put all the weight on the words, made them land in the correct places—bombs inflicting maximum damage. Bombs worked because no one could see them coming, and the resulting explosion of light was a celebration, the fireworks of success.

"How did you get here?" asked Madhu. She knew the parcel would not answer; the girl was breathing too heavily. The air must feel as if it was closing in on her. The tight space was unfit for anything that breathed, let alone a human being. The smell of piss, acidic and thorny, reached Madhu's nostrils. The cage was an oven, and so far it had baked the parcel to perfection. It was time to call the parcel by her name.

"Kinjal," said Madhu, "answer me."

The mention of her name made the parcel flinch. "You know me?" she asked, with utter, stupid innocence.

"Do you want to get out . . . for some air? If you answer my questions, I will take you out," said Madhu. "Now tell me: How did you come here? Who brought you here?"

"I'm here by mistake. Please, my aunty, she was—"

Madhu cut her short. The sequence of events had to be played out perfectly, even if they came out of the parcel's own mouth. Right now, the parcel was processing events by memory, but her memory was influenced by her belief in the basic decency of human beings. That belief needed to be stripped away.

"Did your aunty bring you here?"

"A man brought me . . . he . . ."

"Think about your village. Think about Panauti bazaar."

How well the system worked, this one that Madhu herself had devised. It was up to the procuring agent to drill the parcel's family member for information, for details that could make the parcel understand that she had *not* been kidnapped. In this parcel's case, her aunt, her father's sister, was the one who had cracked the deal. When Madhu had first come into contact with these minors, long before she started working with them, it surprised her how often it was the women in the family who sold the parcels, and not just the fathers, brothers, and uncles. Women were equally responsible for the whimpering and rotting of their own fledglings.

"My aunty took me to Panauti," said the parcel. "She made me meet a man. He was a nice man . . . He told me I would get a job in Bombay."

This nice man had been chosen because he looked like a trustworthy soul. He was small and non-threatening, spoke politely, and was instructed to never touch the parcel. He told her to stay close and get ready for the journey. Was there anything she needed? At Panauti bazaar, the parcel was bought something, a small gift to lift her up and calm her nerves. For a girl from a tiny village outside Kathmandu, the thought of working as domestic help in a city like Bombay was daunting.

"What did your aunty say when she handed you over to the nice man?"

"She was crying . . . She hugged me . . . She told me to be strong."

Had she looked into her niece's eyes, Madhu wondered. Perhaps she had stared straight into those light brown eyes and asked for forgiveness there and then. It was probably the last time they would face each other. Sure, they might meet again in each other's dreams, but, Madhu thought wryly, those meetings could always be washed away. Perhaps the aunty had wished her niece luck. Then the nice man took the parcel to the border by bus. It was his job to know each and every crevasse on the road that lay ahead, which official to bribe, and which border crossing to take and at what time. All along the journey, the nice man had not touched the parcel. His instructions were clear: even if she fell asleep on his shoulder on the bus, he was to look ahead into the cool distance.

Then, with sleep in the parcel's eyes, they crossed over into another country. How useless borders were, Madhu thought. Wars had been fought over them and yet the parcel's entry into her new country was as easy as a game of langdi. For a change, India did not resist; it offered no red tape. As a hijra, it was more difficult for Madhu to get an ID card than for most, but when it came to the parcel, things were as smooth as lubricant. She slid in and was made to wait in a small room in the state of Uttar Pradesh.

"Tell me about the room," said Madhu. "Where the nice man left you."

This, Madhu knew well, was the stockroom where parcels from Nepal—and from the neighbouring regions of India herself—were collected. They were given a decent meal and allowed a good wash. They could mingle with each other freely, because all the parcels had been fed the same story: they were en route to Mumbai to work in factories or as domestic help. Some of them even had sisters or cousins waiting for them in the city, so they would have no problem adjusting to a new place. After they had rested, they were made to stand in a line according to their age. All virgin maal, from nine to twelve years old, they were now examined by new men, given a health check of sorts. During this time, a parcel's instinct might kick in, but ever so gently. She might feel uneasy with the manner in which these new men look at her, the way their eyes scan her body. These were the dalals, the agents whose job it was to choose a particular piece and decide where it would go and for how much. An auction took place in an adjoining room. Whoever paid the best price got the fattest chicken.

"Did you feel . . . the man who took you by train was a nice man?" asked Madhu.

"No . . ."

"Did he touch you?"

"No," said the parcel. "But I was scared of him."

"Why were you scared? Did he hit you?"

"He told me that if I asked for my aunty once more, he would throw me off the train."

"Did you ask for her after that?"

"No."

"Why not?"

"He would push me . . ."

"No," said Madhu. "That's not why."

"He put my head out of the door."

"But why would he do that? Why didn't your aunty make sure he was nice to you?"

"I don't know . . ."

The parcel let out a heaving sob that was less sound, more chest.

"Where did you sit on the train? Was it with other people?" asked Madhu.

She gave the parcel time to settle down, for the spasms to calm. After a minute or so, she asked the question again.

"I was sleeping on a bag . . . behind wooden crates . . ."

"Could anyone else see you?"

"No."

"Were you hiding from other people?"

"Yes . . ."

"Why were you hiding? Had you done something wrong?"

"No, no . . ."

"Who was this man?"

"I don't know . . . He sang a song to me . . . but I did not like it."

"But songs are good," said Madhu. "Everyone likes songs."

"He played with my hair . . ."

After two days, the train came to its final stop at Chhatrapati Shivaji Terminus in Mumbai. Madhu scoffed when the parcel told her about the "big station." It reminded her of the same stupid awe with which Madhu's father called it a "World Heritage Site." Her father had been so impressed with the British that he was still buckling under the weight of the architecture they had left behind. Built in the late 1800s to celebrate the Golden Jubilee of Queen Victoria, it had carried her name for over a century and contained a number of gargoyles frozen in cement, perched ominously high near the clock tower, ready to pounce upon the unsuspecting public at night. A few years ago, the gargoyles had watched as Pakistani terrorists created mayhem, wielding AK-47s like children playing with water guns at a school picnic. Madhu was sure that her father, the sad purist that he was, would have rued the desecration of a World Heritage Site more than the loss of lives. What would he say to the fact that his beloved train station was now the final point of disembarkation for thousands of trafficked girls? How would he respond to that?

At the terminus the agent would have kept an eye out for four women who scanned the platform, looking for men like him. These women worked in conjunction with the railway police to intercept the agents and the maal they were transporting. This recent development was a minor hindrance, but the agents had figured out a way to use the hordes of people who alighted from the train as camouflage. Considering that the station was the final stop for local trains as well as the ones that machined in from the farthest corners of the country, it wasn't hard for the agents to become part of someone else's dream, to attach themselves to a family for a few precious minutes. Once they were out of the station, Kamathipura was just twenty minutes away by taxi.

"Who is Sharu?" asked Madhu.

"My aunty," said the parcel. "You know her?"

"The nice man knew her name, and he gave her name to the man who brought you here by train . . . Do you see what I'm saying?"

It was hard to see in the dark. The dark was for realizations that occurred involuntarily, the way heart valves opened and closed.

"You were told you would work in someone's house as a servant," said Madhu. "Who told you that?"

"My aunty."

"Does this look like someone's house?"

"No . . ."

"Do you think you have come here by mistake?"

It was the final question Madhu asked each and every parcel. There were no mistakes in Kamathipura. Things were topsy-turvy, yes. NGOs did the work of the police, the police did the work of the underworld, the underworld governed the place, children looked after their drugged mothers, and trap doors slid open in roofs. But nothing was a mistake.

The cage itself was a carefully constructed thing. It was a perfect piece of architecture, for it did not cater only to the body. The body was confined within it, but its purpose was to allow the parcel to encounter her own mind, up close. The more the parcel's mind tried to fathom the body's current predicament, the less successful it was, and eventually the brain, tired of holding on, would let go of its own past, like a hand letting go of another from the edge of a cliff, no longer having the strength to retain anything, letting the other body dive into the abyss and disappear.

An hour later, Madhu opened the trap door and helped the parcel down the ladder. So far, the parcel had been cooperative, which meant she had to be aptly rewarded. The reward was a tour of the brothel and a trip to the toilet. Being cooped up in a hot box had made the parcel lose all equilibrium. Coming down a ladder was too much for her, especially when it was the very first movement she was permitted outside of the cage. Madhu had to hold her, steady her walk. The parcel had not been fed since she had arrived, and she was dizzy. But it was still too early for food. Things had to be given to her step by step.

The third floor did not have a toilet. For that, they would have to go down to the second floor. It was about 10:00 p.m., and business was at its happiest. The guard was attaching a fresh garland to the iron grille. He was the pundit of the floor, trying to keep things festive. Two prostitutes walked toward Madhu and the parcel without giving them a second glance. They seemed to be chagrined about something. The parcel could not get out of the way in time—the corridor was too narrow—and one of the women bumped into her and muttered something. Madhu figured their mood had to do with none of the rooms being free. The women must have had clients, but if all the rooms were occupied, they would have to wait.

The door to one of the rooms was slightly ajar. Madhu stopped outside it on purpose. She did not ask the parcel to look; she knew that the parcel's own fear and curiosity would make her take a peek. Inside the tiny room was a tinier bed where two bodies could barely fit. The deed done, the man was buckling his belt while the prostitute adjusted her blouse. She shouted out for the attendant, a teenaged boy, and asked for a box of tissues. The prostitute had done her best to make the place feel homey. Above the bed, in a small alcove, stood a single rose in a plastic vase as narrow as the stem of the rose itself. The rose bent over the mouth of the vase like an old man, so tired it wanted to fall onto the bed.

Most of the other doors they passed were closed. All that could be heard was the occasional thud of bodies hurriedly navigating cramped spaces, and spasmodic male voices. At least those were the sounds Madhu caught. The parcel was probably tuning into sounds from the outside, trying to make sense of a grinding mix of car horns, drunken laughs, women's shouts, and shrill bicycle rings. These sounds lulled most of the residents here to sleep. It was when things were too silent that one had to worry. It might mean that a client was covering a prostitute's mouth with one hand, muffling her agony, while holding a burning cigarette to her inner thigh with the other, slowly moving upward and inward. Noise was good.

The parcel tried to close the door to the toilet but Madhu stopped her. When she squatted to urinate, her thighs were trembling out of sheer weakness. Madhu had to support her once again. She was allowed to wash her hands and face. She drank some of the water in quick gulps, then washed her feet. She was taking her time. Madhu let her. The parcel was doing anything to delay going back to the cage. That was good. It had all been done swiftly and with minimum physical damage.

There was no doubt that what each parcel went through was as traumatic as experiencing war or famine. But Madhu knew she made their suffering less. She gave them a discount. She believed that what she was doing was humane. Half of the money she made from parcel work went to gurumai, and Madhu's share went directly to the parcels for food, medicine, clothes, and sometimes toys. She did not keep a single rupee. For the sake of this new parcel, she was glad she had not lost her touch.

Now that the parcel had drunk water, she needed air. She needed to experience the open world again so that the cage would seem deadlier upon entry. Up one floor Madhu went, until they were on the roof of the building. Padma's watchers were in place, surveying the streets below, keeping an eye on their workers. The women below were not minors and they might have been cage-free, but they were not permitted to move beyond a certain point. They were allowed to stand outside the brothel entrance only so as to draw men in. If they walked even a few yards away from their designated spots, the watchers considered it a sign of escape and swooped down on them, licking their lips in anticipation of the beating that would ensue.

On the roof, the parcel was high enough to get a bird's-eye view of Kamathipura but low enough to smell the gutters. It was the ideal place for her to get an understanding of the topography of her future life. Madhu made her stand near the parapet: first, she would see the back lanes, the spaces between the brothels. Here were garbage heaps that rose three to four feet high. A rat was chewing on a used condom. A crow pecked at something and then let it go. Plastic bags, stale food, sewage, black mulch—it all collided here, much like the sounds did on the street. This filthy bed was deceptive in its softness.

"A girl once jumped from here," Madhu told the parcel. "She thought she could land on the garbage and run away. But she broke her leg instead. They let her remain there for two days."

The parcel turned away. Madhu next led her to the front, where the fourteen lanes were lit up like necklaces. As a young and beautiful hijra, Madhu had foolishly thought that she could use her body to conquer these lanes. But now she had come to loathe the very body she had once thought had saved her. The way it changed shape, without warning, sickened her. It did as it pleased without her permission. Recently, as she had distanced herself from it, denied it the care it so desperately needed, it had revealed further cunningness. The guile that had lain coiled inside it like an intestine was slowly manifesting itself in defeated lumps on the face, on the belly, in discolourations on the arm. But Madhu refused to buckle, to pay attention, for this was just a boring new form of treachery.

It might be too late for Madhu, but she would teach this parcel how to separate herself from her body. She would teach the parcel how to forget that she was human. The body was the enemy. The more you loved it, the more you thought of it as a part of you, the more it blackmailed you.

She looked into the distance at the rest of the city, which kept on functioning as though the red-light area did not exist. It made Madhu wonder about Bombay: Was it more hijra than city? Confused, lost, used by all, looked after by none, she could wear a flower in her hair, but the stench would never leave. Every evening when Madhu watched the red lights snap on and the women and hijras trawl the streets for their livelihood, she knew that Kamathipura was more real than anything else, and that none of its citizens, madams and brothel owners included, were doing sinful work. Not at all.

"We are doing *your* work," she whispered to the people who lived in the buildings that so proudly defined the city's skyline. She could say this with conviction even when there was a ten-year-old girl beside her—*especially* when there was a parcel beside her—because the parcel was proof that prostitution was essential. Without it, the streets would be unsafe. That was the common belief. Wasn't it? That without the flesh trade, people would take flesh without asking? But, scoffed Madhu, contradicting herself, has anyone asked *whose* streets would be safer? As long as the people outside of Kamathipura were not harmed, what happened inside the cages was justified. It prevented rapes. But in order to prevent rapes, parcels were being torn from their homes and raped every minute. One child needed to be kept in a cage so that another could go to school. It was the way the city worked, the survival of the privileged and selfish. Madhu felt anger surge through her. If only she could emblazon the skyline with it; then everyone would see how warped the human mind is. How blind, how bent, how convenient.

Madhu looked through the trees and caught the outline of a statue of Jesus. Freshly whitened and lit, he stood with his arms outstretched high above the convent school walls and looked away from the brothels, just like everyone else. He too had turned his back on Kamathipura; he was facing the future, looking to the high-rises that were sprouting directly opposite him. The only comfort his arms could provide was as a resting place for crows, and even they knew not to stay too long. Even they could smell his disappointment with the people of this city. He looked bewildered by his own ineffectiveness. On the cross no longer, he was free now, but his arms could heal no one. That must be why he was hiding behind the trees. Madhu smiled.

Just when she'd figured that the parcel had had enough air and was about to take her back to the cage, the roof had unexpected visitors. One of the watchers brought a line of girls up for some recreation. These were the older parcels, about twelve to thirteen years of age, who were still held in captivity but were veterans of the sex trade. In three years' time, the new parcel would be a veteran too. After being broken in, she would, on average, service ten clients a night. Even if she were sick for sixty-five days of the year, or if there were floods, or riots, or not enough clients, she would still work for three hundred days each year. She would still service three thousand men in one year, including repeat customers. After three years and nine thousand customers, she would be considered rehabilitated—totally seasoned. She would understand that there was no use in escaping and would be willing to work hard to make money for the pimps and owners. There would be no need for unnecessary burnings and beatings. She would be cage-free. Madhu understood the inevitability of it all.

All she wanted to do was train the parcels not to fight back. Fighting back was like trying to punch the dark. Eventually, one had to stop punching and learn how to see.

"Come here a minute," Madhu said to one of the girls who had joined them on the roof. Madhu had picked the most rotten of them all, the most eaten up. She came to Madhu, but not before she glanced at her watcher for permission. Madhu offered the girl a Shivaji. She lit it hurriedly and inhaled deeply, as though she were inhaling love. Her hand was shaking—she could not steady it—and the shivering lit end of the beedi gave the impression that a firefly was hovering.

"Timro naam ke ho?" Madhu asked the girl in Nepali.

"Aapti," said the girl. "My name is Aapti."

Madhu knew the parcel was watching the girl's shaking hand, the nervous dangling of the arm that was not holding the beedi. It was horizontal, parallel to the ground, suspended as though it was broken. Madhu did not care if the two of them spoke. She simply wanted the parcel to know that this girl was from Nepal too. She wanted the parcel to observe the state the girl was in. There were dark circles under her eyes, and her face was so tired it reminded Madhu of the way the rain lashed the side of buildings and made them lose all colour.

Aapti's hand might be shaky, but her look was not. She stared directly at the parcel.

"You're new here?" she asked.

The parcel slowly nodded. She clearly could not understand how this girl was speaking the same language as her. Aapti looked so different. Madhu could tell that Aapti was twelve, just two years older than the parcel, but they seemed ages apart, separated by a time difference that only Kamathipura could create.

"Come," said Aapti. "Come with us."

She straightened her hand out for the parcel, offered it with a tenderness that took Madhu aback. When the parcel refused, Aapti let the beedi drop to the ground. She took the parcel's hand in hers and led her to the other girls, who were now seated in a row against the terrace parapet. The watcher was administering drugs to them. When the girls got too catatonic, when the cage fever was so high that even the beatings were of no use, the girls had to be given opium. It was mother to them. They suckled to it, were grateful for the care it provided, and continued a lifelong relationship with it. Over time, they would change mothers and move on to heroin for further love and guidance.

The parcel stared at the line of dolls, all in the same position, knees to their chests, waiting for their turn.

"You will be okay," said Aapti. "Don't worry. You'll get used to it."

Madhu stepped in. She had not expected Aapti to try and calm the parcel or welcome her into the fold. That was Madhu's job. The parcel needed to believe that everyone else in the brothel was her enemy. If she did what she was told, Madhu was the only one who could provide her with relief. Aapti's show of kindness, no matter how irrelevant, was a hindrance. Madhu steered the parcel away from Aapti, but then she spoke again.

"It's best not to fight," said Aapti. "Look what they did when I fought."

She lifted her dress, without any self-consciousness at all, and revealed her stomach: a round red mark the size of a cricket ball, the skin rumpled like milk when boiled.

"You're so pretty," Aapti said. "Don't fight."

Then she let her dress fall and in a flash forgot about the parcel. She took her place in the line. The fear of not getting her dose was far greater than anything else. Madhu watched as the parcel followed the movements of Aapti's jangling arm. The sudden jerks, like those of a person trying to swat a fly, seemed to shake the parcel up more than anything else she had seen so far. Perhaps, Madhu thought, this was because Aapti was close to the parcel's age. She could smell the damage.

"Why does she have black lips?" the parcel asked Madhu.

Madhu was surprised; she was so used to seeing the girls with it on that she never gave it a second thought. The black lipstick wasn't really lipstick—it was a thin paste, a creation of Kamathipura itself. No one outside the fourteen lanes ever wore it.

"She has made them black," said Madhu. "On purpose."

"Why?"

"Does it look nice?"

"No," said the parcel.

"So think. Why would you want your lips to look bad? Why would you do that to yourself?"

The parcel was processing Madhu's question. She looked at the girls again. In the dark, their faces were shadows. This gave their lips an even grimmer gloom.

"They make it taste bad. They make sure their lips taste bad," said Madhu. "What do we do with our lips?"

"We eat . . ."

"We eat . . . We chew with our teeth, but what are the lips for?" She blew a kiss toward the parcel, a soft air kiss, rare in these parts. "You see? They don't want to be kissed on the lips. So they make their lips smell. They make their lips ugly."

The parcels never washed their mouths. They cleaned their bodies from time to time whenever they got the chance, but the mouths were theirs, theirs alone to keep dirty. It was the only way they could preserve some part of themselves. It did not prevent men from mounting them, or from tasting them no matter how sour, but it was a deterrent. On any given night, even if it worked once, it worked.

The appearance of these girls was a sign, thought Madhu. She had not meant to do it quite yet, but she would explain to the parcel what her future prospects were. The nature of the place itself, that it was a brothel, was something the parcel would learn naturally, through simple osmosis: the rooms, the men, the smells, the closed doors, the guards, and above all the flesh and skin that was packed within the building permeated through anyone, even the most innocent of minds, and educated them within hours.

Yes, Madhu decided, having these girls on the roof, with neither star in the sky nor cloud, nor the slightest breeze or drop of rain—just hot stagnant air—meant it was time for the cold facts. She would tell the parcel that she had been bought—for fifty thousand rupees.

A thought came unbidden: goats cost more.

During Bakri Eid, goats were sold at a premium, after taking into account their health, weight, and beauty. Sometimes the shape of their horns gave them extra oomph, sending their price to almost two lakhs—four times that of the parcel. But the goats were eventually sacrificed. The parcel would live. Madhu wanted the girl to know this. And for one so young, she needed to start to be acquainted with old age, which crept up so silently, with the grace of a dancer, even though its onset took away all grace, all romance, all movement. Fifteen years from now, at the age of twenty-five, the parcel would feel old. She might not need dentures, or see her hair falling in clumps on the floor, but her bones would ache. After twisting and turning in a cramped space night after night, she would turn arthritic. But she would live. Just like Madhu did.

6

It had been a good night. Madhu had put the parcel back in the cage. She had fed her too, but instead of eating, the parcel had started screaming and could not understand why her screams had no effect. Madhu could tell that her screams were coming from a place she had never known before. She kept looking behind her, something Madhu had not witnessed with other parcels. Did she think there was someone in the box besides her? Another girl, ten years old, also screaming?

When the parcel was tired of screaming, she ate.

Now Madhu was home. Tarana and Anjali were curled up against each other. It was about 2:00 a.m., an unusually early night for the two top earners. In her sleep, Tarana leeched on to Anjali, trying to suck some of her natural beauty. Gurumai was tossing and turning in bed, searching for a position that would give her minimum discomfort. Madhu would have no problem sleeping tonight. She could feel herself falling, the body melting into the floor. But Padma's private mobile phone buzzed its way into her dreams. Not used to having two phones, Madhu at first thought it was someone else's.

"You need to speed things up," said Padma. "My client wants to move things faster."

Padma's words made Madhu feel cold, as if a chill had suddenly crept inside her body and refused to leave. Perhaps it was because she had been taken unawares, in her half-sleep. She got up and went outside as Padma continued talking.

"My man at the station tells me that they're planning on doing a raid. This time it's not just to complete a quota. This new ACP is hell-bent on cleaning the area up . . . Suddenly they are waking up . . ."

Naturally, thought Madhu. Before, property prices in Kamathipura were lower than a pimp's IQ. Now, in the name of real estate, the police would make a few arrests and save a couple of underage girls. They'd work with the government for the betterment of the citizenry.

"The new ACP does not tell his men any details about a raid. It could be tonight for all I know. You need to get her ready."

"But I need time. I need more days. There is a method."

"If I get caught, I may not be able to bribe my way out. Do you have a method for that?"

Madhu put the phone down, grabbed a biscuit packet that had been left on the windowsill, and walked to Padma's. Biscuits were the worst things to eat at night, the most unforgiving. They showed up around the waist first thing in the morning. Good thing she no longer cared.

The parcel had curled into a ball and fallen asleep. Madhu woke her up, gently, and gave her a biscuit. "Eat," she said. "Slowly."

Then she led her down the ladder again, to a floor below. She looked for an empty room. Business was winding up. The room closest to Padma's office did not have a bed. Part of the ceiling had almost caved in, so it could not be rented out. It would work.

"Don't move," she told the parcel.

She went into Padma's office without knocking. She had a job to do. Knocks were for bureaucrats. She would make herself all about action, getting the job done.

"I need one of your men," Madhu told Padma. "There's one in the corridor. I'll use him."

"He's an errand boy, not a pimp."

"He'll do."

The man, in his fifties, was wearing a torn shirt and had stubble so bristly one could clean a toilet bowl with it. Padma called out to the man. She did not use his name, just shouted, "Oi!"

"Is there any alcohol around?" Madhu asked.

Padma handed over some of her own stock. She probably kept it for meetings.

"This is good stuff," said Madhu. "Do you have anything else?"

"Use it."

Only a quarter of the bottle was left anyway. Madhu gave it to the man. He looked over at Padma for permission.

"Drink up," said Padma. "And after you are done with her work, change that damn tube light."

The man stared at the flickering tube light, but it might as well have been his own brain flickering as he tried to fathom why he was being asked to drink. Still, he did as he was told. He drank straight from the bottle but did not put his mouth to the rim. He took large gulps and the liquid didn't appear to burn him. His throat was probably used to it.

"That's enough," said Madhu. She took the bottle from the man and poured some liquor into her cupped palm. Then she sprinkled a few drops on his shirt. He was not comfortable with her touch, but Madhu ignored this and ran her liquor-soaked fingers through his hair.

"Good for the hair?" asked Padma. Even when she joked, Padma did not smile. It was the same dry face with cement cracks.

The man was disoriented. He asked Padma if he should change the tube light now.

"You need to break a parcel," said Madhu.

He looked at Padma quizzically.

"She's ten years old," said Padma.

The man shook his head, shuffled his feet, and shook his head again.

"Morals," said Padma. "Interesting."

"It will take you just five minutes," said Madhu. "It has to be done. Madam will give you five hundred rupees."

The money did not change his attitude. Madhu was impressed. He certainly could use the money, she was sure of that.

"I won't be able to do this . . ." he said.

"You'll have to," said Padma. "Or you'll have to find another place to work."

Madhu could see that Padma was irritated at the man's refusal. It must have made her feel lower than him. A conscience was a dangerous thing to have in Kamathipura. It was looked down upon and had to be trampled, snuffed out as swiftly as possible, the way an honest cop had to be.

"And if you choose to leave, first thing tomorrow morning you will repay the loan I gave you," Padma said.

The appropriate string had been pulled. The man turned to Madhu, waiting to be led to his task.

"Make sure you don't waste time talking," said Madhu as she led him to the room. She herself did not enter. It was imperative that the parcel not see her. The man had to spring upon the parcel out of nowhere. Madhu snuck a quick look: the parcel was standing exactly where Madhu had left her, good girl. The man entered awkwardly. He slid into the room, not knowing where to look. Madhu closed the door on the two of them. These things could not be supervised anyway. But she had to stand outside. It was her job.

She could hear the parcel's cry for help. Then it was muffled. This meant he had put his hand on her. Madhu checked her mobile phone for any text messages from Bulbul. Bulbul loved sending her smiling faces and roses. But there was nothing. The battery was low anyway, so she switched the phone off. Even the phone that Padma had given her needed to be recharged. Both the phones were so small they could fit inside her sari. She wondered what it would be like to have an honest job, a regular one. What if she were a baker or a butcher? What if she were to use her hands to create something that would nourish another human being?

Madhu used her hands in another fashion: to open the door. She entered the room and lifted the man off the parcel. He had an erection and seemed to be enjoying himself. So the bastard had been lying, only pretending not to enjoy young ones. First, Madhu kicked him where he was most vulnerable. The parcel wriggled off into a corner. The man was curled into a ball, just like she had been moments ago. Madhu looked at the parcel. Directly. It was the first time she had made genuine eye contact.

She could see that the parcel did not understand what was going on. But she would.

Madhu slapped the man a couple of times. "Bastard!"

He was in pain and disoriented. Madhu bent down to help him up, and that's when she smelled his breath. It took her by surprise, threw her into a tizzy, and all of a sudden the miserable room turned into the tiny living room where her father sat in front of the TV and watched Doordarshan. Madhu did not want to go there, but the liquor on the man's breath mixed with his own dripping saliva sent her there. She took a step back. The pause meant that the man recovered enough to strike her hard across the face.

"Bhenchoth hijda!" he said.

Madhu staggered, but she coiled back faster than a spring and lashed out at him with her long nails, flailing her arms. Her fingers became needles and one of them got him right in the eye. He moaned, held his eye, and Madhu should have run for cover because the set-piece had gone awry—things had become real. But she didn't run; she stood stock still because the words the man uttered were an echo of the ones her father had once used.

"Hijda hai tu," he had said to Madhu. "My son is a hijda."

Her father had said this under his breath while eating his peanuts and drinking his local booze. He had looked at his wife for support, and she had shaken her head at him—at least there had been some form of resistance from her that night—but that was all. Madhu had longed to take the bottle and smash it in the centre of the room, just to not hear him utter those words. But what could he do? He had been called a hijra, a coward, the worst kind of weakling.

But now that Madhu *was* a real hijra, now that she had accepted her true self, she could fight back. She pounced on the man who was not her father, and also on the man who was. She started pounding him. She sat on his chest, raised both her hands high into the clouds to form a clasped fist, and thundered down on him.

"You're right," she said. "I am a hijra."

It was because she was a hijra that she had more strength than him. She had lost her cock years ago, and with it the ability to ejaculate. When semen is lost, so is strength, or so it is said. But the hijras had pent-up power in cold storage because they had preserved all their semen, kept it all on hold. This moment of fury had thawed Madhu's, and she was grateful that her father was alive, and right in front of her.

"Call me a hijra once more," she said to him now.

Her father mumbled through a mouthful of blood, and even though he didn't say *hijra* again, she punished him, for he was the one who had driven her into the arms of the hijras to begin with. His were the lips through which she had first heard that word, and her breast heaved with such madness that she didn't notice Padma enter the room. Nor did she realize that she had been screaming. A howling spirit trapped in a body she hated sat on top of a body she hated, and Padma was pulling her off the man, who was reduced to a whimper, a wet, scared dog. Madhu gave a blazing smile. Her hair was down, long and frizzy and black, swaying before her eyes, and her bangles were broken, but her spirit was high.

Padma lifted the man and made him leave. If Madhu had been in the Alexandra Cinema right then, people would have thrown coins at her, such was her performance. She composed herself, adjusted her sari blouse. She had temporarily lost sight of her objective, been sidetracked, carried it too far. But perhaps this could turn out even better than expected.

"He'll never touch you again," Madhu told the parcel.

The parcel was still in her corner. She was a stupid moth banging against the wall. Now that the man was gone, her body could not hold on any longer. She released a thin stream of urine onto the floor.

"Are you mad?" Padma asked Madhu. "What is wrong with you?"

Madhu did not answer. Instead she picked up the two balls of paper tissue that had rolled out of her bra and onto the floor during the scuffle. She stuffed them back where they belonged.

"I asked you a question," said Padma.

"You wanted the parcel to be ready," replied Madhu.

Madhu's lips were swollen and they throbbed. She watched the parcel rubbing her own arms and legs. The parcel was trying to scrub herself clean with her hands, lingering over certain body parts longer than others to wash away traces of saliva. Every single parcel did that, but no amount of rubbing could take away the memory of what they had experienced.

In any case, this had been a mere rehearsal. The point was for Madhu to endear herself to the parcel. Now that she had seen Madhu thrash the man who had tried to force himself on her, she would assume that Madhu would help her every single time. But what Madhu could do now was teach the parcel how to *not* resist, to become cold dead weight, lifeless and disinterested, when the man was on top. If the girl was numb, there would be little reason for violence. Resistance brought out the cruelty in men, made them artists who found new ways to inflict themselves on the female form.

The parcel kept moving and every minute or so tilted her head, staring at the floor and then the wall. Madhu knew what she was looking for: a window. Something that opened out into life. From time to time she glanced at Madhu. She did not thank Madhu for saving her from the man, but her manner had changed.

Then she blurted out, "Who are you?"

What she was really asking was: *What* are you?

Who am I? What am I? Those were questions Madhu had asked herself ever since she could form a proper thought, and after all these years, she still became squidgy when she was confronted with them. What should she tell a child? It was simple. You told a child a story.

"Do you know who Lord Rama is?" asked Madhu.

Every hijra knew this story, or had narrated it, and even though it had its link to the great epic the *Ramayana*, the hijras added their own colour of nail polish to it—or remover, depending.

Madhu plunged into the story. It had taken place centuries ago, when the great king Rama was sent into exile. Banished from his kingdom, the much-loved monarch was followed by his people to the banks of a river. This was as far as he would allow his followers to go. The punishment was his, not theirs, and beyond the river, the dark woods beckoned. It would be his home for the next fourteen years. "Men and women," he said, turning to his people, "I want you to go back. Return to your homes." He had to make the journey alone, and no one had any choice but to obey his word.

So fourteen years passed, and Rama became stronger and wiser in seclusion, and when he returned to the banks of the river again, he saw strange beings buried halfway in the ground. Their long hair was down to their waists, and the forest breeze was churning it, making it more alive than bird or beast. "Who are you?" he asked. "And what are you doing here?" The buried ones answered, "You asked all men and women to go back. We are neither men nor women, so we stayed here and prayed for your safe return." Pleased with their devotion, Rama offered them a boon: "From now on, whatsoever you speak, it shall come true."

And that is how men with neither cock nor balls moved from impotence to omnipotence. That is why people believe that if a hijra curses you, you are doomed, and if she blesses you, no matter how the stars are aligned, no matter what your astrologer has predicted, her tongue can make the stars shower luck on you, like divine saliva.

What Madhu did not tell the parcel was what her gurumai had told her. Gurumai had confessed that this might just be a complete concoction; perhaps it was not part of the *Ramayana*. But even though it might have been a fabrication, it was powerful. The hijras had been obliged to keep changing their stories depending on who was in power. When the Mughals were dominant, the hijras were exchanged as slaves, as novelties, and were assigned a value similar to that of gold and horses and land. They were therefore included as part of the booty when a kingdom was lost. But they stayed close to the women and listened for secrets, and they become confidantes to queens, until eventually they rose to the ranks of commanders and diplomats. By carving their bodies, they carved a niche for themselves in both the household and politics. As gurumai would tell her chelas, "Our bodies have been used as lumps of clay. We have been mutilated to serve the needs of men and women. And society thinks of *us* as abnormal. Who is the freak? Us or them?"

When Hindus came into power, the hijras began to flounder. "Until someone had the bright idea of attaching the hijras to that great Hindu epic. I doubt poor Rama ever said those words," gurumai said. But the hijras had empowered themselves, bestowed on themselves the ability to bless or curse—a *Hindu* ability, with Hindu origins.

Madhu had bought the story once. Tonight, in front of the parcel, she needed to believe it again. She could see that the parcel had moved closer to her, not physically, but the story had drawn her in. The two of them were still kilometres apart, but an inch had been won.

"So remember this," said Madhu. "Whatsoever I say, it shall come true. And to you, I want to say just one thing: if you do as I say, you will go through less pain. That is my promise."

Madhu had not sold the parcel a lie. She had told her the truth.

"Now," she said, "let's talk about your name."

"Kinjal," said the parcel.

"I did not ask you your name. I did not ask you your name because you do not have one. Your name is the first thing your parents gave you. And it is the first thing I shall take away. Now your name is Jhanvi. Say it. Say your name."

But the parcel didn't. She needed an explanation.

"Whoever you are, wherever you have come from, you must forget all of that. Your mother, father, brother, sister, everything.

Whatever you were is in the past. From now on, you are my daughter. And as your mother, I get to rename you."

The parcel looked at Madhu for just a second, the way a small animal might, a street cat angry and scared, and then she withdrew again.

"Now I'm asking you again. Say your name."

"Jhanvi," she said softly.

We've begun, thought Madhu. The painting has begun.

"Now tell me your age," said Madhu.

"Ten," said the parcel.

"You are twelve," said Madhu. "What languages do you speak? Do you speak any Hindi?"

"No."

"You will learn."

If circumstances had been different, if Madhu had more time, she would have interviewed the parcel at length. But right now, she had to prevent the parcel from being caught. Madhu's most pressing job was to familiarize the parcel with every nook, every hole, every trap door and false ceiling.

"Come with me," she said.

"Where are we going?" the parcel asked.

"Swimming," replied Madhu.

Madhu could tell that the parcel did not know what to make of her new name. She had come close to realizing what Madhu was telling her, but it was too much for her to digest, so she preferred to remain at the edge of understanding. Even if the name change made some small bit of sense, the parcel had no idea at all why she was being made to stare at a black water tank on the terrace.

She had already memorized all the passages in the brothel. Madhu had been pleased to find that she was a quick learner—even if it was to be expected. She was eager to please because she had realized she could get something out of Madhu. As a result, the corridors and stairways were now embedded in her brain thanks to Madhu's fierce directions. Madhu's voice was ink making new marks:

This door leads to the reception area.

There is a false ceiling here.

To go back to the staircase, turn left, not right.

Never enter this room. It is Madam's room.

This floor is wooden. If you move even an inch, the floor will creak.

"Get in," said Madhu now.

Madhu slid the lid of the water tank to the side. The tank had been "modified" to Padma's specifications. Its mouth had been narrowed, but the workmanship was so good that the change was hard to detect. This synthetic water tank was the most important object in the brothel. It was the safest hiding place, something the police had yet to sniff.

"Go in," said Madhu.

The parcel tried to climb up into the tank but lost her footing. She held her hand out to Madhu.

"Do it on your own. There will be no one to help you."

After a couple of tries, the girl found the lesions that the modifier had made just for this purpose. Once you knew where they were, clambering up was easy.

"I don't know how to swim," said the parcel.

"Then make sure you don't drown. Don't jump in. It's deep. On the side there is a rung. Hold on to it first and then lower yourself."

The parcel got in, wiggled to the side, and was soon out of sight. "Did you find it?"

"Yes." Her voice echoed in the tank.

Madhu shut the lid. The hardest part, she knew, was staying in there with the smell of plastic. It was like being trapped in a large bottle of mineral water in the middle of the afternoon. The air had a hot, flat taste that made you choke. In the cage, the parcel had gotten used to the air in an enclosed space. Now another element had been added to the mix.

Madhu would keep her there for a while.

The parcel could choose to drown herself—Madhu had considered the possibility—but drowning required a lot of depth. The water took you on a journey, allowed you to sink more and more, and the travelling itself made you feel you were going somewhere, to a faraway better place, which made drowning work. But not inside this tank. If she tried to drown herself, her legs would automatically push her off the floor.

No matter how hard the police or NGOs tried to rescue these girls, nature always provided a hiding place, thought Madhu. Previously, when the brothels were informed of a raid, or the watchers saw the police coming, the underage girls were made to climb up on the roof, through a single tile that was removed and then reinstalled. The girls perched there, amidst scattered newspapers and old kites, and the police had never thought to look up until one girl screamed for help. That was when the cops realized that the skies were giving them shelter. Now that the skies could no longer do that, the girls were sent to the depths to hide until the danger was gone. There had been occasions when the police had turned the brothel upside down and could not find a single child. One cop had even opened the lid to the tank, and Salma had laughed at him, just to irritate him and break his concentration. "If I jump in, will you rescue me?" she had asked. Little did the cop know that there was a girl breathing just below him, to the side. The modifications had worked—the mouth of the tank had been narrowed to perfection and the girls turned to fish.

After ten minutes had passed, Madhu lifted the lid and peered inside.

The parcel's dress bloated in the water. "I can see you from here," said Madhu. "You need to hold your dress close to your body. Make sure it sticks to you."

The girl came out shivering. The water was warm, but it made no difference.

"If there is any trouble in the brothel, if anyone ever tells you to run and hide, this is the place you come to," said Madhu. "Do you know who will come looking for you?"

"The po-police," said the parcel through chattering teeth.

"That's right. If they find you, they will not take you back to your family. They will put you in jail. Then Padma Madam will have to give them lots of money to free you. If you get caught, it will be *your* fault. I will not be able to do anything. This water tank is your temple. It is the closest thing to God in this place."

By the time the parcel got out of the water tank, the first light of the day was showing itself. Soft, it promised something new and gentle, but only for the rest of the city. A new day in Kamathipura was just the day before repeating itself with clockwork precision. Shops opened, temple bells rang, children got ready for school, and the men who worked in the sawmills poured mugfuls of water over themselves from huge tumblers. Wearing nothing but their undershorts, they bathed on the sidewalks and got rid of the sawdust in giant splashes, only to be covered in that golden dust all over again.

Madhu had forgotten to carry a towel for the parcel. A mother, she chided herself, would have remembered to do that. "Take me downstairs," she said, and was pleased when the parcel led her there correctly. Good, she had an understanding of the geography of the place. Madhu led her to Salma's room. It was just another tiny cubicle, but it was Salma's. After years of service, she had earned the right not to share it with anyone else. She no longer brought in customers like she used to, but Padma had made it clear that Salma was a lifetime member. This reminded Madhu of her father's college and the professors he used to complain about. They could not be thrown out no matter how outdated and incompetent they were as teachers. It burned his bum, constipated him, and made him cough in fury, until he eventually became just like them, a skeleton in the halls, feasting on the past.

But Salma was not resting on her laurels or taking advantage of Padma's leniency. She worked extra hard, cooked meals for Padma, and even looked after the children of some of the prostitutes while they worked. This morning, she was looking after her own. She was sitting on her haunches in the corridor, hunched over a stove, alongside her three-year-old son. He was an unexpected late entrant into her life. To try to trace the father would have been an imbecilic activity, considering the number of men Salma had been with on a daily basis, and even if she had known who he was, he would probably have beaten her until she got rid of it. Salma was clear that this child, like the one before him, was the only reason she had not killed herself. The rate of suicide was high in Kamathipura, a fact that had prompted Padma to remove all ceiling fans from the brothel. But when the fans were gone, veins were slit—a messier affair. The woman's memory on the ground, so red and wet and stubborn, refused to leave even after the body was disposed of.

Salma could not afford to kill herself. When she was younger, she had given birth to a girl, and she had sent the child away, just as Padma had, but not as far. There was an NGO on Lane Fourteen, and when the girl was two, Salma strode over there and gave the child up on the condition that she could visit whenever she wanted. It was the best thing she had done in her life, and it made her feel human. Now the girl was sixteen, she could read and write English, and she was on her way to college, which made Salma squeal with excitement.

When Salma saw the parcel, she went inside her room, leaving Madhu to watch over the chai and make sure that it did not boil over. The parcel looked at the bubbling stew with anticipation. Then she lowered her head as though she thought she wasn't going to get any, did not deserve it.

Salma came back with a towel. She wrapped it around the parcel.

"She is also your friend," Madhu told the parcel.

Just as Madhu had not revealed her own name to the parcel, she wouldn't tell her Salma's. Names created familiarity, comfort. The parcel needed to see Salma and Madhu as nameless, faceless walls. Once the parcel understood this, a hundred names could be revealed and it wouldn't matter.

Salma bent down and helped the parcel dry up faster. "Go in and wear my nightdress," she said. "It's hanging."

The parcel looked at Madhu. She was asking for permission

to move. This was a good sign. Madhu could tell when her training was working by the small hints the parcels gave off—like steam, they could be felt but were almost invisible.

Salma stooped over the stove again. An old firecracker now, her gunpowder could explode anytime, make her say the most inappropriate things, but when she cooked or made chai, when she was with her children, she became a different woman. She was no longer the petrol-mouthed shrew who set the Marys on fire.

"We have to get some clothes for her," said Madhu.

"You do that," said Salma. "I have this one to look after today. I am taking the day off . . . mother-son time . . ."

She trailed off, like a song fading away.

Madhu glanced at the boy. When she compared her childhood to this little one's, she felt privileged. Madhu had had a bed to sleep on, in the beginning, until her brother was born. At least she hadn't had to sleep *under* one. The toddlers of Kamathipura were given cough drops to induce sleep, then placed under the bed while their mothers worked right above their heads. Sometimes the children would wake up and crawl out from under the bed, and the clients panicked.

At least Salma's son would get an education. He would not grow up to become a pimp. He came crawling to Madhu and tugged at her sari. Madhu wanted to pick him up but she couldn't. Something stopped her. Seeing that, Salma gave her son a loud, splashy kiss on the cheek.

The parcel reappeared, wearing Salma's gown. It was so long for her that she had to hold it up from the sides to walk. Salma took the edge of the parcel's dress and covered her son's face with it. Then she uncovered it again and played hide-and-seek with him. The little one was delighted.

"Where's Guddu?" she asked. "Where's my Guddu?"

Guddu gurgled from underneath the parcel's dress.

"Come on," Salma said to the parcel. "Don't you want to play with him?"

The little boy crawled out from the folds and looked up at the parcel. Madhu could tell that she wanted to lift the boy up; he would be something to hold, something that could not harm her. Maybe she had a brother the same age. Even if she didn't, she needed to feel skin that was warm—the opposite of Salma's and Madhu's.

Madhu wondered how much longer innocence would stay within this boy. It had to leave at some point. But while it was there, everyone fed on it like hyenas—Salma, Madhu, even the parcel. Without realizing what she was doing, the parcel would suck it out of the boy and keep it for herself, store it for the nights to come.

In the afternoon, Madhu left the brothel to allow the parcel to bond with Salma. The parcel needed to be comfortable with Salma; a rapport had to be forged between the two. In case of a raid, the parcel would have to follow quick directions and, more important, once she had settled into her new line of work, Madhu would no longer be there to guide her. Salma would take over.

Madhu needed a break. She had no qualms about who she was now—she had come to terms with her life—but starting this parcel work again had taken a toll on her. On the one hand, she felt she was doing a spark of good—or a particle of good even smaller than a spark—in that she was breaking the parcel as gently as possible, trying to find something to salvage in the gutter.

If Madhu refused to do this work, she would be dishonouring her gurumai. She would be expelled from the community and treated worse than a pye-dog. To re-enter, she would have to pay a fine to the jamaat, the council of hijra elders, which she could not afford, and knowing gurumai, she would ask Madhu to do parcel work again, just to teach her a lesson. The only other option for her was to run away. But where could she go? She could live in a slum. On Tulsi Pipe Road, there used to be a line of hijra dwellings along the railway tracks. Four or five hijras lived under one tin roof. One day, the municipality trucks came and demolished their hutments—just like that, in one shot.

After being displaced from Tulsi Pipe Road, the hijras had to spend weeks without a roof over their heads. This was when the Mumbai rain was more merciless than a Mumbai cop. Some hijras got wet in the rain and never woke up. Madhu did not want to sleep under an open sky, nor did she want to be rat food.

When her brain rattled this way, with thoughts of old age and homelessness, it was a sign that she needed time off. She longed for Gajja. She wanted him to hold her hand. Nothing more. She just wanted to feel the man's roughness against her. She called his mobile, but there was no answer. He must be tending to a patient at the hospital. But what about *this* patient? She could feel it coming, one of those dizzying bouts of self-pity that were so hard to ward off. Even malaria was more bearable. At least with malaria, only the body shook.

She tried him again. No answer. Around her, mobile phones were everywhere. Hearts, brains, and mobile phones—the human body could not function without them. Madhu noted sadly that even the footpath bookseller had a new title, *SMS Se Love*, about a couple who fall in love via text messaging. At the bookseller's feet was an old weighing scale. Some of the pojeet-ives had weighed themselves on it before they knew they were pojeetive, and wondered if the scale was wrong.

Madhu watched a goat trying to wriggle underneath a parked taxi. It struggled to get into the small spot, but finally suc-ceeded. Madhu wanted to join it: she wanted to snuggle up next to it under the car and nuzzle her own beak against its nose. They were both going to be slaughtered at some point. The goat was lucky to go first.

Madhu felt herself sliding deeper and deeper into a hole. The water tank beckoned. Unlike the parcel, Madhu would sink into it and not emerge. The police would find a dead bloated parrot floating on the surface, its beak filled with water, its irrelevant banter gone once and forever.

She shook her head to clear it and picked up her pace. The afternoon heat made snakes of sweat crawl on her back. A gust of burning wind helped her glide through her neighbourhood. When she passed Firdos Milk Bar, the Afghan men barely noticed her. She was so nimble, so desperate to get home. By the time she had reached the kitchen and lit a beedi, gurumai was calling out to her from her bed.

"What's the matter?" asked gurumai.

"Nothing."

"Madhu, how long have I known you?" asked gurumai. "Come." She sat up, feebler today than the past couple of days, and patted the mattress, indicating where Madhu should sit. "Tell me what's wrong."

"Nothing's wrong."

She put her hand to Madhu's chin, just as she had when Madhu was a boy, and raised an eyebrow. It didn't help.

"Where is everyone?" asked Madhu.

The place was strangely empty, given that it was still afternoon. Someone was always lounging around, reading movie magazines or oiling their hair, or tweezing eyebrows and bleaching their stupid face.

"They're all out," said gurumai. "I sent them on errands. There's a jamaat in three days."

The mention of the gathering of the city's hijra leaders increased Madhu's anxiety. "But we just had one," she said.

"I got a call from Bindu nayakji this morning. It's important."

"Is there a problem?"

"She said it was an emergency."

Madhu could tell that gurumai did not want to talk more. When Bindu nayakji wanted something, it got done. She was one of seven nayaks, the most powerful hijra chieftain in the city, and her word on the hijra kingdom was final.

"It's good that we are alone," said gurumai. "There's something I need you to do."

Gurumai removed the key that hung around her neck and handed it to Madhu. This was the first time that Madhu, or anyone else, had been handed the key to gurumai's safe. Gurumai wore it around her neck like a talisman, even went to sleep with it. When she bathed, she took it with her. To see her remove it made Madhu uncomfortable.

"There's an envelope in the safe. Take it out," said gurumai.

The envelope was right on top, old and brown, stiff, almost cardboard-like, as though water had been dropped on it and hardened.

"That is my will," said gurumai.

Madhu tensed and clenched her teeth.

"Relax," said gurumai, noticing Madhu's uneasiness. "I'm not going anywhere. I want you to give this to Padma."

"Padma? What for?"

"I know you don't like her. But liking someone and trusting them are two different things. Things are getting dirty in this real estate race. I want to make sure that my will is solid and cannot be disputed. Padma is going to show it to the same lawyer who has made her will. I'm doing this for all of you."

"Yes, gurumai."

"Do it now. And try not to read it. You'll be disappointed."

Once again, gurumai lifted Madhu's chin.

"See? I made you smile after all," she said.

On the way to Padma's brothel, Madhu noticed that a crowd had gathered—labourers, shop owners, pimps, mothers with children in tow who were going home after school. As Madhu pried through the sweaty mass of people, she heard wailing. About ten prostitutes were standing at the entrance to a brothel. Some were sobbing hysterically, one was lying down on the street itself, while the others were babbling away to anyone who would listen.

"Where will we go?" wailed one. "Where will we go?"

It was a mantra that the woman kept on repeating, with eyes half closed, cheeks dirtied with tears, betel juice at the corners of her cracked lips.

Salma was there too, trying to lift the one who had prostrated herself on the ground in a form of protest. Madhu was shocked: Salma was supposed to be looking after the parcel and bonding with her. What the hell was she doing here?

"Where's the parcel?" Madhu asked.

"Resting," said Salma. "Relax, she's safe," she continued, sensing Madhu's agitation. Then she quickly shifted her focus back to the prostrate woman. "They've been evicted. Last week, they were told the building would collapse if repairs were not done, so the landlord gave them money to stay somewhere else for a week. Now they've come back and the brothel is locked up. Choothiya banaya!"

It was a villa-type brothel. The number on the archway was 007, but there was no Bond, no second-grade agent even, to come to anyone's aid. The main door had a shiny new lock on it and wooden panels had been nailed across the windows to prevent anyone from getting in. All the prostitutes' belongings were stacked up neatly outside the main door: steel trunks, one on top of another; three wooden cupboards with so many scratches you'd think they belonged to cats; cooking vessels; plastic bags full of chappals; and makeup kits. One of the cupboards displayed a poster of Shah Rukh Khan, and even he gave a doleful smile. Some of the women already seemed to have resigned themselves to their new fate; they were going through their belongings silently. But the one on the ground was refusing to get up. Salma yanked her arm, but she repeated the same phrase for all to hear: "Now we have nothing . . ."

Salma bent down and whispered something in her ear. The young woman's histrionics began to fade. Slowly, she gathered herself and went to one of the steel trunks.

"Let's leave," said Salma. "Slip away quietly."

"But I need all my clothes. I need—"

"If they see you go with me, they won't let you leave."

"Let me take something . . . please."

Madhu saw how it was breaking the woman's heart to leave behind what had taken her years to accumulate. She pulled herself together and quickly rummaged through her belongings.

A cop arrived, and the crowd slowly receded into their own lives. Nothing was ever their problem anyway; this was just an unexpected piece of entertainment on a sweltering afternoon, Madhu thought. But then, a surprise: the prostitutes were not going to let them off the hook so easily.

"It's bhadwas like you who are doing this!" an older whore screamed, pointing to a couple of middle-aged men who were on a cigarette break. They were part of a small unit that manufactured umbrellas. "You madarchods are fucking us!" Madhu guessed that the men had no clue what she was insinuating. Still, the whore might be old but she was not mad. Gurumai was right: the brothels were being shut down by landlords, and small-scale industrial units were being set up instead. It was impossible to get such cheap rents elsewhere in the core of the city, and so the sex workers were being tricked into leaving.

Madhu watched as the men gingerly threw away their cigarettes and climbed up the stairs to their little workshop, which had once been a brothel. But the old whore would not let them go without a fight. She picked up one of the chappals from the plastic bag, a fat green rubber one, and flung it at the man. Her anger had sharpened her aim: it landed straight on his neck. The man began to abuse her but knew better than to inflame an already injured soul, and slunk back to his umbrellas.

Madhu turned to leave. It seemed that Salma would be occupied for a while, and Madhu was concerned about leaving the parcel unsupervised for too long. But then, a new group entered the fray: Marys armed with pamphlets and good intentions.

"Yeshu ban jao," said one of the Marys to the old prostitute. "Embrace Jesus."

The Mary was accompanied by a South Indian woman, a former brothel madam named Aruna, who had converted to Christianity. The Marys had taken many prostitutes into their fold, and a few of them were "cured," while many still worked. Christianity was the latest craze in Kamathipura. Madhu likened it to the fervour with which bell-bottoms had grabbed the red-light area's thighs in the late 1970s and early 80s. Back then, every young Nepali sex doll in the district owned bell-bottoms, which made her burn hotter in the eyes of men.

Now it was the message of Christ that everyone was wearing. And what a perfect opportunity to convert people into the religion, to help them get acquainted with Yeshu, when they were jobless and homeless and hurling obscenities at the police.

"Don't touch me!" said a prostitute to a cop who was trying to calm her down. "Cowards! You are working for my landlord!" she screamed, pointing to the umbrella factory. Madhu knew she had meant to point to 007. Then, probably anticipating that if she continued to abuse the cop she'd get a tight slap, she became docile: "Please help us. Only you can save us!"

At last, Salma was done waiting. She ordered the young woman to march. She slung a bag over her shoulder, but Aruna stepped in and blocked her path.

"It's not a bad thing that you have lost your home," she told the young woman. "Maybe it's a sign that you must do something else." She held out a pamphlet.

Now that she could see the young woman up close, Madhu understood why Salma had chosen her. She was pretty and would be an asset to Padma's brothel for sure. Salma's intervention was business mixed with a pinch of compassion.

"Take this," Aruna told the girl.

There was a photo of Jesus and a lamb on the pamphlet. A bright light shone from Yeshu's head, radiating in the general direction of the lamb and falling on the hay instead. Madhu wondered why the hay needed light.

"She can't read," said Salma. "You're wasting your time."

"We can teach you," said Aruna. "There was a time when I couldn't read either. Now I can."

"That's great," said Salma. "Now go suck a cock."

Madhu, Salma, and the girl started walking at a brisk pace, but the former madam followed. She sensed that this girl was still young and vulnerable.

"Why do you want to stay in this line?" asked Aruna. "We can help you find good work. I used to be in this line but then I came out of it."

Salma turned to the young woman and said, "When your cunt is as old and shrivelled as hers, you can also leave this line."

Aruna was trying her best to stay calm and focused. "I work at the centre now. I work for Prem Nagar. We are rehabilitating sex workers."

"There's nothing wrong with us," said Salma. "We don't need your help."

"Look," said Aruna. "We have our meetings in a room that is just across—see?"

"Leave us alone," said Salma.

"Maybe she doesn't want to go with you."

"Why don't you ask the girl?"

"What's your name?" Aruna asked the girl.

"Yes," said Salma. "Even I would like to know that."

"Ekta," said the young woman.

"Ekta," said Salma, "do you want to come with me and work, or do you want to go sing bhajans with this woman?"

"We don't sing bhajans. We are Christians. We have prayer meetings."

"Do you serve popcorn also?"

"I'm done talking to you. Let the girl speak."

Madhu watched with a mixture of amusement and sadness. Part of her wanted to rush back to the parcel; if anything happened to her, Padma would skin Madhu alive. On the other hand, this battle between Salma and Aruna was too delicious to abandon. The two women fighting over Ekta—one for her flesh and the other for her spirit—was a reflection of the parcel's current state, the way she hung in the balance. Except that Madhu was in charge of flesh *and* spirit. Because it was impossible to salvage both, she was trying to relinquish one in the hope of preserving even a whit of the other. She wished her task was as clear-cut as Salma's or Aruna's.

Salma squeezed Ekta's hand. "Say what you want. Speak the truth."

"Leave her hand," said Aruna.

"Look, Ekta," said Salma. "You can pray in the brothel also. You can do sex work and, if you like, pray during your free time. But prayers don't fill your stomach."

"We will empower her!" said Aruna. "We will teach her how to stitch, how to—"

Salma cut her off. "You want to be a tailor?" she asked Ekta.

Somehow this helped Ekta make up her mind. "I'll go with her," she said, gesturing at Salma. Pleased with the victory, bristling with energy, Salma decided to properly introduce herself to Ekta.

"My name is Salma," she said. "I'm glad I found you."

Aruna accepted defeat but tried a parting shot: "If you ever need me, I'm—"

"She won't. But if *you* ever decide to start whoring again, I have an empty bed next to mine. In the meantime, say hello to Jesus for me."

Aruna gave Salma a look of disgust. As Aruna retreated to her prayer meeting, held in a small room sandwiched between a cigarette shop and a milk bar, Madhu's attention was caught by a man who was talking to the cigarette shop owner. He had been slyly sipping chai as he watched the prostitutes' drama outside the brothel. It was Umesh, the real estate agent who had recently paid gurumai a visit.

"As if I need *her* to talk to Jesus," barked Salma, pointing at Aruna's back. "As if without *her*, Jesus doesn't love me. If he wants to love me, then love me. I've never lied about who I am." Then she pointed to a new building on Bellasis Road. "It's buildings like this one that are making us suffer. You think the people who will come to live here, you think they are any less sinful than us? The women who sleep in these buildings, they are also whores. How many of them actually love their husbands? How many of them actually *want* to sleep with their men? We both do the same thing. Only I do it better," said Salma.

Madhu followed Salma's outstretched, accusatory hand. In the red-light area, these new buildings were called "The Towers." Many of them were as yet uninhabited, and the dark grey cement walls gave them a ruthlessness that made Madhu queasy. They seemed to grow in the dark, in illogical spurts, seeming so far away from completion one moment and then suddenly gaining height overnight. And the towers were not just in the east; they were coming up from behind Madhu as well, surrounding Kamathipura on all sides, giant sentries advancing, blocks of cement thousands of metres tall with rectangular holes in them for the windows to come. To Madhu, they looked like the teeth of smiling sentries.

Her eyes left the buildings and moved on to something closer, to a notice that was pasted on a wall right in front of her:

Free Bird Treatment Camp
Prabhu Towers 9 a.m. to 7 p.m.
Call us to save the life of birds
365-day bird help line

Suddenly, Madhu started laughing. Right before her eyes, at least ten women had been rendered homeless, tricked into an even darker future, when as tenants, they had had every right to be treated fairly; right before her eyes, a young prostitute had been enticed into a futureless future; and here was some chooth ka dhak-kan, some complete cunt-lid, offering a workshop to save birds.

Birds!

Why not her? What had Madhu done to be overlooked so completely?

Were birds worth saving because they could not tell their stories, tell of the cruelty and injustice they had encountered over the years? Or was it because it was possible to fix them, bandage a wing or two, and then make them fly away, out of one's life forever?

"What's so funny?" asked Salma. "Why are you laughing?"

We cannot be fixed, thought Madhu. And we will never fly away.

7

Madhu handed gurumai's will to Padma, then headed back to the cage. Salma had allowed the parcel to play with her son for a bit, but had then put her back in lock-up. All Salma had wanted was a playmate for her son, and once he had been returned to the NGO, the parcel was no longer needed. This worked beautifully for Madhu: the parcel had been allowed to breathe, then a chokehold had been put on her all over again. When Madhu shone the flashlight on the parcel, she noticed that the soles of her feet were swollen. She must have been kicking the cage bars. But she was calm now, defeated and totally receptive.

"There was a girl like you once, a long time ago," said Madhu. "After just one week, she could not remember her mother's face. Do you remember your mother's face?"

"Yes . . ."

"Touch the bars," said Madhu. "Put your hands on the bars." The parcel was hesitant. Madhu could see she thought she was going to be beaten, but of course Madhu would do no such thing. Beatings were primitive, such a waste of time.

"I will not hurt you. Hold the bars with both hands."

The parcel did as she was told. She gripped the bars tightly, her small fingers encircling them. The parallel lines of the bars in front of her face as she peered through them were much like the two lives she would have from now on—her past and the present—and the two would never meet.

"Each time you think of your mother, I want you to hold these bars and ask yourself one question: What feels more real, your mother or these bars?"

Madhu could see that the question was making the parcel sink. It was travelling down through her body faster than anything she had ever imagined. How far away her old life must seem.

"I asked that girl, 'Why can't you see your mother's face?'" Madhu continued. "She said it was because she was scared. But that wasn't true. Her mother could not show her face to her daughter because *she* was ashamed. Even I would be. Even I would not show my face if I had sold my own daughter."

It was essential for Madhu to let the parcel think about this. She had added another ingredient to the mix, another herb or poison, depending on the way one looked at it. Madhu knew there was no difference between the two. In the right dose, a poison could be used to one's advantage. It was a secret that gurumai had shared with the young Madhu. She used to put drops of a substance in Madhu's eyes to make her pupils dilate, and it had made her eyes widen like legs and flutter like butterflies.

She let this new piece of information simmer inside the parcel for a few hours. And all that time, Madhu sat there in the loft, saying little, allowing the parcel to ask questions, but never answering them. The minute the parcel shrieked or showed signs of hysteria, Madhu asked if she would like a visitor, and the thought of the slithery thing in the cage silenced the girl. At times, she tried to stand up, but the cage did not allow her to do so fully. It ensured that her back was bent, another element of the design that was intentional. If in the water tank she turned to fish, here she was a bent plant, being cut down to size.

Finally, the parcel managed to go to sleep with her arms around her knees, and Madhu was pleased. The parcel had learned a valuable lesson: she was the only person who could provide comfort to herself. Madhu knew there would be times when the parcel's heart would beat madly inside her breast, and she would have to let it go to town. It was best if she understood that anxiety or panic or any cry for help would be met with deafening silence, which in the end would only accentuate the cry, make it all the more ear-splitting and useless.

Madhu could now see the parcel without the flashlight. She enjoyed being cooped up with the girl, and her eyes were gaining the accuracy of a sniper's. She could clearly see the goodness in doing this work. If she hadn't been here, the parcel would be bloodied and bruised by now, with the smell of pimps on her. In Madhu's hands, the lie was being taken out of her—the thought that she would be free anytime soon. That was the true poison. Through the bars, Madhu tried to pet the parcel—not by touch, but with a gentle gaze over the contours of her body. In sleep or in wakefulness, the parcel had someone to share the terror with at least.

———

Around three in the morning, the parcel woke with a jolt. Madhu had dozed off too, on the ground near the foot of the ladder, and the sudden rustle above her head startled her awake. She rose immediately; there was work to do.

After the two of them had a quick chai on the floor below, it was time to go shopping in Barah Gulli. Every Friday, from 3:00 a.m. to noon, Lane Twelve transformed into a bargaining paradise. There were many names for it: Midnight Market, Sab Kuch Market and Chor Bazaar Ka Bhai, or "Brother of the Market of Thieves," which alluded to its more famous sibling, Chor Bazaar, on Mutton Street. Madhu would buy clothes for the parcel at Sab Kuch Market, but for footwear, she would go to another midnight market, the one on Dedh Gulli, which had become a shoe lover's utopia. Madhu smiled when she thought of the Nike Air shoes that Bulbul had bought a year ago—shoes that might have been stolen by professional shoe stealers from outside a mosque or temple in the city and eventually sold to a vendor. The Nikes forced Bulbul to walk faster—she felt she *had* to—and she looked like a demented jogger in a sari, traipsing on the moon.

At the entrance to Lane Eleven, Madhu recognized an old woman who was looking after two children. She was affiliated with one of the brothels, and her job was to keep the children entertained if the clients had no one else to leave them with. There was a younger woman beside her, wearing black tights and a pink top—the last showpiece left.

Madhu turned right to Barah Gulli, walking alongside coolies carrying large TVs in cane baskets on their heads. They dropped them off at a repair shop that had so many TVs stacked on top of each other that Madhu wondered how the owner managed to work on even a single one. At the entrance to the playground, two men lay on a handcart and shared a beedi. Their knees touched, and they both stared at the sky, blowing rings of smoke that disappeared before they could fully form. Here, even smoke had a miscarriage.

As soon as they entered the playground, Madhu could sense that the parcel was taken aback by the commotion. Normally, the place was lit up by halogen lights until dawn, but tonight the lights were not on; perhaps they were not working. All Madhu saw were the beams of flashlights moving horizontally and vertically, directing her to the dozens of vendors displaying their wares. The parcel should have been accustomed to the darkness by now, but clearly she was dazed: she almost walked into a roller on the ground. By noon, once the vendors had left, the roller would be used to flatten out the dusty earth again, leaving no trace of what was happening right now.

Madhu loosened her grip on the parcel to test whether she would let go of her hand. She didn't. So they carried on, walking by the man selling washing machines and old computer screens, past empty glass bottles, the majority of which had once held Chivas Regal and Red Label whisky, and past ceiling fans that lay flat on their backs on the ground. It seemed more and more brothels were taking Padma's cue and removing the most common means of suicide. When the lights shone on the fans, they resembled deformed metal insects that had once been alive. Next came the typewriters, reading glasses, binoculars, world maps, pens, refills, remote controls, gumboots, mirrors—so many mirrors, some with minor cracks, and others just empty frames—harmoniums, and stethoscopes. But the most popular vendor here was the one who sold crutches. He sold them cheaply, but they were sturdier than any house in the area. In a place where beatings and injuries were more common than a sneeze, the support his crutches offered was beyond measure.

Gajja was here too, but Madhu did not go near him. This was business time for him. He took medicine from the hospital whenever he could, especially cough drops and some high-voltage painkillers, and sold them. His clients were mainly prostitutes who were addicted to the cough drops or used them to lull their children to sleep while they worked. Gajja guided them on the proper dosage and what to feed children before they took them. Sometimes the mothers took the cough drops too, and their children would crawl around the edge of the bed, trying to wake them up.

The parcel stopped at exactly the spot where Madhu normally did: the record seller's stall. Even after all these years, Amitabh Bachchan was still the centrepiece. The vendor was a huge fan. His son had worked as an extra in some of Bachchan's films. The vendor had his own flashlight, which he shone on the album covers: *Sholay, Deewaar, Zanjeer, Silsila* . . . *Sholay, Deewaar, Zanjeer* . . . He went back and forth, cover to cover, directing Madhu's vision. Even though he was talking to another man, and not paying much attention, the light fell directly on Bachchan's face.

Madhu was starting to feel displaced by the beam of the flashlight. The record seller was merely using it to light his merchandise, but the brashness of the glare, the nakedness of it, the way it shone like the headlight of something approaching, forced Madhu to turn inward, toward her past. She locked eyes with Bachchan's and thought of her father's radio churning out the tunes of Kishore Kumar and Mukesh—the real voices behind some of Bachchan's lip-synching—woeful melodies filled with loss, or something much deeper than loss: an emptiness so vast that Madhu felt she carried acres and acres of nothing inside her.

With each note, she had imagined being lowered into a coal mine, where the air became closer and only the sound of her breathing remained. She had wanted to cry, scream, anything to get rid of the nothingness, to give it form, but Kishore Kumar and Mukesh stole her voice and only made her more barren.

It was only when the *women* sang that the tears had come. It was only when the women ached for their men that Madhu had ached too. How she had revelled in that ache. How it had lifted her. The despair was so beautiful, it was the most freeing experience she had ever had. It was a glorious stream of tears, from eyes to bridge of nose, until her tears had fallen into another world, where they were appreciated.

Even now, Madhu still played one song from her father's collection in her mind again and again. She sometimes hummed it to herself and only realized she was singing when she was halfway through it. She had seen the entire movie that featured the song only once, but she knew exactly how the hero, Amitabh Bachchan, held the green-eyed heroine, Rakhee, in his arms in a land full of snow. Amitabh told his love, "Sometimes I have this thought that you have been made for me. Sometimes I feel my heart has this thought that you are my destiny." When Madhu had heard those lines, she realized for the first time that a *heart* could have thoughts. That was when she'd had her first longing, not for sex, not for anything dirty, but just to be held by a man. And any man whose heart could think would be the one for her.

In the movie, Rakhee is married off to the character played by Shashi Kapoor instead of Amitabh, and Rakhee sings that same song again on her wedding night, but she is still singing it to Amitabh. Shashi Kapoor does not know this, of course. He is madly in love with her, and she is in love with someone else—which all made sense to Madhu, because love is about *not* having. The moment she had seen that movie, she had become Rakhee, and she imagined herself in pink lipstick, nose ring, and flawless skin, the red vermilion a mad streak of passion running through her forehead, trying to split her head into two because she could not have her man. Even though her husband was holding her, delicately removing her ornaments one by one, she only longed for her lover, and she sang to Amitabh, who was far away, and said to him, "Sometimes my heart has this thought that you were made for me."

Years later, when Madhu looked back on this moment, it occurred to her that even in her dreams, she did not get her man. Even in her dreams, she did not get love. Out of the hundreds of songs that the radio had sent her way, this was the song that had entered her blood and changed it from B positive to O positive. She had become a universal donor, had given herself to all, because she understood that she belonged to none.

Madhu was brought abruptly back to the darkness of Barah Gulli by the sound of a police siren. No—it was a toy jeep a little boy was playing with. The parcel was staring at the boy, who was tugging at his father's shirt, asking him to buy the jeep. His other choice was a toy ambulance. Perhaps it was fitting, Madhu reflected, that they sold police jeeps and ambulances here. One had failed to protect, and the other had failed to rescue.

Suddenly she didn't feel well. Familiar bile rose in her stomach and up her throat. All at once, she felt there was so much acid inside her that if she were to spit it out, she would disfigure the loveliest of faces. She had to get out of there, away from Amitabh and Rakhee, but she hadn't completed her task and bought any clothes for the parcel yet. She simply did not have the strength to shop.

On most days, she managed to keep the piercing reminders of the past at bay by wrestling with them, by crushing them to the ground until they stopped thrashing about and behaved. Tonight, however, the parcel was watching her, and it made Madhu feel uneasy—what if the parcel saw Madhu weaken? It would send the wrong signal. No, Madhu could not allow that. Both master and slave could not be frightened. The parcel needed to be placed back in captivity until Madhu regained her balance.

Madhu turned and was heading back to the brothel with the parcel when she saw Salma talking to a vendor and handing him a huge carton of condoms. This was one of Salma's regular gigs: she would convince the Marys to give her free condoms for the safety of her co-workers, and then she sold them in Barah Gulli. Of course, no one in Kamathipura cared for the condoms, so men from outside the district bought them for a pittance for personal use.

Madhu asked Salma if she would buy clothes for the parcel. Salma shrugged her shoulders and took the girl's hand.

The minute Madhu stepped off the playground, the halogen lights snapped on. She started running.

It seemed to Madhu as if she had been running ever since she was a child. Trapped in the wrong body, she had felt the panic take over time and again; it still did, insistent as ever, rumbling through her like a tabla, *dhakadhakadhaka*. Would it never stop? Was it possible that things were getting worse, that the ruptures in her sense of the present were much larger somehow? The gaps had to be bigger, she thought, for the past to permeate her with such velocity.

Running would not solve anything. Neither would time. Time did not heal. Time was not money, either. It used to be. Now time was wrinkles. Time was wobbly knees. A spasm in the back. Muscles freezing out of shame. Time made Madhu remember more. For forty years she had lived inside this body. No matter how much she accepted who she was, she was still afraid. She was still angry. She still wanted answers.

She ran past the diabetic ghosts who swayed to and fro outside Geeta Bhavan. She could see them clearly, even if they were ghosts, because they were just as scared and angry as she was. They were angry at the gulab jamuns they ate, and they were scared because they no longer had any effect on the living. Just like Madhu. She had no effect on the living. She had no effect on her own family.

She waited on the bridge, past the banana seller, on the forty-seventh step.

Her brother finally arrived, the pathetic little goat. She imagined him with a jutting chin, just like her father's. There he was, sending out cigarette smoke as though it were a coded message to the elite in the city.

Barah Gulli had put Madhu's body on alert. She was hyperventilating. If she'd had a stethoscope to put against her breast, it would melt, such was the heat inside her. She was so heavy right now that even the crutches in Barah Gulli, the ones that supported lives more miserable than hers, would not be able to bear her weight this morning. She knew it was not Amitabh and Rakhee who had put her in this mood.

It was the sight of the bloody flashlights.

———

After she had become a regular in Hijra Gulli, after Bulbul and she had become closer than sisters even, Madhu's father took him to a holy man. This man, Madhu was told, was a great seer. He would be able to provide a cure. No matter how many times his father slapped him when he walked on his toes or giggled with a limp wrist, he could not be corrected. Once, when Madhu had come out of his bath, he had worn his towel around his chest, covering his breast, instead of around his waist. He did it out of modesty, but he also liked the way it made more of his thighs visible. The gesture was innocent, natural, and yet it had earned him a slap. Afterwards, his father decided to take Madhu to the holy man.

When Baba saw Madhu, he held his hand, closed his eyes, and said to Madhu's father, "This boy needs your love. Great misfortune may befall him if you do not look after him." Madhu's mouth fell open. His father asked Baba if he could give Madhu a sacred thread to help him mend his ways. "Change will only come through your acceptance," said Baba. No thread was given.

Madhu and his father walked to the bus stop in silence. Madhu's father did not utter a single word on the bus either. For a few hours, Madhu thought that something would melt in the man and he would treat Madhu like a human being. That night when his father ate, he sat next to Madhu. When Madhu's mother put the first chapati on her husband's plate, as she always did, he broke it in half and gave one piece to Madhu. "Eat while it's hot," he said. His voice was still stern, but Madhu could make out a tremor in it.

As usual, his father was the first to finish the meal, and he rose from the table, put on his spectacles, sat by the window, and stared at the road. This was his silent thinking time, when he'd ruminate about history, his meagre salary, his mediocre students, their lack of discipline, and the politics at the college, which he would then complain about to his wife before bedtime. But that night he spoke: "Madhu, come here." So Madhu joined him by the window. But then his father was silent, lost in thought again. Maybe he just wanted to stare at the traffic with his son, or perhaps he wanted Madhu to go to Geeta Bhavan and get some sweets, even though it was the end of the month, when he was always short of money. Madhu's mother piped up and asked Madhu what Baba had said. And Madhu lied: he replied that Baba could understand the father not accepting the son, but what about the mother? Madhu had never had the guts to tell her how he felt, that after his brother's birth, whatever love had once come his way was gone, directed toward his brother. Whenever he tried to put his head in her lap, she was always holding her other, normal, son.

That night, his mother did something unusual. She put Vijju down and held Madhu close. She told him that he was the first born, and first-borns are precious, and Madhu should never forget that. "Don't take your father's words to heart," she said. "Understand his position. They make fun of him at the college."

"Why?" asked Madhu. He knew why, but he hoped his mother would lie.

She told him the truth. "Because they have seen you. You behave like a girl. We may be poor, but as a teacher he commands respect . . . and you are taking away the one thing that he has. Can you not find it in your heart to listen to him?"

She said this *while* holding Madhu, while mother's and son's bodies were pressed together. In that hug, Madhu was trying to convey all the emotions he felt, and as she spoke, he realized she did not understand him at all and never would. Just then, his father called out to him again.

"Madhu . . . ," he said. "I think . . ." He was finding it hard to speak. "Madhu, I . . . I want you to know that I . . ."

Madhu got up and went to the window. He was willing to wait for his father's words. For the first time in his life, his father was talking to him, man to man. He waited with a patience that could calm any fear.

That was when the lights went out.

His father's face turned dark. It was a power shortage; there had been one a month before too. Madhu's mother got a flashlight and shone it around their tiny flat. It lit the calendar on the wall, one with a precious pink baby on it. Madhu's father, distracted by the power cut, turned away from his son, mumbling about the papers he had to correct.

Fifteen minutes into the blackout, there was a knock on the door. Madhu's mother assumed it was one of the neighbours—the same woman who had come over during the previous blackout to make sure everything was okay. She was a recent widow who just needed an excuse to visit. Without looking through the peephole, Madhu's mother opened the door. The next second, the flashlight fell to the floor and she moved a few steps back. Madhu and his father ran over, and Madhu picked up the flashlight and shone it in the direction of the door.

The beam lit gurumai's face.

"May I come in?" she asked.

Madhu shook so violently, he feared he might cause cracks in the floor.

"Who are you?" his father asked. Madhu could detect the tremor still in his voice, but now there was a new note of hardness.

Gurumai refused to answer.

"May I come in, please?" she asked again.

She was cordial, gentle, and confident. She was so centred, Madhu felt as if a towering presence was standing at the threshold. It was his mother who confronted gurumai first.

"You have the wrong house," she said. "There is no newborn here."

Gurumai looked straight at Madhu. Even though it was dark, even though the flashlight in Madhu's hand was only lighting parts of gurumai's sari, his mother's face, and his father's hands, he knew gurumai had homed in on him.

"I'm here for *him*," said gurumai. "I'm here for Madhu."

Just then, their widow neighbour opened her door, and Madhu's father hurried gurumai in. His need to keep face tricked him into letting a hijra into his home.

"What do you want?" he asked.

"How do you know him?" asked Madhu's mother.

Then gurumai uttered the line that would seal Madhu's fate.

"I know him because he is one of us," she said.

In the short pause between these words and her next ones, Madhu's childhood disappeared. In that short space, a vacuum opened up and swallowed his future. Then he remembered what gurumai had told him almost a year ago at the chai stall: *I will take care of things.*

"You need not worry," she told Madhu's mother. "I am not here to claim him. It is against our code to do that."

"If you ever touch my son . . . ," said Madhu's father, his hand trembling, his face fuming.

But gurumai did not move. She became even calmer.

"That is not your son," she said. "That is your daughter."

Then she turned away and went out the door ever so gently. Madhu saw her walk back through the corridor and turn right, toward the stairs, but he heard no footsteps.

Vijju had slept through it all. For a child who shrieked all day, who was a hyena in the wind, he was too silent, too content, Madhu thought.

That night, Madhu's father drank his cheap liquor in silence while Madhu shivered. When the power came back on, Madhu's mother turned off the lights. The truth was too bright to behold. No questions were asked of Madhu. His mother lit incense sticks and circled the picture of Shiva, clockwise and anticlockwise. The incense sticks were the only source of light, a dotty red glow, but even they were too bright for his father, who got a headache and swallowed his pills. Madhu pretended to go to sleep, afraid that the questions might begin at any minute.

He had been right. As soon as he feigned sleep, the questions did begin. He could hear his parents whispering, not out of concern for him, but because what they were discussing was so private and shameful, they were worried that the wind might carry it to their neighbours.

"I don't know what to do," said his father. "We can't even afford to send him to boarding school."

"It's okay," his mother replied. "It's okay. God will help us. He will change."

"Forget him. What will happen when our younger one is older? No one will marry him. They will see Madhu and decide that both brothers are effeminate."

"I will pray harder."

The next morning, the neighbours came with their questions and concerns. They came as though someone had died. Where was the watchman? How does the hijra know where we live? This is a decent building. We may live next to the red-light area, but *our* lights are white.

These were not questions, but veiled condolences for a failed son, and thin threats. With their clean eyes, they scanned the flat and made Madhu's father feel even smaller. He never let anyone enter his home, and now they had not only entered the flat but had taken a peek into the worst moment of his life.

Madhu was in his school uniform already, so he left. But he did not go to school. That was the day he went to Hijra Gulli, to the narrow lane that would liberate him and make him reborn.

Gurumai took him in and told him that there were two conditions a person had to fulfill to become a true hijra. One, he had to be accepted as a chela by a hijra guru. That condition would be easy to meet since gurumai was more than happy to accept Madhu as her disciple. Two, Madhu would have to be sculpted. Only a hijra who was emasculated was truly liberated, and she enjoyed a higher status in the hijra hierarchy than one who was not.

"A hijra is one because of the *soul*," gurumai told Madhu.

If the soul truly wanted to be a woman, wouldn't it naturally reject the penis? It was a natural progression, the falling of the penis and testes, like leaves when seasons changed, except that this change was permanent. Gurumai had known hijras who lost their minds because the operation had not been done. They went mad, literally, and became obsessive about objects. One hijra, she told

Madhu, had started stealing hair from the slums of Dharavi, where they hung hair to dry in the sun so they could export it to foreign shores to be used as wigs and hair extensions. This hijra stole the hair and brought it all to her small hut, where she chewed on the strands and tied them around her waist and neck. Until the poisonous blood was removed from her through the operation, she had continued to behave in this manner.

Even now, it was hard for Madhu to think about her operation. As she stood on the bridge, she could smell the disinfectant that had been applied. One hijra performed the operation, while another hijra was assigned to take care of Madhu's every need afterwards. That was Bulbul. She had been through it herself. But in Bulbul's case, even after the operation, she continued to behave irrationally, and gurumai said that perhaps all the poisonous blood had not seeped out of her.

What Madhu recalled about her operation was culled from her own hazy memory and from Bulbul and gurumai. It was important for her to take these bits and pieces and weave a tapestry for herself, because this had been the moment of her transformation. Her own memories about the event came in sudden convulsions, much like the physical convulsions she continued to experience long after the operation, when she'd suddenly wake up and her body would remember a thing or two.

About a month before the operation, Madhu was asked to stop wearing male underwear. He was given two pairs of panties instead. Bulbul made him tuck his penis between his legs and wear both panties at once so that he would get used to not having anything down there.

He was told not to look in the mirror anymore.

"You must forget the old face," Bulbul said.

A week before the surgery, he could have no spicy foods, no booze, and no drugs. Bulbul would have ganja once in a while because she was just as nervous as Madhu was. He was put on a healthy diet and all expenses were taken care of by gurumai.

"No problem," gurumai said. "You're my child now."

During this time, Madhu often thought about his parents. On the one hand, he was glad that he had run away from them. It was clear that he and they needed to be apart. But it hurt him that he had not been found. He was only a short distance away from his home, and he wondered if his family had even bothered to search for him. Was his disappearance the answer to his mother's prayers?

Thank God for Bulbul. She was the one thing in life that gave him joy. In those early days and nights, their friendship kept on blossoming, and she showered Madhu with praise about his skin, his eyes, his thighs—what a feast men would have. She said she was jealous. Madhu was jealous too of this person Bulbul was referring to, because Madhu couldn't see her. He was still a boy, still his father's son.

When Bulbul was high on ganja, she was funny. She would talk about the law, which she had a great interest in, particularly as it applied to the hijras.

"Madhu, Madhu, Madhu," she would say—she always said Madhu's name three times after she had swallowed her golis. "Do you know that castration is a criminal act under the Indian Penal Code?" Then she'd giggle. "To become who I am, I had to break the law." She laughed so much she fell to the floor, and lifted her sari to show Madhu how empty she was. All that remained was a small fleshy hole. Madhu laughed too—out of terror.

The day was approaching. Then the night was coming. Then it was the midnight hour. And then it was 3:00 a.m.

Madhu's pubic area was shaved. After her bath, she was asked to remain bare and to step inside the secret room. Four hijras were waiting in that room, and one of them had the key to Madhu's future: gurumai.

She was one of a dying breed, a dai-ma, a midwife who had performed more than a hundred operations. She was the gatekeeper who delivered Madhu from one life to the next, from humiliation to freedom. Only one person had died under her knife. "He did not have the will to live," said gurumai. "He was weak."

Madhu could not afford to be weak. There was no turning back.

Did he have second thoughts? Of course he did. He fluctuated between yes and no, went back and forth, up and down, shivered the way a tube light shivers just before coming on to full brightness. He thought he was making a mistake.

What Bulbul had said scared him—he did not want men to feast on him. Yes, by then he was well aware of what happened in the brothel, but the thought that his body was going to be tasted bothered him. He wanted love, to be acknowledged, to have someone run his fingers through his hair, or kiss his cheek. He told gurumai he could not go through with it.

"That's fine, my child," she said. "You can go home anytime you wish."

No one stopped him. No one tried to cajole him into staying. Even Bulbul seemed relieved. She told him he could come visit her whenever he wanted, even if he chose to remain a boy. That was enough for Madhu. At least he had made a friend. He decided to leave before they changed their minds.

He ran to the stairs, and even though he knew he would get the beating of his life from his father, he kept going. But then, something happened. Not a riot or bomb blast or gang fight—nothing of that sort. Bombay hadn't yet become its savage sister. It was bubbling and brewing toward its new avatar, but hadn't fully imploded.

What happened is that Madhu slipped.

On his way down the stairs, in his confusion and fear, he slipped. He did not even make it to the street. His ankle did not break, but it was swollen.

He waited at the bottom until Bulbul came down to go to the laundry.

Madhu could barely walk. He could not even rest his foot on the ground. Of course, Bulbul could not take him home to his parents, or she'd get into trouble. Madhu would have to stay there until his ankle healed; then he could leave. But he knew what everyone else knew: this was meant to be. He had not even made it to the street. The ice on his ankle only proved the fact that his fate was locked and frozen. There was such a thing as destiny, and it came—like an angry, forgotten ancestor it came—to remind Madhu of his future.

A week later, he found himself in the operating chamber with gurumai, Bulbul, and two other hijras. They were the same age as gurumai but looked much older. They were in that room because of their physical strength. They were the manliest hijras Madhu had ever seen.

Gurumai offered a prayer to Bahuchara Mata. She held the knife before the picture of the goddess and asked her to bless it. Madhu tried not to look at the knife, but he could not help himself, so gurumai held it behind her back.

There was a small stool in the room. Madhu took his place, with Bulbul behind him. When Bulbul had been on that stool years ago, she had been made to bite her own hair. Madhu's hair was not long enough yet, so he was given another, more effective, option. Gurumai placed the picture of Bahuchara Mata before him. In the picture, she was riding her rooster, as always, and the trident in her hand was shining.

"Hold her," said gurumai.

Madhu waited for someone to hold him. Bulbul was behind him, but neither she nor the two old hijras moved.

"Hold the Mata," said gurumai.

Madhu realized that gurumai was talking to him. She was not referring to the Mata as a picture. Bahuchara Mata was *here* and gurumai wanted Madhu to hold her. As soon as Madhu took Mata into his hands, two of the hijras tied a thick nylon rope around his waist and pulled hard from either side until he could barely breathe. This was done to prevent the blood from flowing to his groin.

Anaesthesia was for the weak. Madhu would have to depend on the goddess.

"Is she smiling?" gurumai asked.

Three days earlier, Madhu had been given a picture of the Mata and asked the same question. Now, if Madhu found she wasn't smiling, the operation could not proceed. It would be fatal. It was not up to gurumai to make the call. It was up to Madhu.

Madhu thought of his father as he looked at the picture. He could not see Mata's face; only his father's face appeared. His father already knew Madhu's life would amount to nothing—and perhaps he was right.

"Yes," said Madhu. "He's smiling."

No one questioned why Madhu had called the Mata a "he."

Gurumai then took another string and tied Madhu's penis and testes with it. The two old hijras spread Madhu's legs from either side and held him down.

Gurumai began chanting in a low, guttural whisper, "Mata, Mata, Mata, Mata, Mata . . ."

The two old hijras joined in. Their voices were just as hard as gurumai's. They were building a tempo; they were in harmony with each other. Bulbul completed the mantra. Her voice, even though it was much higher than the others, merged seamlessly. But above them all, Madhu heard another voice. It was distinctly male and it was not chanting Mata's name. It was a wail coming from the outside, from the street. Madhu thought he was hallucinating.

He started chanting, "Mata, Mata, Mata . . ."

He stopped looking at gurumai. He knew what she held in her hand. Madhu felt something. A bite. Something bit him. Hard.

Then he felt hot blood trickle down his legs. His first period.

The blood gushed and he wailed. But he had been trained to stay conscious. This was where Bulbul came into play.

"Look at Mata," she reminded him. Under no circumstances was he to close his eyes or fall asleep. But Mata's picture slid from his hands. Now the fight was on—a wrestling match between Bahuchara Mata and her sister, Chamundeshwari. One sat on a rooster and the other on a lion. One sister gave life while the other terminated it—at least that's what the other midwives believed. But not gurumai. She was in complete control of the situation.

It was all about letting the right amount of blood flow out of Madhu's body. Making the correct slice was just part of it. That was why those who wanted to get castrated preferred gurumai to doctors. The doctors of Nagpada and Madanpura would perform the operation, but terrified of losing the patient, they immediately stitched the wound up. They failed to grasp the significance of the ceremony, whereas gurumai knew how much blood to drain out. She could *see* the impure blood leave the body, every trace of it, while the hijra balanced between life and death. To ensure that all of the poisonous *male* blood was expelled, Madhu had been willing to risk death. He had tasted death more closely than any other human being alive.

"When you are no longer scared of death, only then are you liberated," gurumai had told him. Nirvan, the ultimate liberation, was a state of mind.

When gurumai thought it was time, she stopped the flow of blood. Hot oil was poured over Madhu's absent genitals and a small stick was placed there to keep a hole open so he could urinate. He knew he would not be urinating anytime soon because he had sweat pouring down every inch of his body. The smell of antiseptic pervaded the room as the two old hijras wiped the blood from the floor.

More hijras from the household streamed in. Madhu's life was in the balance. They started clapping loudly, chanting Mata's name with a fever that made the room boil. They ensured that Madhu did not slip into a coma. Bulbul kept opening Madhu's eyes again and again. There was an army in the room.

To this day, however, Bulbul maintained there was no one else in that room besides her, the two other hijras, and gurumai. She insisted that the four of them had done all the clapping. To Madhu, it had felt like there were thousands there.

Madhu's forty-day period of healing began. His wound was not stitched closed. More sesame seed oil was applied by Bulbul.

All she did in those initial days, the poor thing, was make the oil hot and apply it. Madhu was given black tea and told not to force the urine out. He was so weak a fly could have crushed him.

He lay in bed all day and night. He was forbidden from looking into a mirror. He had forty days to forget the old face. The most important dictum of all was that he was not to see a man during his healing period. So he could not look outside his room. On the third day, or it could have been the tenth, he was given rice, which he threw up instantly.

"Good," said Bulbul. "Whatever impurity did not leave through the blood is leaving through the mouth."

He was bathed, but to do this, Bulbul made him sit on a stool, propped him up against the wall, and poured water over him. He could not bear the feel of water on his skin. There were days when he cried bitterly, cursing himself for being born. In addition to his own cries, he repeatedly heard the cries of another, the same wailing from outside that he had heard above the sea of chants during his operation. Now that Madhu was more lucid, he could decipher a name in that cry: Hema.

A man was shouting out a woman's name, stretching it out for kilometres, making it the longest name in the world. There was so much anguish in his call that Madhu simply had to ask Bulbul who he was.

"That's Gajja," Bulbul said.

And that was how Madhu fell in love for the first time. He was fourteen years old and he fell in love without even looking at the man's face. It was the wanting in Gajja's voice that did it, and what he learned of Gajja's story.

Gajja had been in love with a prostitute named Hema and had been ready to marry her, to take her away from Kamathipura. He would give her respect and had promised to never bring up her past. There was just one problem: the girl had been bought by the brothel madam for a reasonable sum and had yet to pay out that amount, which was beyond Gajja's reach. But he sold his little hutment and offered the madam something close to the actual amount, promising to pay the remainder, and the madam agreed. It was a miracle. The act of kindness would perhaps give her a seat in heaven—not a front row seat, just a tiny spot somewhere.

But fate has a cruel way of poking its nasty nose into other people's happiness.

For about a week, Hema was wracked with high fevers she could not shake. Gajja took her to a doctor at JJ, where he worked, and was told that she had dengue. She died shaking in his arms. A mosquito had ended what could have been a glorious union.

Gajja had to be pried away from Hema's body. The madam and the other prostitutes had to literally tear him from her arms. Even though Hema was dead, he lay next to her for hours, asking her to wake up. He kept asking for a garland. He would not budge until someone got him a garland.

A garland was yanked off the entrance to a nearby shop and given to him. Gajja placed it around Hema's neck. He married a dead woman. He had shown everyone that love could be found in places of horror. But afterwards, he started drinking heavily, wandering the streets and wailing Hema's name. When Madhu heard Gajja's story, he regained some of the faith in men that his father and the boys at school had made him lose.

On the fortieth day after the surgery, Madhu was ready to be renamed. Receiving a new name was part of the initiation ceremony. Normally, the guru had to take the initiate to the hijra leaders of Bombay, who would then assign a name. But when it came to the hijra code, gurumai was willing to make transgressions—she housed hijras who begged, who blessed, and who prostituted all under the same roof. She was a dai-ma and could bend the rules like a magician bending the wind. Madhu was free to choose any name he wanted from a list given by gurumai. The feminine names—Lucky, Dimple, Rani, Chandni, Lekha—made Madhu's mouth water. But he decided to retain his original name. It was the only thing that had been with him since his birth that was not a lie. Madhu. He had hid in that name for years and it had kept him safe.

On the fortieth day, Bulbul brought him tweezers to pluck whatever hair was on his face, but he was already hairless. Castrated so young, he would surely blossom into something full and feminine—there was no doubt about it. He was bathed again and Bulbul dressed him like a bride. She bejewelled him, parted his hair in the centre, and applied mehndi on his hands and feet.

He was ready to look in the mirror.

Electricity shot through him. Someone had taken a plug point, connected it to his rectum, and released a current so beautiful, it slit him open. He was staring at a lioness with a flowing mane. He could feel the adulation from gurumai. The envious stares from the other disciples covered his body like bruise marks. The two old hijras were happy for him, though—they had helped in his creation.

At 3:00 a.m., they went to Rani Baug. The zoo had the only natural body of water in the vicinity. The watchman did not stop them. Gurumai had been using the zoo for years. She lit an oil lamp and placed it on Madhu's head. There, amidst the chattering of birds, they performed a final puja for Bahuchara

Mata. Milk was poured over Madhu and then into the water.

"You are free now," said gurumai.

Madhu was no longer cursed. He was now a she, reborn as a hijra. She could now channel Bahuchara Mata.

That night in the zoo, not a single animal made a sound. There were no roars, bellows, or trumpets. All the hijras could sense the presence of something otherworldly. More than anything, they could sense that Madhu had been set free. The animals were in cages, but Madhu had transcended her body. Neither man nor woman, she had found a place among beasts.

8

Before dawn came, Madhu was gone from the bridge. She had to leave. Once light arrived, it made the sight of her parents' home unbearable, and her hungry gaze felt all the more shameful.

Madhu hoped Salma had bought the right clothes for the parcel and not dressed her up like a prostitute. Why waste time? Why delay the inevitable? That was Salma's way of thinking. But to Madhu, the right clothes had a purpose: they were meant to highlight the parcel's innocence and purity for that first client, the way white fabric gave an aura of calm and cleanliness to the wearer.

On Sukhlaji Street, she noticed the van that operated as a mobile Ayurvedic clinic for the residents of Kamathipura. An old man sat inside the van and promised cures for arthritis and incontinence, but at this time of morning he attracted only pojeetives.

Madhu was anxious to return to the parcel in the loft; she needed the motherly darkness. She made sure it was always night in the loft; the hot air always stank, but the light was in her control. She was in charge of its emission, what it exposed, what it concealed. To Madhu, there was nothing natural about sunlight. It lit up things too savagely, without the slightest regard for her sensibilities, especially when she stood on the bridge. She did not want to see her parents' faces, or her brother's for that matter. She hadn't seen them in decades. Silhouettes were all she could handle.

She observed the parcel for a few moments as the girl slept. Then Madhu leaned back and rattled the cage bars with her legs.

"Get up!" she shouted. "Up!"

The parcel leapt up, almost hitting her head on the roof of the cage.

"What's your name?" Madhu asked. "Tell me your name!"

"Kinjal," said the parcel.

Madhu reached through the bars and gripped her neck.

The parcel realized she'd made a mistake. "Jhanvi," she corrected herself.

"How old are you?" Madhu was ferocious. She had spent the last two days drilling facts into the parcel, and still the girl had answered the very first question wrong.

"Twelve."

"What village are you from?"

Madhu could tell that the name of the parcel's village was on the tip of her tongue, but she knew she was not supposed to speak it.

"I was born here. I'm not from any village."

"Don't lie to me. I will take you to the police station right now. Then you'll tell me the truth."

"It's the truth . . . My mother was from Nepal, but she died. I was born here."

"Do you go to school?"

"No."

"Why not?"

"I don't . . . I help here . . . I clean the place."

"That's good," said Madhu.

She suddenly changed roles and was no longer the interrogator. Of course, when a cop questioned you, the truth came out like watery shit in a matter of seconds, but the parcel had done okay. There was one thing left to do. She opened the cage and let the parcel out.

"Now hide," said Madhu. "You have a ten second start. If I can see even your shadow, you'll be sorry."

No sooner had the parcel slipped down the ladder than Madhu went after her. She could see the parcel getting inside the water tank. Once she was in, Madhu peered over the top. The parcel was still. Just as Madhu had taught her, she held her dress to the side of her body so that it didn't bloat. Madhu was satisfied. The girl could not be seen.

Sometimes raids lasted for a couple of hours. The parcel needed to get used to staying in there for that long. Madhu set herself down and prepared to wait for dawn. Her thoughts returned to her pitiful addiction. What if Bulbul or gurumai or even Gajja found out about Madhu's habit of voyeurism on the bridge? Deep down, did she somehow hope she would find her way back into her family's life? That was as laughable a venture as parcel work. Earlier, the parcel had been moving in her sleep, jerking an arm and then a leg, like dogs do when they lie on their sides, close their eyes, and dream they are running. The parcel was running too—running back to her village at night, wherever it was. It was hard to watch, which is why Madhu had woken her up with such cruel voltage.

Madhu's father had had a chance to change Madhu's future, and history, by accepting his son—but he could not. He studied history, but he dared not make it. Madhu prided herself on doing the opposite. By wiping out the parcels' past, she was wiping out history. So who was more powerful now: Madhu's father or Madhu?

When she came into contact with the parcels, Madhu felt that God had a purpose for her. She connected with them. She could feel their terror better than anyone else. She knew that if she made their world smaller by sledgehammering their dreams of being rescued, she'd help them. It made her sick, how they turned to God in their cages. She thought back to her early days in Hijra Gulli: the sooner the truth had hit Madhu in those early days—that her family had not bothered to look for her after she ran away—the faster her world had started to shrink. And the more confined her world got, the less she had needed her parents or her brother. That is, until a few years ago.

That was when a single new bridge had weakened her—the JJ Bridge, connecting Byculla to VT station. Even though no pedestrians were allowed on it, she had walked on that bridge one night after a few pegs with Gajja. She'd just drifted there, the way dust drifted. As she climbed up, she saw the Mahanagar Blood Bank to her left and reflected that she was not even allowed to donate blood. To do so, you were required to tick a box for male or female on the medical form. If neither was ticked, the doctor could refuse to take your blood, even if you were giving it for free. This had happened to Madhu. Gajja had called her to give blood to an accident victim, an acquaintance of his, but when Madhu showed up, the doctor sent her away. All her life, her father had made her feel like an aberration, a nonentity, and now a doctor had supported that view.

But the harder parent, Madhu now realized, had been her mother. She had been the most difficult to fight because she was in no one's corner. Too cowardly to oppose her husband, she had secretly given Madhu bits of comfort, like scraps of food slipped under the table as though Madhu was a deformed child hidden away from sight.

Madhu's new hijra family had seemed to offer her the acceptance she needed and deserved, and she had not minded paying the price, allowing truck drivers to enter her with the same recklessness with which they drove on highways. She once told Bulbul that so many truck drivers had entered her she should have "Horn OK Please" tattooed on her arse.

Now she realized that she had left home only to fall into the illusion of freedom. The veil had lifted. She saw that she had chosen to live with a group of people who were as unwelcome in society as lice in hair. Her father's scorn had been replaced by society's.

The screech of a taxi snapped Madhu out of her thoughts. It was the voice of reason telling her to wake up and accept her life once and for all. The harsh sound was pushing her to accept the harsh truth. The parcel would have her sounds too, thought Madhu: the footsteps of Padma Madam walking with a client toward the cage; the squeaks of the cage door opening; the hurried breath of the client, his hungry anticipation wetting the stale air in the loft; the vocabulary of the trapped and eternally hunted. But before these entered the parcel's life, Madhu needed to introduce a different sound. She picked up a stick that lay on the floor and tapped it against the water tank a couple of times. This is what the cops sometimes did to check if the tank held water or was being used as a hiding place. Madhu tapped and waited. The parcel did not respond. Madhu was pleased. The tap was a simple, unassuming sound, but it was one that the parcel would recall many years from now, as an old woman.

It was always the simple things that hurt. Wounds could be subtle, silken beings.

Madhu went back in her memory to that night a few years ago when she had met up with her one steady love, Gajja, and drank too much with him at the hospital. Later, instead of returning to Kamathipura, she had gone in the other direction, toward JJ Bridge. Regret had made her go there. Her beauty was fading faster than the dye on cheap fabric, and her hijra family was no longer fulfilling her. The sisters she had bonded with had been traded to another guru like cattle. Of course, Bulbul was always there for her, but even she was getting gloomy. Gajja was a constant in her life, but the need for intimacy was leaving her fast, and she knew it was hurting him. She was desperate to stand on that bridge—she didn't know why, she simply knew it was necessary.

That night, she had looked down over the side of the bridge at the Suleiman Usman Bakery. A little farther ahead, she saw a building named "Fancy Mahal." It was so close to where she stood, she could almost touch it if she leaned across the gap. The traffic below, on Mohammed Ali Road, was abuzz with motorcycles beaming rude shafts of light at the minarets and meat shops. No, jumping was not an option. One needed energy for suicide. She was beyond that; she was already dead.

That was when she had confessed a dark secret to herself. She had faced up to a thought that had been growing underneath the regret: Even though her father had been hard on her, hadn't he become more calm after their visit to the holy Baba that day long ago? Hadn't Madhu's father invited Madhu to join him at the window that night to stare at the traffic below? He might have been humiliated by Madhu's presence in the family, but his struggle with that feeling was human.

Madhu stared at the grey cement of Fancy Mahal and wondered what would have happened if gurumai had not shown up at her home. For the first time, standing on that bridge, Madhu saw clearly who her father was: a struggling history "sir," teaching uninterested students about the British, or Akbar, or whatever the syllabus told him to teach. With his short, thin frame, he would have been blown away by the wind to the Department of Failures were it not for that heavy brief-case he carried around to ground him in importance.

What if Madhu's father was not an insensitive man? What if Madhu's mother was not a coward? What if Madhu had read them wrong? Had his mother not shed a tear or two? Had she not on occasion stepped in and taken a blow that was meant for Madhu? Why hadn't Madhu thought of that before?

That night on the bridge, she had concluded there were no answers . . . Just as there was no answer now as to why the parcel was a shivering wet mass of fear in the water tank. *Why* was the disease. Madhu had convinced herself of this time and again, drilled it into her skull with the same urgency that construction workers were drilling holes into the pavement of Kamathipura. *Why, why, why* . . . If you said it long enough, or loud enough, thought Madhu, you could see the ridiculousness of the question. There was no answer.

And yet, it turned out there *was* an answer.

When Madhu was in her thirties, she had stopped doing sex work. She was sick of it. But gurumai had not given her permission; the businesswoman in gurumai would not let her do so. Madhu refused anyway, so a barber was called and her head was shaved to humiliate her. It was a huge blow for a hijra to have her long tresses lopped off. She was also asked to pay a fine of ten thousand rupees, which she could barely afford. Yes, she had been allowed to retain half her earnings, but Madhu had always been too lenient with cash. She fed dogs, she gave prostitutes train fare to go back to their villages, and she had once even given a client his money back *and* something extra because he wanted to buy a cycle for his son. She bought the parcels dolls and books and colouring pencils, and she had bought Bulbul an entire collection of Kishore Kumar hits, which she regretted because Bulbul played them all day long. Madhu could afford to be this generous because her arsehole was functioning beautifully. It was nothing short of a lugubrious wonder. Even when the Mumbai stock market crashed, her gand-hole was raking it in.

She had been the toast of Kamathipura, a rare bird in a cage. Literally. Gurumai had asked a laundryman around the corner from the brothel, a man whose father used to work in the theatre as a lighting assistant, to affix some lights to the bottom of the brothel window to illuminate Madhu above. She had felt like a work of art. Actress that she was, she used the light well, letting it warm her legs and stream its hot glow right up her thighs, revealing just enough, but never more. There had once been over five hundred hijra sex workers in that one lane in Kamathipura, and Madhu could easily say, with utmost humility, that she was among the most beautiful. In the prime of her life, she had been so voluptuous and fiery she could burn a man with a single stare. One of her clients had been a doctor, a respectable ENT specialist, who drove to Madhu in his wife's old Fiat. The car would always stall three minutes away from the brothel. "It's my wife's way of saying, 'Don't go,'" he told Madhu.

"So why do you come?"

"Because you are unlike anything I've tasted."

He showered money on her. He'd stand up while she slept naked on the bed, take a handful of ten-rupee notes and let them fall over her like rose petals—except currency did not die and had a scent more fragrant than that of any rose.

Hers was a simple game. First, she would demean her clients: "You are not big enough or hard enough. Take your prick and go home to your wife. You can never satisfy me." That was all it took to inflame a man's ego. The most fragile thing in the world, the ego of the male species, was so easy to belittle. In response, the men took her with the force of a gale, and she did her precious drama: "Oooh . . . aah . . . I have never been . . . Oh my god . . . stop . . . Don't stop . . . No, please stop." Sometimes the choothiyas were so drunk they *thought* they were fucking her in the arse, but all she did was put cream between her thighs and make them come in seconds.

Then something had changed. The first sign she was aging came when she started hemorrhaging internally. She had used up all her reserves, and when her body was more honest, more in touch with its mortality, it started remembering things. After all, she was a Sherpa of the flesh. The mind could not be relied upon. It had the ability to make up stories, good or bad, and warp memories to suit a purpose, but only the body told you what had truly happened. The body could make up nothing. It stood witness to all the things she had done and every sensation she had felt. She decided to cross-examine herself. She told her mind to shut up and put her body in the witness box.

Six months after her head had been shaved in front of the hijra leaders, gurumai had asked Madhu if she would start prostituting again. Madhu said no, but it was a softer no, the no of a child begging its mother for something. Gurumai, against her better judgment, granted Madhu her wish. Madhu became a badhai hijra, one who sang and danced at weddings, and soon she accompanied Bulbul and Sona to her first "blessing."

The blessing was held in a middle-class home. On the day of a wedding, even a dungeon like that house shone. Sona played the drums and Bulbul sang. They had taken a portable tape recorder with them to play the cheapest item songs, which was gurumai's idea. The world was changing; tradition had to take a back seat to hip gyrations.

Madhu was not a dancer. She simply put her arms to her sides and started swaying. The whore in her made the men notice. She did not want them to. In fact, she was scared and self-conscious about having to dance.

As well, the happiness surrounding her was getting to her. She was in the presence of "normal" people on a day of tremendous joy. She was standing in someone's middle-class living room after years and years of banishment. It felt like another planet. She could not bear the smell in that home because it did not smell of sex and urine. It was so clean, she thought she might gag on the cleanliness, and on all those fake smiles tolerating her presence.

Bulbul's singing made her feel even worse. The words Bulbul sang were all her own:

Oh look at this rickety face
Look where it is placed
On the body of a woman
Who once was a man
But is now neither, neither, neither.

Madhu had never seen Bulbul at work and she marvelled at her skill. She was using her hands so subtly, to highlight her face. Even a mediocre painting could pass for a masterpiece for a second or two if offset by a frame, and that is exactly what Bulbul's fingers were doing: providing a second or two of authentic femininity, a mere drop of acceptance in the ocean of time.

But the women who were gathered to watch thought Bulbul was mocking herself. They were giggling like a bunch of ten-year-olds at someone who had just got her first period. When Madhu looked at the bride's face and saw that she knew nothing of a hijra's pain, it irked her that just by being born in the right body, this young woman had avoided all that Madhu had gone through. Madhu realized that she had stopped swaying and that her gaze was locked on the bride's smile.

"Don't stare at her," the bride's mother told her. "Don't look at her face. You should know better. It's not good."

Madhu was so startled, she started swaying again, but she could not digest the mother's words. Madhu knew that if she opened her mouth, she was asking for trouble, but her own mother's words came searing through her memory: *"Why can't you just listen to him?"* That was it.

"What's not good?" Madhu asked the bride's mother.

"Hah?"

"Why can't I look at her face? What's the problem?"

Sona suddenly stopped drumming and Bulbul tapered off into silence.

"You should know," said the mother. "It's unlucky. She will be unable to bear children, just like you."

How warped the human soul was. This woman had allowed Madhu into her home on her daughter's wedding day because she was superstitious. And so, in her mind, the hijras were extorting money from her, preying on her fears. Instead of being part of a historic tradition, the hijras had been pushed to the fringes and were left sitting on the margins the way flies sat on the rim of a plate, unwanted, circling the perimeter to find a way back in, but never succeeding. Money was not given to them as a reward for their skilled performance. Money was given to drive the hijras away.

"Do you know why I cannot have children?" Madhu asked her.

The woman had by then realized the folly of her assault. She had simmered down, but Madhu had awoken.

"I cannot have children because I have nothing," she said.

Then Madhu lifted her sari and started to remove her panties. Bulbul placed her arm around her, but Madhu shook it off; she could not stop. She put her own arm on Bulbul's shoulder instead, used her as support, and tugged her panties down her legs. Then she lifted her red sari, which spanned the room like a flower, opening its petals for all to see—except that there was nothing. The flesh was so barren, it showed no signs of life except for a cigarette burn made by a truck driver long ago.

She stood there with her sari hoisted for what seemed like an eternity. In lifting her sari, Madhu was also using it as a shield to cover her face. Then the silence was shattered by the bride's cries, and the men of the house drove the hijras out. Madhu had ruined the happiest day of the bride's life. She was told to go die.

When gurumai heard of this, she told her three hijras to keep quiet. This incident could not reach the ears of the hijra leaders. She felt sorry for Madhu, and also was resigned to the fact that Madhu had changed. Madhu herself could not understand why she had acted as she did that day. She was thus relegated to begging, and Bombay Central became her adda. From a dhandhewali to a badhai hijra, and now a mangti, one who begged, she had experienced all three roles that a hijra could play. Her income crashed, her stomach lost its tautness, and lines started to appear beneath her eyes—hot, sorrowful bags that swelled with madness. Her body was no longer ravaged by men—and let alone, it talked even more.

Madhu was sure that the parcel's body was talking to her this very instant. She carefully slid open the lid of the water tank just a sliver and shouted, "If anyone's in there, come out!" She listened for a response but heard nothing. Once her eyes adjusted to the light inside the water tank, she saw the parcel's quivering silhouette. That quiver was the second question the body asked, after *Why?*—*What if?* That was the second sign of internal bleeding: the slow, ruinous feeling that in some way perhaps she was responsible for her fate.

Around the time Madhu was reduced to begging, when her body was no longer worshipped by men and had all the time to speak, it made her ask: What if she had not run away from home? If she had not run away, perhaps her father would have accepted her. The acceptance would not have been whole-hearted; it would have been a quiet resignation, the way one accepted falling hair. Father would have inched toward son. Each time he smelled the girl trapped inside Madhu, it would have rattled him, but his own worst fear, of public gossip, had already come true. In time, acceptance would have set him free.

The more Madhu had stared at the walls of Fancy Mahal that night on the bridge, the more she had believed this to be true. Cars passed by but no one stopped; she camouflaged herself well into any darkness. Even her sari clung to her, assisting her in avoiding detection.

She allowed herself an awful thought: Gurumai had laid a trap for her. Gurumai was not her benefactor, her guardian, as Madhu had thought. Her own disastrous need had prevented her from seeing gurumai's true face. And Madhu had chosen her current life because of her own stubbornness. She had become more and more uneasy as crows cawed and dawn arrived, and the only thing moving was a small Pakistani flag attached to the minaret of a mosque. The satellite dishes on the tops of buildings yawned, bored at her pain.

It was then that she had looked directly into the apartment across from her. As lights came on, she had seen a family waking up. Together. The father gently leaned down to wake his boy. The boy wiped his eyes and begged for more time. The mother carried her little girl in her arms to the toilet. It was all so simple.

A great calm came over Madhu. Then, an even greater sickness.

She had become visible. The father, a man with a long beard, had spotted her. He came to the balcony, where he was joined by his wife. Madhu and this couple were only feet away from each other. Both man and woman looked at Madhu. They said nothing. They knew what Madhu was. They did not shoo her away. They allowed her into their family, to stand in the shared calm of people who loved and respected one another, and for that Madhu was grateful.

Instead of going back to Kamathipura that morning, she had gone to step forty-seven on the bridge closest to her family's home. That was the first time. And that's how bridges had become her nasha. No wonder her brother now stood on his balcony so often in the middle of the night. No wonder he couldn't sleep. That shadow, that feeling on her brother's skin that something was watching him, judging him, that was Madhu. It had taken her years to get to this point.

Dawn came and Madhu felt strong. She told the parcel to come out of the water tank. The girl had endured the process well. As Madhu dried her off, she saw that the water had pruned her hands into those of an old woman's. The water was doing its job. It had hidden many parcels. Now Madhu was certain that this parcel would be her last. Unlike water, which took the form of the vessel that contained it, Madhu would no longer allow herself to be shaped by others. It was time to reclaim what she had lost, what had been taken from her.

Once Madhu was done delivering the parcel, she would put on her finest outfit, a salwar kameez with a gold border, she would take meaningful strides toward Geeta Bhavan, where the diabetic ghosts would egg her on, she would climb up the stairs to her former home, and she would knock on the door. In the dark, just like gurumai had. For a second time, a hijra would visit her home. But this time, her brother would open the door.

9

It was always night in Kamathipura. Days were a mutation of
night. When dusk came, the hijras appeared like stars and
stood in clusters, lit up. Roomali looked extra white tonight,
while Devyani stood erect on the public toilet roof and peered
into the distance like a sentry from a different era, on a fort
tower, alert for an enemy onslaught. Devyani's error was that
she was looking for the enemy outside the boundaries of
Kamathipura, when the real-estate vultures were already inside.
Among the hijras, only Madhu noticed the small bulldozer
parked on the other side of the public toilet. It hadn't been
there when she returned home the night before. That a bulldozer had come in so stealthily in the middle of the night,
without so much as a sound, meant something.

Madhu tried to tell herself she was just being paranoid.
Gurumai would never sell. The bulldozer must be for the structures surrounding Hijra House. Just as the hijras were a thorn
in the face of society, the building they lived in would serve as

a reminder that they could not be disseminated easily. They were scar tissue, and they would somehow endure.

Madhu knew that the gathering of the hijra leaders was in one day, and that fact was weighing on her. Even though the gathering was not in Kamathipura, gurumai was having the brothel cleaned in case one of the leaders wished to visit. But Madhu knew that would never happen. The hijra leaders looked down on sex work. It brought shame to the hijra community. No leader would ever enter Kamathipura. Still, gurumai insisted on employing some retired female prostitutes to clean the brothel anyway, and they were busy scrubbing the walls and floors so hard that neither prostitutes nor brothel would have any skin left.

Madhu kept her mind on the task at hand. The parcel needed her attention. She needed to be made ready. As Madhu walked toward Padma's brothel, it occurred to her that nothing could destroy Kamathipura. Its structures could be demolished, but it could not be destroyed. She was experiencing the same thing with the parcel. The parcel would die and then re-emerge in an altered form.

When Madhu arrived at Padma's brothel, Salma told her that the parcel was in her room. The girl had been running a fever, so Salma had given her a Crocin.

"We need to do something," said Madhu. "Have you forgotten?"

"No," said Salma. "I'll fetch the parcel."

When they came down to join Madhu in the street, the three of them were greeted with a surge of unholy noise. The pimps of Kamathipura had suddenly turned pious. It was their monthly cleansing too, and they were singing bhajans in praise of Sai Baba. They had paid money to the owner of Café Faredoon and requested that he feed the poor on their behalf. A long line of the destitute had formed outside the restaurant, where they waited to be fed mutton biryani paid for with rape money. One pimp had cymbals in his hands and was striking away with such fervour, he was convinced he had been forgiven.

Salma and Madhu parted ways, Salma muttering about needing to go to Bachuseth Ki Wadi. This was a kebab place known all over the city, and next to it was a string of tailors. After the government had shut down dance bars, many of the bar girls had moved to the suburbs and resorted to prostitution, or had gone back to their townships. Tonight, the tailors of Bachuseth Ki Wadi were having a sale of second-hand outfits, ones that the bar girls had sold back to them for a pittance. Some of the bar girls were still around, working in a dance bar or two that managed to operate clandestinely. Madhu sometimes watched them arrive at the dance bar in taxis; they'd slip through the back entrance like pretty robbers.

Tonight the street lights were brighter than usual. Madhu smirked when she read the street name: Nimkar Marg. The name change was a pathetic attempt at giving the area an air of respectability. Someone must have felt that *Nimkar Marg* was less dirty than *Foras Road* or *Kamathipura*. As if by changing a name, the area would be different, thought Madhu scornfully. Name it anything—the area would always have the screams of whores whizzing around, looking for someone to listen. Screams could not be fooled. Screams did not pay attention to street names.

A lone white bull stood below the flashing neon sign of a mobile repair shop. Madhu felt the parcel slow down as they passed; she stared at the whip marks on its skin. Bloody lines ran deep across the beast's back and belly. Madhu imagined the same arm coming down in the same arc each time the bull slowed down. The parcel ran her fingers along the bull's skin, tenderly avoiding the lines.

Madhu had never seen the parcel this way. Perhaps the bull reminded her of something, or someone, and she was trying to speak to it. She flicked a couple of flies off a wound. Then she looked at Madhu, wanting to stay there for a bit. Madhu paused and let her tend to the bull. The parcel drove the flies away again and then blew on the bull's wounds, determined to provide some relief. When Madhu looked at the parcel's eyes, she saw that they were watery. Madhu sighed. It was perhaps the last act of kindness the parcel would perform. Once she was opened, the kindness would leave, just like the flies she was driving away.

As Madhu went to lead the parcel away from the bull, a police van passed by. It stopped a few feet away from them, outside a newly erected police booth. Madhu guessed it had sprouted there to make the normal citizens of the area feel secure. On the police van, painted in white against dark blue, were the words "Crimes Against Women Children and Senior Citizens Call 103."

Madhu read the words again, just for fun. Here she was, right in front of the van, with a parcel that was going to be opened up as though she were a birthday present. The bull was now moving its head in the parcel's direction in appreciation for the girl's efforts to drive the flies away. It had stopped twitching. But now Madhu was getting wary. Two cops got out of the van and went to a chai stall. A third cop came out of the police booth and started talking to the other two. He looked in Madhu's direction. Madhu smiled at him, then reached out to place her hand on the parcel's shoulder. The girl had moved toward the bull's mouth and was mumbling something to it.

Luckily, the busyness of the street kept things normal. A prostitute was holding an old man by the hand and helping him cross the road. She was being abused by another prostitute, who accused her of stealing her client. A goat followed the old man across the street. A motorcycle veered to the side to avoid the goat and slid instead into an empty cot placed outside a barber's shop. People rushed to the rider's aid.

The parcel looked up at Madhu. Then, she made a run for it.

She shot away, a terrified bullet in the direction of the cops. She shouted for help and one of the cops turned, and for a moment, Madhu's heart beat faster. But then the cop was distracted by his colleague who was trying to move the crowd away from the fallen rider. The parcel was only a few feet away from the police van.

Suddenly Salma stood in the parcel's path, blocking her like a dam. She swooped her away into a side street, and Madhu followed. The two of them stood silently in front of the parcel. Madhu saw the colour fading from the parcel's face—hope was leaving the way the sun left an evening. The outing had simply been a test to see if the parcel would try to escape. Salma had been stationed there all along. Madhu had wanted to check if the parcel could be trusted, if enough fear had been instilled in her. But the poor thing had done what most girls did: she had seen the cops and tried her luck.

And like the parcels of the past, she had failed. Like all parcels, this one had to be punished.

On the way back to Padma's, Madhu did not admonish the parcel in any way. In fact, she stopped at a bhel-puri vendor and treated the parcel to her fullest meal yet. The parcel could hardly eat a morsel. Madhu sensed that she was terrified. Each time Madhu looked at her, she flinched the way one flinches in anticipation of a tight slap across the face. But Madhu did nothing of the sort. When they reached the loft, the parcel got into the cage like a well-trained animal petrified of its owner's whip. She was about to say something to Madhu, but Madhu just smiled at her as she closed the cage door, which rattled the parcel even more, pushing her back into silence.

Madhu was playing things cool on purpose; her nonchalance was certainly going to make the cage smaller that night. Sleep would come to the parcel in fits, and each time the parcel woke up, her dread would grow. She'd have time to reflect on the futility of her escape attempt. The night would also give Madhu enough time to think about a method of punishment. Physical punishment was out of the question because that would damage the parcel. Madhu had to keep her fresh. But there were ways—there were always ways.

Gajja unknowingly provided Madhu with one when he called her the next morning and asked if she would go with him for an afternoon show at New Roshan Talkies. Madhu was so taken with the idea that popped into her head, she did not bother to ask which show. She hadn't been to Pila Haus in a while, but she hoped the tattoo woman was still outside New Roshan Talkies.

That afternoon, she collected the parcel on her way.

"I live here," said Madhu, pointing to Hijra House as they passed by it. "All my sisters live in that building."

Next to the public toilet, Bulbul was playing carrom with a young chap, a budding gangster. She kept giggling after every shot she made, holding her mouth, mocking herself for how inept she was at the game.

They passed the blue mosque and then reached Two Tanks, where the sound of steel clashing into steel reminded Madhu of the time she used to work in Gaandu Bageecha—the Anal Gardens. When she saw the gardens a few minutes later—an abandoned ground just opposite the scrap houses, an arid place with cement blocks lying around—she held the parcel's hand tight; a reflex when remembering the unpleasant. After Madhu had defied her gurumai and stopped sex work, after lifting her sari and flashing the bride's mother, after begging work made her slip into an even deeper depression, she had slid even lower and come to Gaandu Bageecha to regain some of her lost glory. Her beauty no longer visible, her false sense of power gone, she would smoke a chillum near the small statue of Ganesh outside the gardens. Then, sufficiently numb, she would wander through the gardens in search of clients.

In the mornings, the ground was used for minor political gatherings. Activists practised speeches on people who would never vote. Starting at about five, the gamblers arrived to play cards until dusk. After that, it was Madhu's turn. She would stand against the far wall of the gardens in the devil dark with a small flashlight and snap it on and off three times in quick succession. That was her signal. She then clapped three times, the shrill hijra clap, to warn people. She did not want them coming to her thinking she was a woman.

Only the junkies came. Sometimes Madhu did not even get paid. Sometimes she got roughed up by young men who called her a freak. But on other nights, she'd get a man who was honest enough to pay for his relief. She no longer brought pleasure to anyone—not for a moment did she fool herself. She brought the men some relief, that was all. She was slightly better than a bowel movement.

She did not use condoms because the men did not want to. If she insisted on condoms, they would go to someone else. Sometimes the junkies were so clouded that she would have to go through their pockets at the end of the session to collect her payment. She never cheated them. If anything, she felt pity for them and gave them a discount while they were sleeping. She was so lonely by then that she'd lay down next to them after her lovemaking—she liked to call it that—while they were unconscious and hold their bodies close to hers.

This was when Gajja had yanked himself out of her life for a while because Madhu had pushed him away. She felt she was no longer worth looking at. So after spending the day begging at Bombay Central, she'd go to the gardens and hug anything male, anything with a beating heart. Some of the men were gentle in their sleep. They were like children. Some cried in their slumber, making random sounds of ache and home that ricocheted against her breast. When the men made those sounds, Madhu sat up against the wall, placed their heads in her lap, stroked their hair, and studied their faces in the stingy glow that spilled from an old street light. Some had so many lines in their faces; others had a few teeth missing. She started connecting with them as they slept. Awake, they were of no use to her, but asleep, they were allowing her to mother them. It gave her the strength to go begging the next day.

She'd never had any ambitions to be a mother and adopt children the way some hijras had. But now she discovered that she had quietly harboured this hope, keeping it buried inside her because it was one more thing that would be laughed at. She believed that sometimes life gave you a lesser version of a dream, and it was up to you to take it. So she took it in her arms, and she cradled those junkies as if they were her own flesh and blood. Even though some of them had abused her while they were inside her, once they passed out, all that remained was her caress and their breathing.

She spoke to them while they slept, told them things she had only told Bulbul, about how her father used to hide her from the neighbours. Whenever someone from the building would stop to chat and Madhu would answer in his feminine voice, his father would finish Madhu's sentence and send him away. When Madhu was a boy, he'd had a girl's voice, but now that she was a hijra, she had the voice of a man. She just didn't get the joke—or maybe she did, and so did her junkie children. But unlike her father, they never passed judgment; they never wanted her to become invisible. Gaandu Bageecha may have been arid, more desert than garden, but it gave her some shade, cooled her down when the hot sulphur of failure was eating her bones. It was during those nights, when she kept her palm on the foreheads of her little junkies, that she felt for the first time in her life that she had the power to bless. She had dropped her beauty, renounced it the way a snake lets go of its skin, and now in the role of mother, the force of Bahuchara Mata was flowing through her.

She did not do any hocus-pocus or chant mantras. She simply thought about the story of the young Mata traversing a jungle in Gujarat and being pounced upon by a band of thieves. To protect her dignity, the Mata had sliced off her breast and placed it as an offering before the thieves. This act of mutilation had resonated with the hijras over the centuries. By mutilating herself, she was honouring herself. The Mata had sacrificed her womanhood in order to preserve it, just as the hijras let go of the male in them to become channels for the Mata. But what had the Mata been trying to say in that forest? What was the young Mata discovering for herself? That she was a woman, even without her breasts. As long as her soul was intact, her body could be massacred ten times over. So Madhu, against a wall in Gaandu Bageecha, with a sweet junkie in her lap, moved beyond self-mutilation into compassion. The force of the Mata was gentle and eternal and made no distinction between junkie, truckie, servant, or labourer. Birth had not made Madhu who she was now. The lack of touch had. So she would give to her little junkies what had been denied her, and when she placed her hand on their heads, she felt something swell inside her. It was not love, because love was something slippery—it could be caught but then it slid away. What she felt, and imparted, could not be caught to begin with. Each night, after a quick fuck, she would put her children to sleep and walk back home to Hijra Gulli. She was one of the rare few who had discovered why the arid ground in Gaandu Bageecha was called a garden.

Now, as she walked alongside the parcel in the daylight, Madhu found it strange to be staring at the same ground. It was occupied only by a small boy trying to fly a kite. He had no string, but he was holding the kite by its ears and trying to send it up. Seeing the kite go limp, he picked it up, and ran with it. Then he stopped abruptly and looked around, not knowing what to do with so much space.

By the time Madhu and the parcel got to Pila Haus, they were both thirsty. Madhu ordered a watermelon juice for both of them outside Pestonji Building. The parcel would need strength for what was about to happen.

Madhu surveyed the area. Pila Haus, like Kamathipura, had become a version of its former self. Originally called "Play House" because of the high society plays that had once been performed here, it was now a hub for B-grade films and two Chinese dentists, Dr Wang and Dr Tang. There was an Afghan dentist as well, with a fish tank in his window that contained three fish named after his three wives; and Dr Sharma, who was new and had a miniature Indian flag embedded into a denture as a window display. It was Dr Sharma who had refused to treat Madhu. Dr Wang had taken a look at her teeth instead and told her that in China, during his great grandfather's time, eunuchs were respected and worked with the royal family.

Today, Madhu was not here for her teeth. She found the woman she was looking for. Deeba was seated cross-legged in her sari, looking more like a fisherwoman than a tattoo artist. Laid out before her were designs sketched out on white chart paper covered in transparent plastic: demons, rats, Krishna, a light bulb, and a black butterfly. For years these were the images she'd engrave on the arms and necks of her customers. She took requests, depending on her mood, but she would never copy a design from somewhere else.

"Trying to run away last night was wrong," said Madhu to the parcel. "Do you understand?"

The parcel nodded her head and looked away from Madhu, licking the line of watermelon juice from her lips.

"If you do wrong things, there are always consequences."

This time, the parcel did not nod. She looked straight at Madhu, but there was no insolence in her look at all. She seemed to be making some sort of plea. Madhu's mention of consequences had made her realize that retribution was on the way, and it made even the smallest dash of bravery ooze out of her.

"If you make any sounds, if you do any drama, if you attract any attention, you will really suffer. That man who attacked you, I will not protect you from him again. So make sure you go through this well, and if it pains you, remember that the pain has come because you tried to escape."

The parcel looked around nervously, unsure of what her punishment might be.

Madhu led her to Deeba. "How are you?" she asked.

"It's slow today," said Deeba. "How is Bulbul? Did her man come back?"

Madhu smiled. Of course he did not come back. He never would. Bulbul had his name inscribed on her back, thinking it would draw him back. She just looked like a package that had been rubber-stamped. Fate sealed.

"I have a customer for you," said Madhu, indicating the parcel.

"Want a butterfly for her?" asked Deeba.

"No." Madhu did like the butterfly. One wing was longer than the other, as though it had realized something and was reaching for it.

"Why do you have rats?" asked Madhu. "Who would want a rat tattoo?"

Deeba showed Madhu the outside of her ankle. A snarling black rat with spiky teeth was tattooed there.

"When I first came to Bombay, I used to sleep on the road. A rat bit me so badly, I almost died. To cover the mark, I made a rat. Customers like the story when I tell them, and then they want it too."

"Tell Deeba your name," Madhu said to the parcel.

"Jhanvi," the parcel replied. Madhu nodded. This time she had not made a mistake.

"That's what I want. Write her name on her forearm, so she never forgets it."

Deeba patted the ground next to her. The parcel looked at Madhu with new understanding, her eyes even more pleading. If that look could work, Madhu would have been jelly ages ago. Deeba inserted brand new batteries into her clunky apparatus; it had a dull needle at one end.

"I sterilize it each morning on the chaiwala's stove," she said to the parcel. "So don't worry."

The needle whirred like an angry mosquito. Whirring and buzzing, it spiralled its way into the parcel's skin, reminding her never to run, that even if she ran, she would never manage to escape because her name was now stamped on her arm for her and all the world to see. It was the only passport she would ever get. This name might not have that much power now, but in time it would gather so much weight, her right arm would be heavier than the left.

Madhu held the arm down and steadied the parcel. The whirring continued, the blood dripped, and no one cared. Only the DVD seller glanced their way, through the curtain of horror films that dangled on strings from the roof of his shop. By the time the tattoo was done, the parcel's skin was red and raw. Madhu was reminded of the white bull the parcel had tried to soothe.

Now the parcel had whip marks of her own.

The two of them waited for Gajja outside Roshan Talkies. The cinema was showing an Ajay Devgan movie called *Gundaraj.*

A man was standing in the lobby with a switch in his hand, which he pressed every few seconds. The resultant ring of the bell reminded everyone that it was show time.

"Balcony! Balcony! Balcony!" he announced.

Madhu bought the parcel boiled eggs from the vendor outside the theatre and hoped that the munching would distract her from the pain. Her mobile rang: Gajja was already in the lobby and wanted her to hurry up. When they arrived, Madhu could see that Gajja was surprised.

"This is Jhanvi," Madhu said. "Jhanvi, this is my friend Gajja. Nice name, no? If you add an *n* in the middle, it gets even better," she said with a wink.

Jhanvi stared at Gajja's face but said nothing. Neither did Gajja.

By the time they got to their seats, the theatre was full. For a weekday afternoon, Ajay Devgan had pulled in an impressive crowd. Large fans blew air in Madhu's face. She opened herself to the fans and closed her eyes.

"I wanted to talk to you alone," said Gajja.

"So talk," said Madhu.

Moments went by and she heard nothing except the squeaking of Gajja's chair as he adjusted himself. She opened her eyes.

"Tell me . . . ," she said.

"I have to go back to my village," he said. "The Parsi doctor I work for is retiring. The new one hates me. He wants to get his own people in."

"So get another job . . ."

"I'm done with Bombay."

We are not done with Bombay until Bombay is done with us, thought Madhu.

"I want to watch the movie," she said instead.

She did not want to think about Gajja leaving. He was not her lover anymore, but he was the only man in her life. Gajja and gurumai were her two gods. One was kind; the other was confusing in her kindness.

"I want you to come with me," he said.

Gajja had been her first. She had been a virgin until he made Madhu his, and Madhu could not have asked for a better man. That much gurumai had allowed her. She could pick the man who would make her a woman. For two years after her castration, gurumai had nurtured her, fed her. Madhu did not have to do a thing. Every month she was stripped and made to stand in front of a mirror. She and gurumai felt utter glee when her hips grew, and her breasts showed themselves, and her hairless body glowed with youthful pride. She could urinate properly and there were hardly any signs of scarring. Gurumai was the perfect midwife.

If only Madhu's mother could see her. Madhu had made herself into a beautiful girl and could not be mistaken for a boy. A reversal had taken place, and she fantasized that she would be accepted by her parents now. That's how stupid she had been. Whenever she mentioned this to Bulbul, Bulbul would nod her head in encouragement, but she was the most transparent person in the world and Madhu could see her doubt. One day, Madhu told Bulbul that she wanted to go home to see her mother. Would Bulbul accompany her?

"Why do you want to go home?" Bulbul asked.

"I . . . What if they came looking for me but couldn't find me? I'm their child. They must be worried about me. It's been two years."

"Doesn't that tell you something?"

"You don't understand. Maybe they went to the police and reported me missing but the police did nothing."

"We may be hard to find, but . . ."

"I'm a girl now. I'm . . . Just look at me . . . You said I'm pretty. Am I not pretty? Were you lying to me? Tell me the truth."

"You're pretty, Madhu. You're very pretty."

"Then come with me. I just want them to know I'm alive."

"They know."

With quivering lip, Bulbul told Madhu that her mother had already spoken to gurumai. She had tracked Madhu down. She had not rested day or night; she had scoured the streets for gurumai with venom even snakes would die from. She had gone to the police and reported her son missing, but the cops were looking for a boy in a school uniform, not a girl in a sari. Madhu's family was not rich—they had no donations to make—so even though Madhu was on the missing list, and the police could have found him if they really wanted to, his case was treated like a missing shoe or key.

Eventually her mother had come to Hijra Gulli. Gurumai had not denied that Madhu was here. "You can call the police," gurumai said. "But it has already been done."

"What has been done?"

"She is one of us now."

Bulbul said that when Madhu's mother heard that, she went into a trance. She sat in front of gurumai in total silence. Neither one spoke. Each took in the other's presence.

Over the years, Madhu had made herself believe that information had been exchanged during that silence, about her, from one mother to the next. *My son likes sugar on his chapatis. My son is an Amitabh Bachchan fan. My son likes to be held tight and told that he is not useless. Sometimes my son stares at traffic for hours.*

While her mother would have given gurumai the past, gurumai would have offered the future:

Your daughter is fulfilling her destiny. She has a sister named Bulbul. She has a new mother now, one who cares for her.

That's why silences were heavy. The words accumulated like the dead, body upon body, until there was a stinking heap of corpses and the smell in the room was too bold for anyone to bear. So of course, Madhu's mother had to leave.

Where was Madhu during this time?

She was in the operating chamber, locked up, recovering.

In the years since, her mother had never come back. Not once. Yes, Madhu had lost her genitals. But wasn't Madhu the same person inside, the same soul who to this day had not found solace? It is said that a mother's love is pure, that when a mother prays for her child, the universe listens. Madhu had discovered that mothers were just as debauched as the rest. In her opinion, the halo needed to be taken off their heads and placed in the gutter, where all halos belonged.

When Madhu learned about her mother's visit, she begged gurumai to let her go home. For the second time, she asked for permission to leave.

"You can go," gurumai said, "as soon as you have repaid the loan."

"What loan?"

Gurumai spat her tobacco into her spittoon and asked Bulbul to fetch her account ledger. She opened it to a page labelled "MADHU" in bold. Underneath her name, there was a list:

- Saris
- Bangles
- Jewellery
- Food
- Hand mirrors
- Makeup
- Nail polish
- Rent
- Chappals
- Salwar kameez
- Table fan
- Bulbul's gift

Gurumai had even charged Madhu for the new table fan she had bought. Madhu had complained about the heat, and the fan had been purchased for her comfort. But Madhu could never get a single breeze from that fan. No hair of hers had moved because of it.

Madhu had no clue what "Bulbul's gift" had been, but she knew why Bulbul had to be given one. When a new hijra was inducted into the fold through the Nirvan ceremony, the hijra attending to the inductee had to be given a gift. Without Madhu's knowledge, Bulbul had been given two new salwars, new chappals, and a gold bangle.

Gurumai said she had not even listed the fee she would have to pay to the hijra elders on Madhu's behalf, as she did for every new member. The conclusion was clear: Madhu was no better than a slave who would have to crawl her way out of debt. When Madhu asked Bulbul why she was not wearing the gold bangle she'd been given, she looked at Madhu as though she was stupidity multiplied by eternity. The bangle was locked in guru-mai's treasury for safekeeping. This was business. This was Bombay. It had not become the financial capital of the country by twiddling its thumbs.

Madhu's mother had given birth to her. Gurumai owned her.

So at sixteen, Madhu started repaying the loan. She chose Gajja, a drunken man ten years her senior who had a shattered heart and barely remembered who he slept with. She chose love. Love opened her legs. It was manufactured love, no doubt. It was imagined; it was hoped for. It was, in reality, just a smelly tongue down her throat and a hard one up her behind, but Madhu made it something else. To this day, it had lasted.

But now she had to tell Gajja that she could not leave Bombay with him.

She had been in the wild too long. The normal was terrify-ing. The normal was being a man's something, as opposed to a nothing. She had been invisible so long. Any form of respect-ability would give her shape, start putting her back together. But what if the parts didn't fit? What if, in her new avatar, she turned out to be even more peculiar?

She was fine. She was content with what life had given her. That was the lie she held on to in the cinema hall.

The parcel had fallen asleep against her shoulder. The pain must have knocked her out. Madhu looked at the girl's face. It was so still in the light that glanced off the movie screen, it almost made her want to stroke the parcel's cheek. On her other side sat the man she cared for. In this darkened hall, she felt slightly human. Perhaps it had to do with the name of the the-atre: Roshan. It had brought a little light into her life. Chhotti batti—that's what the parcels used to be called anyway.

The parcel breathed against Madhu's arm. Thin streams of air from those tender nostrils tickled Madhu's skin: touch without being touched. Even Gajja had fallen asleep. His snore was disturbing the couple in the row ahead. The woman turned her head and looked at Madhu, hoping that she would nudge Gajja to stop.

Madhu would do nothing of the sort.

Instead, she smiled at her. It was not an apology, but a form of ownership. This man was hers. Let him rest, he had earned it. This child too.

The woman smiled back.

She had mistaken Madhu for a woman. For ages, Madhu had tried to embrace womanhood, but her desperation made her stumble and she had become a pathetic parody. In this moment, Gajja and the parcel had made her complete.

Madhu truly believed that a woman did not need a man and a child to be complete. Yet she suddenly felt proud. She was giggling inside, skipping, jumping, doing all the things she had been too ashamed to do as a boy on the school playground.

She was with her family.

She pressed her nose against Gajja's stubble and took in the scent of booze and hospitals. It was the warmest smell she knew. She had to be careful not to wake them up. The minute they woke up, this feeling would stop. They would become real.

Some relationships lasted a lifetime; hers would last for the remainder of this movie. Sometimes life offered you a lesser version of a dream. She chose to take it.

10

When Madhu returned from the movie, the mood in Hijra House was tense. The day of the jamaat always made gurumai scowl. She had told Madhu many times that had it not been for the fact that she ran a brothel, she would have been a nayak, one of the seven hijra leaders of Bombay.

When gurumai was much younger, she had openly questioned the council's refusal to acknowledge that hijras were involved in sex work. Her argument was simple: Offering blessings in exchange for money was a predatory act. It thrived on people's superstitions and fears, and there was no proof that the blessings worked. So why were the hijras who did this work considered respectable when their income was built on a lie? On the other hand, prostitution was real. It was as honest a job as butchering or baking. "And it works," she had joked, much to the amusement of some of the younger hijras. But her views were not entertained.

Gurumai's anxiety was not helped by the fact that all the members of Hijra House were glued to the TV that afternoon.

The whole nation was in an uproar over a recent crime. A billion souls were passionately demanding the blood of three men who had raped a bride on her wedding night. One of the men was her neighbour. Until last night, everyone had wanted the rapists dead. Now a new solution had been proposed.

"Castrate them," said the female lawyer on TV. "Let the animals live. Don't kill them. Let them live."

There was applause from the studio crowd. A politician who sat next to the lawyer agreed. He was pushing for the reinstatement of an old law, formed during British rule, that would allow rapists' penises to be severed.

"Perhaps the death penalty is not enough," he said. "Maybe castration is a bigger deterrent. These people need to be humiliated. Make them hijras."

When she heard that, gurumai's back slumped, as if there were no vertebrae holding her up. "What they're saying is that our existence is a fate worse than death. I don't think they will ever understand us," she said.

Madhu silently agreed. The debate shouldn't become about hijras, but when *would* the third gender come first?

"Shut that shit off," said gurumai, when the program broke for a commercial.

Madhu glanced at her. Gurumai was determined to look her best today, but she was struggling. The sweat on her face gave her away. Strands of her silvery hair stuck to her forehead, and there were heavy, wet stains under her armpits. She had told Madhu that she did not want to take Dr Kyani's painkillers because she had to remain sharp for the council meeting later on. And now the debate on TV was depressing her as much as it was Madhu.

Madhu was as hopeful as everyone else that the accused would pay for the vileness of their act. But in the pursuit of justice, why were the hijras being spat upon? For her and her sisters, castration was a pathway to a higher life. It's what gave them respect. It also bothered Madhu how much coverage this incident was getting: a *bride* had been violated on that most sacred of nights. But what about ordinary women on ordinary nights? Or indecent women, perhaps, like sex workers? Or hijras? What happened when less-than-ordinary souls got violated? Why not create a furore then? Why let their pain slide away like rainwater into a gutter?

"Ladies and gentlemen, let me bring your attention to the hijras, women, and children of Kamathipura," she would have said if she had been on that show. Here, in Hijra Gulli, everyone had a hideous memory or two lying around in their pockets like small change. And, like small change, they were considered insignificant.

Just as Madhu was about to sink into a pool of gloom, guru-mai asked her to massage her legs. Even though Madhu was tired, the physicality of the task started to ease her mind. The purrs of pleasure that came as every drop of Ayurvedic oil seeped into gurumai's calves, calmed Madhu as well. Somehow gurumai always managed to settle her down. But that feeling quickly dissipated when Umesh showed up with his real estate woes.

"Forgive me," said Umesh. "I should have called."

"I'd offer you some chai, but you won't be staying long," gurumai said.

"What I have to say will only take a minute."

"Then why say it at all?"

Umesh looked around the room. He noticed the incense sticks, the thin white smoke curving toward the ceiling.

"You had the place cleaned?" he asked.

"Yes," said gurumai. "In your honour. I had a feeling you'd be back." She offered Madhu her other leg. Now the left calf needed looking after.

"The stables are going to be shut down," said Umesh.

At the mention of the stables, gurumai's calves tightened. Madhu doubted that Umesh understood that the stables of Kamathipura had a special place in gurumai's heart. Very few people knew that she had slept in the hay on her first night in Kamathipura with the horses for company.

"The inspector paid a surprise visit," he said. "He found that the horses were too thin and were stepping in their own shit and urine."

"Many humans also step in their own shit and urine. What's your point?"

"The builder I work for is buying the stables."

"Congratulations," said gurumai. "Would you like a laddoo?"

"Look . . . ," said Umesh, trying to contain himself. He shuffled about, searching for his next words. Gurumai was skilfully pricking his ego with the edge of a dai-ma's knife, but he was taking it better than Madhu would have expected. He must really want Hijra House.

"We have also acquired the steel mills at Two Tanks," he said. "And I'm here to make an honest offer."

"I don't doubt your offer," said gurumai. "You are honest about buying, and I am honest about not selling. I'm not saying this to get a higher price. This is not just our home; it's our grave. We will die here."

"Then why not die richer? We are not asking you to relocate. Once the new building comes up, you will have flats to stay in. You and your chelas can still live here, but in better conditions."

"Please don't insult me by making such a statement."

"You will have it in writing."

"Like the residents of Bachuseth Ki Wadi? Once the new building went up, no one wanted to live next door to prostitutes and bar dancers. We are allowed on paper, but never in people's hearts."

"If that's how you feel, we can consider giving you a small unit on the side."

"Look at him," gurumai said to Madhu. "We have not even moved in and already he is throwing us out!"

"I can offer you a crore for this place. You and I both know it is not worth that much."

"Then why offer? Why do you need this hole?"

"Because this hole is causing an even bigger one in our pocket. There are two builders fighting to get a contract to redevelop Kamathipura. Whoever gets a seventy per cent majority can go to the government and bid for the contract. We have spent a lot of money on bribes so the contract doesn't go to the rival builder. But even bribes have an expiry date. So this place is important to us."

"The only time they need us is when they want us to leave," said gurumai to Madhu.

Then she moved her leg away from Madhu and sat up straight. "Go tell your builder he does not have my vote."

"I'm sorry to hear that," said Umesh. "If you do change your mind, you have until tonight. After that, there's nothing I can do."

"I appreciate your concern."

"All I'm saying is that the horses in those stables have been standing in their own shit for years. Someone finally noticed."

Gurumai spat the tobacco she was chewing into her spittoon

as a last word to Umesh. He left, disgruntled but not defeated. There was a sly grin on his face.

"He's too confident," said Madhu. "He knows something."

"He can know how to make his own mother come. I'm not selling."

Although she kept her mouth shut out of respect, Madhu was convinced that gurumai was in no condition to attend the jamaat. It had been months since she had walked down the stairs of Hijra House. And indeed, halfway down, her knees buckled and she started coughing; Bulbul quickly borrowed a chair from one of the carrom players outside. After sitting for about fifteen minutes, gurumai finally managed to get into the waiting taxi. Madhu and Bulbul climbed in beside her.

The building where the jamaat was being held was called "Lucky Compound," and even though it wasn't in the greatest shape, it was definitely more fortunate than its namesake in the suburbs, a newly built structure that had suddenly collapsed one night. This original still-standing Lucky Compound had been given as a gift to the hijra elders. Only the elders knew who the benefactor was, and gurumai often said that if she could find out who this person was, she would approach him with a business venture. She wanted to open up franchises, like the McDonald's that had sprung up a short distance from Kamathipura, on Bellasis Road. Her idea was to open small brothels that could be duplicated in all the main metros. Then she'd have a business card that she could stick up the bums of the elders. Perhaps they'd finally accept that prostitution was just as respectable as other hijra occupations. For now, she was entering the jamaat on unequal footing. If she hadn't been a dai-ma, she'd have been asked to stand in a corner and would have been given no respect at all.

Madhu had attended many gatherings before, and she could sense that as the hijra leaders got older, their hunger for respect increased. As their bones turned brittle, money and power were the only forms of calcium that worked. Each of the seven hijra houses of Bombay was represented: Haji Ibrahimwala, Poonawala, Dongriwala, Bhendi Bazaarwala, Lalanwala, Lashkarwala, and Chaklawala. Each clan had one leader, the nayak. But above all of these mighty chiefs was one supreme commander: Bindu nayak, leader of the Haji Ibrahimwala clan. Her clan was considered the most superior of the lot, and the hijras of that house walked with that knowledge in mind.

The nayaks were seated in a closed circle on the ground. The rest of the hijras—scores of them crowded around their leaders—were never allowed to be part of the circle. They had to remain outside it. They were the debris. Madhu could not help but stare at one of the leaders, Kanta nayak. Her stomach was so large, one could have mistaken her for being pregnant if only she did not look like an old man. Gurumai always remarked that Kanta nayak needed two chelas around her at all times, one to carry the sagging skin on her jowls, and the other to support her belly. But her eyes were as sharp as a moneylender's.

"*You* seem to be doing well," Madhu heard Kanta nayak snidely remark to Samira nayak, referring to the jewellery the latter wore. Even though all the nayaks lived in the same building, sometimes they did not communicate with each other for weeks, focusing only on matters pertaining to their own clan. They were always locked in a silent power struggle, and a jamaat was the perfect venue for each to try to establish her supremacy.

"Maybe it is destiny that has brought us together tonight, for I have some disturbing news," said Bindu nayak, addressing those gathered. "But first let us get a few matters out of the way."

She started with one of Kanta's chelas, who had been blacklisted six months ago for abusing her guru. She had spent the intervening months begging near the airport and was in ill health. She wanted to be readmitted to the clan.

"Munni, stand up," said Bindu nayak.

From among the group of hijras, a lanky figure rose. She looked ashen, an effect heightened by the fact that the other hijras had put on makeup and she had not. She wore her hair in a bun, but it was still dishevelled, stubborn straw.

"Munni, what do you have to say for yourself?" asked Bindu nayak.

All the hijras stared at Munni. Madhu shivered. It was a hijra's greatest fear to be asked to leave the house she had sworn allegiance to. She would become an instant pariah.

"Speak, my child."

Munni had nothing to say. She started shaking. The hijra next to her was clearly disturbed by her silence but was afraid of reaching out to her on account of the nayak Munni had offended. It would be interpreted as an insult.

"Munni, your offence was that you threw your guru's spittoon back into her face. Then you called her a fat pig," said Bindu nayak.

The offence was always stated aloud so the rest of the community could understand what constituted a punishable offence. It was also an opportunity to make Kanta nayak's shame public. That was how Bindu nayak ruled: through humiliation.

"What do you have to say, Munni?"

Munni finally found the courage to look up at Bindu nayak. Her eyes were teary and bloodshot. She folded her hands together in Kanta nayak's direction. There was no question about her sincerity.

"Kanta, do you take her back?" asked Bindu nayak.

"I'm sorry," said Kanta nayak. "But after what she has done, I cannot accept her."

"I understand," said Bindu nayak.

Bindu nayak looked around the room. A hijra's future would be decided in the next few minutes.

"Do we have any takers for Munni?" asked Bindu nayak. "What can you do, Munni? What are your special skills?"

Munni looked too underfed and tired to remember. She seemed defeated, like she'd already surrendered to the possibility that she would be spending another six months on the streets, without a roof, without a master.

It seemed no one was willing to take her.

"Fine," said Bindu nayak.

She motioned to a disciple of hers, who took a steel tray and placed it at Kanta nayak's feet. A red cloth lay in the centre of the tray. Madhu watched as Kanta nayak put her hand underneath the red cloth and raised it an inch or two. Apparently, there was an adequate amount of cash under the cloth, because she nodded her approval.

Bindu nayak was the only guru who could accept this miscreant now, and she had showed her magnanimity. She had accepted a hijra who was of almost no value. Munni stood rooted to the spot, waiting for the next move.

"Deen, deen, deen," said Bindu nayak.

Although these words were usually spoken only when a

person was being initiated into the hijra community for the very first time, Bindu nayak used them to signal a fresh start.

"Munni, you are my disciple now. Come, my child."

Munni rushed to her new mother and melted in her arms. A hijra had been traded. The jamaat was off to a forgiving start.

Next, there was an argument about territories.

Kanta nayak accused Samira nayak's chelas of begging near Bandra station. Samira nayak said that she did not remember ever agreeing *not* to send her disciples there. After some bickering back and forth, Bindu nayak decreed that it was Kanta nayak's domain, thus helping her save some of the face she had lost. To appease Samira nayak, Bindu nayak told her that her disciples could work on the trains themselves, all the way up to Bombay Central. They were free to charm the passengers on the Central Line for the next fiscal year. After that, the contract would have to be renewed.

"Just one rule," said Bindu nayak. "Don't flash any of the passengers. In Virar, one hijra lifted her sari when a woman refused to give anything. She turned out to be a cop's wife. The hijra got the beating of her life. Also, it's not good for our image. So no flashing."

"Flash your tits instead," said Kanta nayak.

"Much better," said Bindu nayak.

"By the way, there's a new shop in Dongri that sells the cheapest padded bras. The quality is great. I've asked him to make neon ones."

Before things got out of hand and raucousness set in, Bindu nayak motioned that she wanted to speak. The volume came down, and only the moths banging into each other around the sizzling tube lights could be heard.

"I'm disturbed," said Bindu nayak. "Rumours are being spread about the hijra community." Then she looked straight at gurumai. "Do you know anything about this?"

"No," said gurumai. "Should I?"

"There is word that you have been using Hijra House as a shelter for pojeetives," she said.

"So what if I am?" gurumai said defiantly. "If we don't look after our own, who will?"

"Your intention is good," said Bindu nayak, surprisingly gentle in her tone. "But why invite an outsider to see what you are doing? Why invite a real estate agent to hold the hand of a dying pojeetive?"

Oh no, thought Madhu. Gurumai's plan had backfired. She had tried to shock Umesh into never coming back to Hijra House, but what had happened had reached the ears of the hijra elders. What game was Umesh playing?

"The person who gave us this building now thinks we are also hiding pojeetives in our rooms. Your antics with this agent, whoever he is, have caused us great discomfort."

"His name is Umesh," said gurumai. "And he is a troublemaker."

"What does he want?"

"We are one of the few buildings preventing his builder from getting a seventy per cent majority of the property in Kamathipura."

"Thanks to him, *we* have been asked to take a test by the owner of our building."

"What test?"

"To see if we are pojeetive. It's just a pressure tactic . . . He thinks we will influence you to sell. All these builders are connected."

"I'm sorry you have to go through this," said gurumai. "But I'm not selling."

"Are you sure?"

"As sure as a pojeetive is of dying."

Somehow Bindu nayak did not mind the sharpness of guru-mai's tone. If anything, she seemed to admire her resilience.

"Then we will support you," said Bindu nayak. "And to show our support, we will continue the night's festivities at Hijra House."

For the first time in history, the seven hijra nayaks entered Kamathipura. They graced Hijra Gulli like spiritual souls finally blessing the cursed and the wretched. It made Madhu want to throw up.

But there was no doubt that the presence of the nayaks was giving the hijras of Kamathipura some hope. Old enemies were making up, hugging each other outside on the street, sharing cigarettes and laughter, exclaiming that they really only had each other to count on. In Madhu's eyes, the lane that had once boasted more than five hundred hijra prostitutes suddenly regained its lost glory. It was experiencing a major boost of power, a heroin shot so beautiful that everyone felt it at once. The clattering of bangles, the flip-flop of chappals, and the exaggerated fluttering of eye-lashes was all a unified effort to defy God. The caricature that was each hijra's face, the smudged red lips, the white powder, the pockmarks, were a challenge to Him. That which He had given, they had altered. In creating them unequal and tainted, God had left in them a hunger to look beautiful, a need so fierce, they were ready to skin doves and wear them on their faces.

Upstairs, gurumai finally had her wish: she was smoking a chillum with the seven nayaks, and even though this was not an official gathering anymore, all the nayaks were seated in a circle, and gurumai was part of it. She was finally *inside* the circle. Madhu was happy for her. But she could tell from gurumai's watery eyes that she was taking too much opium. The other nayaks were sharing a chillum, but Bindu nayak had given a special chillum to gurumai, just for her use, and it was making her heady in more ways than one. Madhu was worried that gurumai would embarrass herself in front of the nayaks. The last time she had overdosed on opium, she had hallucinated and had been severely constipated for a week.

Gurumai saw Madhu hovering and motioned for her to come close.

"Padma just called me," said gurumai. "Why aren't you answering your phone?"

"I want to be here," said Madhu. "If you need anything."

"Go to Padma. Something's come up."

"But I want to stay . . ."

"Go," said gurumai.

"Go easy on the opium," whispered Madhu. "Please."

"You are a good child," said gurumai, patting Madhu's cheeks.

She said it with the generosity of someone who is high, but also with love, and that made Madhu want to stay even more. But she knew better than to argue with gurumai in front of the nayaks.

"I need some golis," said Madhu. "For my work."

Gurumai gestured for Madhu to take some from the small bowl by her side: tiny opium pills that went by the names of Chandu and God's Dream.

As Madhu walked down the stairs, the absence of men on the stairwell pleased her. The brothel felt like a home when hijra arseholes were on strike. When hijra arseholes had a "No Entry" sign posted on them, the real arseholes had nowhere to go—the men simply skulked away, not used to being rejected. None of them would dare to abuse a single hijra today. There was an army of hijras in the street, their bodies sticking unusually close to each other. Glued together by the tasty desire for revenge, they were ready to inflict pain upon man, that terrible thing they were almost born as.

Bulbul was chewing on some kebabs outside Hijra Gulli, forsaking her diet for the night. Madhu took a couple of pieces from her, and a swig of alcohol from a hijra she had never seen before. As she chewed, some strands of mutton got stuck between her teeth. By the time she was done removing all but the last tiny one, she was standing face to face with Padma in her brothel. She let the mutton strand remain. She respected its spirit. The goat it once was must have been a fighter.

"The client has paid the advance on the parcel," said Padma. "So get her ready."

"Tonight?" asked Madhu.

"No, the day after tomorrow."

"But . . . then what was so urgent?"

"The client wants a photo of the parcel."

Padma took the phone she had given Madhu and punched in a mobile number. "Do you know how to send a photo from the mobile?"

"Yes," said Madhu.

"Then get it done. And remove everything from the phone."

In one swift stroke, Padma would recover every single rupee she had spent on the parcel. On the first night, the parcel would fetch Padma at least ten times her cost, and yet the parcel would remain a slave for years.

They were in Salma's room. Madhu had dressed the parcel up in clothes that Salma had bought for her at the midnight market. The lighting in the room was too dim, the surroundings too bleak, and Madhu was having a hard time trying to make the parcel look fresh. She looked young, but the skin underneath her eyes was sunken. This was the first time a client had asked for a photograph. Normally, flesh was flesh.

"Do you know why I'm taking your picture?" asked Madhu.

"Yes."

The firmness of the parcel's reply surprised Madhu and made her snap the picture almost involuntarily. The result was a bit hazy.

"You want to show it to someone . . . ," said the parcel.

"Who?"

"A man."

"That's right," said Madhu. "Now sit still. You are moving."

But the parcel was not. It was Madhu's hand that was moving, struggling to get the right composition for the photograph. She took two more shots and noticed how the parcel was staring straight into the camera, without any shyness or fear. She was trying to say something to Madhu, or to the man who would finally see the photograph. Tonight, the parcel had a different quality.

"Why are you doing this?" asked the parcel.

"Quiet," said Madhu. "Sit still."

The phone's battery was dying and Madhu was frustrated.

"Please," said the parcel. "Tell me."

It wasn't the first time a parcel had asked Madhu this question. But the coldness in her voice was new. She had stopped pleading. She just honestly wanted to know.

"I'm trying to take a picture," said Madhu.

"You will not help me this time," said the parcel.

"I will," said Madhu.

A final click. She got the picture she needed. It was the size of a passport photograph, but it captured the parcel's entire body. There was no emotion on her face, just the facts: black hair, black eyes, and so on. The photo was ordinary and had a grainy look about it. It gave the impression that this girl was somewhere far away. It also suggested that there was an aura of simplicity about the girl—she did not know too much or think too much, and would perhaps not offer much resistance.

Satisfied, Madhu took out an opium pill from the pouch in her sari.

"I want you to take this," she said. "I want to see the effect it has on you. I will give it to you again when you meet the man. It will help you stay calm."

But the parcel wasn't listening. "In my village, there was a girl . . . three years older than me. She had to get married to an old man."

"You're not getting married."

"I will get married many times," said the parcel.

"Yes," said Madhu.

Then, not knowing what else to do, Madhu showed the parcel her photograph. "Here," she said. "This is the one I will be sending."

When the parcel saw it, she stared at it for a few seconds. Then she slowly reached out, took the phone in both hands, and placed it in her lap. It was as though she was talking to herself in the picture, telling herself she would be fine. It was a moment of intense concentration between two girls. The girl in the photograph was the one who would be hurt, but the girl sitting on the bed was the one who would feel the pain.

The opium had the desired effect on the parcel. She was calm and relaxed. If Madhu timed things correctly, the parcel would be sufficiently numb on the night of her opening, still show some signs of life as per the client's needs, and not remember everything afterwards.

Madhu did not even bother putting her back in the cage. She left her at the foot of the ladder just below the loft. The girl's eyes were half closed and there was a slight smile on her face, as though she had just heard the chirp of her favourite bird, or her mother's voice calling out to her, telling her that lunch was ready. She had made no movement apart from a single tilt of the head in the past hour. There had been no hallucinations. She took well to the drug. She was drowsy, with the simple illusion that perhaps life was worth living.

It was the same illusion that the hijras of Kamathipura were perpetuating with their camaraderie that night. Lane Five was celebrating as well—perhaps there was a wedding. Four drummers and three keyboard players dressed in glittering gear were playing at a thunderous volume. Despite the heat, the drummers were wearing white gloves. Young men danced around the band, their faces stupid and full of glee, their shirts sticking to their backs with sweat in thick blotches. One of the men was dancing with money clenched between his teeth. He held both his hands high, with forefingers pointing upward, while he swayed from side to side. He took the money out of his mouth and circled it over the head of another man, as women watched from behind window grilles only a floor above the street. Madhu could hear the drumming all the way back to Hijra Gulli.

Then there was another sound mixed with the distant drumming.

Someone was wailing. Madhu stopped walking. She stood still and tried to block out the band. There was no mistaking it; it was not one person, but a chorus of crying—hysterical shrieks of loss that only hijras were capable of.

She picked up her pace and rounded the corner. Men had left their carrom boards to crowd around the staircase to Hijra House. They were trying to peer in, but the dank darkness and a swarm of hijras blocked their view. Madhu pushed through them all and rushed up the stairs. She passed hijra after hijra, but not one familiar face. No one talked to her; no one told her a thing. Her mind, frantic, jumped straight to Bulbul.

But Bulbul was on the floor, wailing the loudest, along with Anjali, Tarana, Sona, and Roomali. Devyani was standing against the wall, stone-faced. Madhu asked Bulbul what was wrong, but Bulbul was too delirious to answer. Then Madhu saw the broken bangles on the floor: shattered fragments of blue and red and yellow.

Madhu's heart stopped; she knew what that meant. But she kept moving ahead, toward the nayaks. Bindu nayak stepped forward and tried to embrace Madhu, but Madhu brushed her away. She wanted to get to the body. She wanted to see it for herself. She did not want anyone to tell her anything. Not a word. She wanted to see.

Gurumai was lying on her back, her mouth slightly open, her eyes closed. Madhu reached for her, but hands held her back. Only a foot away from gurumai, Madhu collapsed like a weak sapling. A pathetic stillness gripped her. Someone propped her up but she rejected their help. She stood on her own, rising from the ground like someone a hundred years old.

The nayaks were suffocating her with their stares and concern, hovering around gurumai with the bent necks of vultures. Behind Madhu, her sisters were shrieking, but she herself was not capable of making a sound. Then the smell woke her—the many scents mingling in the room, of liquor, sweat, and sweet perfume. The smell shocked her into movement. She took one step forward and touched the body.

Gurumai's stomach was the first part she touched. Maybe it was because gurumai was her mother. She noticed that gurumai's hair was dishevelled and knew she would not like that at all. Madhu lifted her head and adjusted her hair, and in doing so, felt a whisper of breath come out of gurumai's lips onto her forearm. Perhaps gurumai was trying to tell her something. Or perhaps it was simply the remainder of a word, the second half of the last word gurumai ever spoke. Half formed, it had to come out.

It was meant for Madhu.

"It is God's will," said Bindu nayak. "It is God's will. May God keep her safe." She came over to Madhu, but Madhu curdled at her touch, and she knew that Bindu nayak sensed it. Confused, she raised her head. Gurumai might not be breathing, but there were still hordes of hijras in the room who were, and their breath was twisting Madhu into shapes she had never felt before.

"We will have to proceed with the burial tonight itself," said Bindu nayak as gently as possible. "All the nayaks are here. She would have liked us to perform the rituals."

"What happened?" asked Madhu. "How did she . . ."

She could not use the word yet. She did not want to.

"We don't know. That's the beauty of her death," said Bindu nayak. "But what a night to go on. In the presence of all the nayaks. Even I would wish for a death like that."

Madhu watched, too dazed to process what she was witnessing.

A bucket of hot water lay at gurumai's feet. The nayaks tied white pieces of cloth around their hands and began to wash the body. None of the disciples was allowed near gurumai. She had seven children but not a single one of them was cleaning her.

"I want to do this," said Madhu. "Let us do this."

"If the nayaks are here . . ." Bindu nayak shook her head. "She was our most respected dai-ma."

Gurumai's naked body was covered with a green cloth. Madhu wanted the cloth to be removed. Gurumai had been born a hijra and she was proud of it. If she'd had her way, she would have walked naked every day of her life, her body a reminder of the maker's cruelty and imperfection.

"I will stand naked before God," she had once said to Madhu. "If He also lowers his eyes in shame, just like humans do, then I will know that hijras are a mistake. But if He looks me straight in the eye, then we are the perfect creation, higher than man or woman."

Bulbul placed her hand over Madhu's eyes and wiped them.

"Don't cry," she said through her own curtain of tears. "If you cry, what will happen to the rest of us?"

"I'm not crying."

It was true: Madhu's eyes were burning, not crying. She was incensed at not being allowed to send her own mother home. She moved closer to the body. Bindu nayak stopped tending to gurumai and signalled for the others to continue.

"I hear you have a man who works in a hospital?" she asked Madhu. "Can he get us an ambulance to transport the body? Once the sun comes up, we cannot bury her. We will have to wait another day."

"So wait," Madhu said. "Let the body stay here so people can come and pay their respects."

"Those who matter are here already."

"To you, perhaps," said Madhu.

Madhu could see that she was trying Bindu nayak's patience, but she wanted to keep gurumai with her another day. She wanted to sit alone with the body. There were so many things she wanted to tell gurumai. So many questions remained unasked and were sitting on her chest like giant crucifixes.

"Call your man," said Bindu nayak.

"Why not use the cars you came in?"

"We want the nayaks and body to all travel together."

Madhu dialled Gajja, but when she spoke into the phone, her voice cracked. When it vaporized, she passed the phone to Bulbul.

Now that the body was washed, Bindu nayak took off her chappals. She handed Madhu one.

"Here," she said. "This much you can do. You start."

All seven disciples removed their footwear and stood in a circle around the body. Madhu was the first one to strike. She raised the chappal high above her head and brought it down on gurumai's stomach. After three strikes from her, the rest followed. They beat gurumai's body and cursed it for being a hijra. Their beatings were a warning for her never to take rebirth as one. Madhu flinched as she did this. In all her years, she had never raised her hand to gurumai, and now they were chastising her when she was not capable of emitting a single word in reply. Bulbul stopped hitting gurumai and fell over the body, taking a couple of beatings herself. Madhu quickly pulled her away.

When Gajja arrived, gurumai's body was taken down the stairs and into the night.

The carrom players and steelworkers were still out there, but the hijras formed a barricade around gurumai, preventing them from having a look at the body. This was the reason hijras were buried at night: as the soul left the body, it was the duty of those left behind not to let the look of strangers defile it. One look by man or woman, one sneer or disgusted glance, and the soul was trapped again.

Gajja looked at Madhu, and she gestured that she was okay. He sat in the front with the ambulance driver and urged the nayaks to hurry because he needed to get the ambulance back to the hospital as soon as possible. The nayaks sat in the back with gurumai. Once again, Madhu was left out in the cold, a reminder that hierarchy, not love, ruled her world. It should have been Bulbul and her in there, sitting on either side of gurumai, holding their mother's hand. Instead, she and Bulbul were trailing the ambulance in a taxi.

When had gurumai breathed her last? Was it when Madhu had been taking the parcel's picture? Was that why Madhu's hands had been so shaky? Could she feel gurumai's longing for her, the need to be comforted during those last few breaths? Madhu's brain was a tangled nest of thoughts, and yet events were moving so quickly, so smoothly.

Through her haze, Madhu was surprised to see that a grave was ready at the cemetery in Nariyalwadi, waiting for gurumai.

But then again, Bindu nayak owned five graves in this burial ground, including one for herself. She had bought them years ago, when graves were cheaper. Now graves were real estate too, resold at a higher value. Sometimes cemeteries reused old graves, dumping one body on top of an older one.

The ambulance stopped outside the graveyard gates.

The nayaks pulled the stretcher out and laid it on the ground. There were no flowers for gurumai. Madhu would have liked to put flowers on the cloth that covered her. This was all so plain, so ordinary for someone as dazzling as gurumai.

At last it was the disciples' turn to take over. The final walk would be theirs and theirs alone. The nayaks took the cloth off gurumai's body and propped the stretcher up vertically, so that it looked as though gurumai was standing. Madhu then placed herself directly in front of gurumai, and allowed her to fall into her arms, as one would accept a child. Behind gurumai, Devyani took the place of the stretcher; Madhu then made gurumai stand erect against Devyani's tall figure.

Now Bulbul and Madhu stood on either side of gurumai while Tarana and Anjali tied gurumai's ankles with a thin rope to Bulbul's and Madhu's. Gurumai was now propped between Madhu and Bulbul with her arms around their shoulders, the three of them like bosom friends coming out of a bar. In this way, holding their mother up, they walked gurumai to her grave, tall and respectful, her eyes closed but her body moving forward.

This was how gurumai had wanted to go. In her final moments on earth, she refused to lie prostrate on a stretcher. Even in death—especially in death—she would walk, upright in bold defiance. Hijras might be forced to live in shame, but they went to their graves better than anyone else.

Madhu could feel Bulbul shuddering in the dark, breaking into tears and then regaining composure again, until they stood before the yawning hole that would soon accept their mother. It would be dawn soon. Madhu took one hard look at the person who had shaped her, who had forged her destiny, who had sculpted her body with one stroke, whose hug was more true than that of her real mother, who had made her feel she was worth something when she did not have a friend in the world, who had taught her how to make a man come, and come again, who had fed her rice and dal with her own hands, who had looked so deep into her eyes that Madhu was convinced their bond went back lifetimes, and who had had the courage to tell her parents who she really was. Madhu loved gurumai, and would continue to do so, but not in the way humans experience love. Madhu loved her the way the wind loved the trees. She was visible only because of her.

Madhu moved away and watched gurumai enter the ground.

The next morning was the most silent that Madhu had ever lived through.

Gurumai's bed was empty. Her crumpled bedsheet was still warm, and for a second, Madhu almost convinced herself that gurumai had gone to the toilet to relieve her bladder. But the sheet was just a piece of cloth, a reminder that a cheap wooden bed could outlast a human being.

Madhu was confronted with the mess of the previous night's gathering: empty chai glasses, whisky bottles, steel plates with mutton crumbs, chewed-up chicken bones, and cigarette butts strewn over the floor like a holy offering. This was all that remained of the last night of gurumai's life. Madhu and her sisters were part of that debris.

After taking their baths, Madhu and the others put on white saris and walked through the rooms, sipping chai, picking up cigarette butts and sweeping the floor. When it came time to clean up gurumai's bed, Madhu could not bring herself to do it. That crumpled bed was gurumai's last imprint on earth. If she straightened the sheet out, she would wipe the slate clean. She ran her fingers along the sheet again, lightly, not erasing its texture in any way. It had felt gurumai's skin more than any of them had. If gurumai's spirit was contained in there, Madhu wanted to access it.

But then, suddenly, she moved away. The sheet was reminding her of how gurumai had looked the night before, with eyes closed, facing the ceiling. Madhu had never seen her so soft, almost childlike in her nakedness. The more she tried to push gurumai out of her mind, the less successful she was. Gurumai's face kept appearing before her—her face and neck, as though they were the two most vital parts of her body.

And that is when it dawned on her. How could Madhu have been so stupid?

There had been no key around gurumai's neck last night. Who had the key to the safe? Someone had taken it.

"Bulbul," she asked, "where's the key?"

Bulbul was slumped on her small stool, staring into the mirror.

"Where is gurumai's key?" she asked again.

Bulbul did not answer. Her mind was somewhere else. Her mobile phone was on the dressing table. Madhu picked it up. Bulbul had taken a photo of herself. The whiteness of her sari had added a spectral hue to her already silvery skin.

"Bulbul?"

"He wants me to send him my photo . . ."

"Who?"

"He sent me word after so many months . . . I finally got a message from him . . . I'm so relieved . . ."

Madhu glanced over at the radio on the window ledge.

"He wants to see what I look like now. He wants to show me to his parents."

If only Bulbul could see herself now, with her eyebrows arching in the middle, twitching with hope, then diving downward into total misery. Today of all days, Madhu had to tell her the truth. Today, she had to shatter the illusion and tell her there was no way Bulbul's man could send her messages through the radio, because the radio was not even on.

"The radio is not working," said Madhu. "See . . . there aren't even any batteries in it."

She opened the small hatch where the batteries were normally placed and showed it to Bulbul, who took the radio in her hand and caressed it.

"It's been good to me," said Bulbul.

"Bulbul, you have to listen to me," said Madhu. "Please. I'm your friend, your sister who will never lie to you."

"I thought you would understand."

"I do . . ."

"You're just as bad. You stand on a bridge for hours . . ."

"What?"

"You stand on that bridge . . . where you lived . . ."

"What are you talking about?" Madhu's voice rose. "What would I stand on a bridge for? Do you think I'm mad?"

"No," said Bulbul. "I don't think you are mad at all. Neither did gurumai."

Madhu stared at Bulbul, but she was not even looking her way. She was trying to find comfort in her own reflection. Madhu felt dizzy.

"Gurumai knew?" she asked, more to herself than Bulbul.

"We saw you one night, standing next to the banana seller . . . You were looking at your old balcony."

Bulbul got up from her stool and put the radio back on the ledge.

"You believe your family will take you back. The same way I believe my man will come for me."

"Why . . . why didn't you tell me you knew?" asked Madhu.

"It was not the right time," said Bulbul. "But it is now."

"What do you mean?"

"One mother is dead," said Bulbul dully. "Maybe it's time for you to return to the other."

Madhu thought about that wisp of air she had felt on her forearm last night when she touched gurumai's body. She had no doubt now that it had indeed been gurumai's last word. She had not imagined it. And now she was able to grasp what the last word had been.

Return.

That's what gurumai wanted Madhu to do. Gurumai's last wish had not been for herself; it had been for Madhu. She did not want her child to be an orphan. Of all people, it was Bulbul who had confirmed this. Madhu felt a tenderness for Bulbul rise within her suddenly, like it had when the two of them first met.

"You really think I should go back?" Madhu asked.

"Will standing on that bridge bring you peace?"

"But what if . . . what if they . . ." Madhu struggled to finish her sentence. She could not bring herself to ask the question. So she decided to ask a question that Bulbul *would* be able to answer. "What did gurumai say? When she found out?"

"She said nothing," replied Bulbul. "Neither of us spoke about it."

Until now, thought Madhu. Until gurumai's final breath.

Madhu decided she would return to the one who had brought her into this world. And she would have to do it now. If she thought about it too long, she would lose the courage to take this step. Yes, it would have to be now, in this moment of despair and madness brought on by gurumai's sudden passing.

Madhu's mother was old now, but still breathing. Madhu was certain that she had kept her mother alive by standing on that bridge for hours. She had stalked her mother with her love. All those nights she stared at the balcony, she had been providing oxygen to a woman who had made the mistake of holding her breath and spitting her child out of her womb and her life.

Now she would have the chance to take Madhu back.

It was a Monday afternoon. Because it was a public holiday, the family would be at home to witness the reunion.

Usually when Madhu exited the red-light district, she felt like she was doing something illegal, like crossing a border without a passport, or breaking quarantine while infected. Today, however, she felt nothing of the sort. She was no longer a hijra; she was no longer Madhu Chickni. She was a boy in short pants again, and a girl caught inside that boy, like a parrot in a cage. When she passed by Underwear Tree, she noticed a row of new underwear, freshly washed and hung out to dry. This was a good sign: newness. A sign of prosperous beginnings. In the little hut below Underwear Tree, she caught a glimpse of her face in a small mirror and was shocked to see something rare: a smile. Perhaps gurumai herself had etched it there with her crafty old hands.

Apart from that smile, gurumai had also given Madhu clarity. Madhu's naked hatred for her father had blinded her to the real person she needed to make amends with: her mother.

Her father could be excused for not understanding her, she thought. But wasn't her mother the true custodian of Madhu's soul? Gurumai had merely done a touch-up on Madhu's body, to keep it in sync with the soul—the hijra soul that lived in the womb for nine months. Madhu's mother *had* to have known who Madhu really was.

Madhu thought of going to the forty-seventh step to calm herself. But no—there was no need for that. She told herself to believe, to not be a coward. Bulbul had made her believe, and gurumai was giving her the strength to race toward the ones she loved, the ones who would take her in. She would enter their lives again, the way a humble ray of light enters a dim hallway.

At last she was face to face with the building she had once lived in, the concrete of her youth. The footpath was still the same shambles it had been back then; the only difference was that new holes had appeared. She stood at the entrance, astonished that she had made it this far. The long corridor that led to the elevator was unmanned; the watchman's stool was empty. She gathered her wits and went straight to the elevator. She would have preferred to take the stairs but her legs were jelly. She hoped she would not collapse when her brother opened the door. Or would it be her mother? Or, even better, *him*?

Her father, who had spent many sleepless nights on account of her, she would forgive with the might of saints. Even if he had become a jibbering-jabbering lump of flesh whose mind was gone and whose eyes could barely see, she would sit by his side and feed him. She was used to caring for the dying.

If her brother was married, she would get along famously with his wife, and if there was a child, she would be in a unique position to be both uncle *and* aunty.

The door was the same, with the same brass nameplate. Nothing had changed.

Her heart was so unabashed in its excitement that there was no need to ring the bell. The way it thumped was announcement enough. But she rang the bell anyway. Perhaps her family would think it was the butcher or the vegetable vendor or the postman. In a way, she was a postman delivering good news of love lost and found. Her sari was the white envelope, and she herself the letter, her eyes the ending and the beginning.

Come on. She had waited too long. The time was ripe. Guru-mai had died so that Madhu could come here.

The door did not open.

She cursed herself for not bringing gifts. She should have brought something, some token.

Maybe no one was home.

That was fine. It was providence: maybe she was meant to buy each member of her family a present. She was a sailor who had returned from the wild seas. Of course she should bring them something from her travels.

She took the stairs down. Rather than being disappointed, she was still delirious with the thought of her return, her new-found bravery sparkling inside her.

As she left the dimness of the corridor and entered the street, she came to a sudden halt. A short woman was limping toward the entrance of the building. Madhu was hit by a force greater than any strong wind. There was a rush of memories, a warm smell, a voice singing to Madhu when she was little. The woman was clutching a small grocery bag that contained vege-tables, her arm wrinkled with age.

It was her. And she was with her son, the one she cared for.

The son walked right behind her, talking on his mobile phone. Madhu froze. She quaked with love, was filled with the desire to rush into her mother and take that grocery bag from her hand. She almost screamed out, "Ammi, Ammi, Ammi"— three times, as if she had won a prize. But before the words could leave her mouth, her mother looked right at her, and Madhu's mind careened out of control.

Her feet staked roots in the ground out of terror. Then her mother moved past Madhu, as did her brother. They moved past, but then her mother looked back. She stared at Madhu's face. Madhu could hardly believe it. After more than twenty-five years, their eyes were meeting again. Her mother came to Madhu, stepped forward, and placed something in the palm of Madhu's hand.

Then she turned away and entered the building.

Madhu stared at her palm. It held a five-rupee coin.

The coin throbbed in her palm, pulsating like a mistake, shivering with the truth. She had been mistaken for a beggar, and that fact shot through her belly, the shame of it trickling down her legs as she ran home.

Kamathipura took her back without so much as a whimper. What a fool she had been to think she could abandon it. But this time as she stood outside Hijra House and looked up at the building that was her abode, she recognized it for what it truly was. The balcony where she was once put on display, with jasmine in her hair and fake jewels around her neck, was diseased in daylight. Hijra House had given her asylum, but it was not her home. She was a patient there, much like Bulbul and the rest of her sisters. Over the years they had stood outside, like clothes on a laundry line, hoping that the wind would take them away, whisk them to a better future. They were delusional. And she was the most delusional of them all in thinking that her mother would take her back.

She did not feel like climbing the stairs. She felt like going down, descending into the earth. She walked away from the building, without any aim at all, the stray dogs reminding her that even they had someone to lick, unlike her. A blind beggar was limping next to her, his silver eyes deep within their sockets. He had his arm on another man's shoulder, a begging partner who sang praises of Allah into a flower-shaped microphone and urged the faithful to give alms. Even the blind beggar had someone to guide him and speak on his behalf. But not Madhu. She was truly alone. As she walked, she remembered the scent of someone who was just as alone as she was, someone who, like her, had no mother any longer, no family. No one. Her cage was the only place Madhu could be right now. She needed its history, the cries of past parcels stuck on the walls, their dainty feet thrashing against the cage bars.

She climbed the ladder that led to the loft and lay down beside the parcel. She did not mimic the parcel, but she saw that they were two bodies in sync, both wanting to curl into a ball and disappear into oblivion. The coin was still in Madhu's palm, a reminder of how unrecognizable she had become.

In a year or two, no one would be able to recognize the parcel either.

Madhu remembered another parcel who had been held captive in the brothel for three years. The only movement she had been allowed during that time was from cage to brothel bed to toilet. Hundreds of clients later, when she was finally offered daylight, she trembled. But what no one expected, or perhaps even cared to think about, was what would happen when she saw her face in a mirror. After three years, she had become someone else. She was all of thirteen, and three of her front teeth were broken, and her scalp showed through thin strands of hair. She started screaming at the mirror, begging to know where she had gone.

How wise she was. Unlike Madhu.

Madhu had stared at the mirror every single day and tried to beautify herself, and in doing so had masked the person she had turned into. If she had not looked at herself for a year or two, she would have been shocked into seeing exactly what her mother had today: a dilapidated face struggling to retain the slightest form of dignity. A body and face that had emerged from her mother's womb was now worth five rupees in pity. Madhu would have seen that.

The foolishness of her act made the silence in the cage unbearable.

"Do you think your mother sold you?" she asked the parcel.

As the parcel's body moved a little, it gave off a strong odour, but Madhu knew it was the cage itself that reeked.

"Tell me," said Madhu.

"No," said the parcel.

"How do you know?"

"She was my mother . . ."

If Madhu had had the strength to smile, she would have. Her work was complete. The parcel spoke of her mother as though she was in the past. The fact that she believed in her mother was irrelevant. Why could Madhu not work that same magic on herself? How could she have fallen for the very illusion she had protected the parcels from?

"You shall meet the man tomorrow," said Madhu. "You are ready."

She wanted the parcel to react; she wanted her to cry. Then Madhu could be of some use—and she desperately wanted to be of service to another human being. But the parcel gave her nothing. The girl was silent, and in her breathing there were no signs of panic. Her breaths were even, while Madhu's were fast and sour. She could not console anyone. She was left gripping the coin again. She scurried out of that hole and down the ladder, a rat on the run.

Back at Hijra House, Madhu sat in a corner, dazed, watching Bindu nayak opening gurumai's safe, and wondered how she had allowed Bulbul to talk her into such madness. But it was not Bulbul's fault. She was just a sound, a sudden, startling noise that frightens a person into pulling the trigger on their own gun. The gun had always been in Madhu's hand and it had always been pointed at her own temple. Bulbul was just the sound.

"Stand up," Devyani whispered to Madhu. "Bindu nayak's getting angry."

Madhu did not care about the hijra chieftain. She rose not to appease the nayak, but because gurumai's safe had finally been opened. Bindu nayak had taken the key from gurumai's neck while cleaning the body the night before and had brought it back to Hijra House. She wanted to open the safe in front of all the disciples so there could be no accusations later on.

A list was made of gurumai's bangles, jewellery, and cash. There were also some photographs. But no will.

"There's no will," said Bindu nayak. "Do you know if she made a will?"

Madhu was careful not to speak. This afternoon she had acted without thinking and it had cost her everything. Her last ounce of self-respect had fled from her. She was determined not to falter again. If she told Bindu nayak about the will, that it was with Padma's lawyer, Madhu would be offering the information in blind trust. She would stay silent and let the consequences play out. Later, she would get hold of the will, and if it was in favour of her and her sisters, she would bring it to the table.

"If there is no will, then everything has to be distributed equally," said Bindu nayak. "I leave it up to you to do that. As the senior-most hijra in this house, Bulbul will be your new guru."

"But Bulbul . . . she's not . . . ," said Anjali.

Madhu respected her for not completing the sentence.

"She's not capable?" asked Bindu nayak. "Even if that is true, I will be overseeing the matters of this household now. She will report to me."

Bindu nayak kissed Bulbul on the forehead, placed her palm on Bulbul's head, and blessed her. Bulbul remained unperturbed, neither happy nor sad. She might as well have been anointed as a fly on the wall.

Bindu nayak took Madhu aside. "As you know, nayaks cannot condone sex work. It is unfortunate, but that's the way things are. You are closest to Bulbul. I will stay in touch with you. I am counting on your co-operation."

Then Bindu nayak, a royal guest who had graced their home and touched their weary foreheads, left. Madhu did not know why her co-operation was needed. What did Bindu nayak mean when she said she could not condone sex work? Did she expect Hijra House to become a beauty parlour?

Madhu shook her head. Her more immediate concern was the contents of the safe. There was one item she especially wanted, that would be hers and hers alone. It was wrapped in a cream cloth, but she could see its shape. It was pushing through, wanting to be uncovered.

She reached out and felt the cold grey metal of the knife in her hands. This had been the instrument of deliverance for her and many other hijras from far corners of this land. It would be hers now. From now on, it would always be with her wherever she went. Just as a rooster carried Bahuchara Mata through the heavens, this knife was gurumai's vehicle. Gurumai would have wanted Madhu to have it because she was her most successful patient.

She held the knife on the edges of her forefingers. It had perfect balance. There was not a single blood stain on it—a sure sign that gurumai had had no blood on her hands when she castrated young men. It had never been polished in all those years and it still had a shine—not the way gold or silver gleamed, but there was a hint of brightness, as though the blade had been dipped in a full moon and remembered the taste.

Madhu now had something from both mothers. A knife and a coin. But she did not know what to do with either.

12

The night before a parcel was to be opened, Padma always performed a small puja. It was to ask for forgiveness for what was about to ensue. It was also a plea to the gods to provide the parcel with fortitude. Madhu surveyed Padma's office. There was a menu of Hindu gods on the wall to choose from— if Padma was out of favour with one, she could turn to another. She had been silent for a long time, her eyes closed, and it was making Madhu edgy.

Suddenly, she asked Madhu a question: "Why do we need men to protect us?"

She opened her eyes and looked at Madhu, waiting for an answer. But Madhu knew she was not supposed to give one. They were not equals. If Padma had asked gurumai that question, it would have been different.

"All of this has happened because of one man," said Padma, indicating her brothel as she circled the incense stick around the small idol of Ganesh. "After my father died, I was looked after by my neighbour, who cared for me as her own. Then her husband decided it was better that I become a prostitute. Everything that has happened to me since, has happened because one man failed to think I was worth anything."

Madhu thought, but did not say, that one man had failed to accept Madhu too, and the effects of that were beyond what she could have imagined. Her future, and Padma's, had been decided by men. The two of them were not so different from each other.

"I was spared from TB, only so that my cunt could be put to greater use," said Padma. She said it with a sting that made Madhu sit up straight. "Even when a good thing happens, it happens for the greater bad. Remember that."

The incense stick in Padma's hand was shivering.

The opening of the parcel, Madhu realized with new clarity, was just an excuse to perform the puja. The puja was not for the parcel, it was for Padma herself. She was crying for her own peace, battling against the things that had been done to her.

"My husband was a good man . . ." Padma started coughing, perhaps because her throat was not used to speaking well about someone. "He asked me once how I could deal in underage girls when I had been through the same pain."

Padma looked around the room, and Madhu recognized in her a lost soul scanning her surroundings for answers, trying to find them anywhere, but fully knowing the futility of her undertaking. A tube light, or a rickety wooden chair, or a cracked tile in the floor, or the peeling paint on the ceiling could not provide answers. The only thing on offer was the abject emptiness of those objects. They were just as empty as Padma and Madhu.

"The thing is," Padma continued, "I couldn't answer my husband's question. You see . . . you do it once and something dies in you, and then you keep it . . . that feeling . . . from growing back again, until you have won. And what can I say? I'm Padma—I always win."

Padma's nose wrinkled, the incense smoke tickling her nostrils. "I think he passed away because he realized he could not change me. After he died, I gave my girls away. I don't even have photographs of them. Sometimes I remember their faces."

Her daughters must be grown women now, with children of their own, and here was Padma trying to recall their faces as little girls. But so what? Everyone in Kamathipura was holding on to a good memory, something that made them feel human and gave them pain beyond measure. Madhu steered the conversation in a different direction.

"I need gurumai's will," she said.

"Of course," said Padma.

Madhu was relieved that Padma didn't seem to view Madhu cutting her short as disrespectful. If anything, Madhu was humbly reminding the old doyen that sharing private moments, opening up to others, only brought you more misfortune.

"The lawyer has gone out of the city. He'll be back in a week," said Padma.

"A week? Can you tell me where his office is? I need the will."

"I will call in the morning and find out," said Padma. "Now let's focus on the parcel."

"I need that will. Bindu nayak is capable of anything."

"Who's that?"

"The leader of Bombay's hijras."

"I'll do what I can," said Padma. "Your gurumai was a special soul. I will make sure her final wishes are fulfilled."

"Thank you," said Madhu.

"Now make sure the parcel is ready by eight tomorrow night. And don't decorate her. Just make sure she's clean."

"No flower in her hair?"

"No," said Padma. "There will be a priest at hand to perform rituals. He'll do it."

"A pundit? What for?"

"The man who's buying her, he's very rich. He's also a pojeetive. His pundit told him that if he takes a young virgin, he will be cured."

"The client told you this?"

"He had to when I asked why he wanted a photo of the parcel. It was for the pundit to see if the match was good. People will believe anything their pundit tells them," she sneered.

Once again, Madhu's mind was spinning. In all her years doing parcel work, this was a first. The belief about virgins wasn't new; it was an ancient one, from long before the pojeetive existed. The idea was that disease was an impurity, a curse thrust upon a man's soul, and it could only be cured by purity, by a man locking himself upon a young one, sucking up her energy, using her as an antidote. But Madhu had never seen it being put into practice.

"What about a woman pojeetive? Does she get to fuck a young man?" Padma asked bitterly. "Once again, the woman is being sacrificed. Things will never change."

No wonder they call it the "Maharog," thought Madhu. The mother of all diseases had forced people to practise a "cure" as violent as the disease itself. It forced Madhu to see the parcel in a completely new light: she was now a bottle, a pill, a potion to be consumed.

But Madhu said nothing and made her way home, her heart heavy, her mind reeling from the senselessness of it all.

Madhu and her sisters' first night without gurumai was spent listening to the radio. They all lay in the dark, not speaking, just crying. Gurumai's empty bed had a fresh sheet on it. It looked so cold, without any creases at all, until Bulbul could take it no longer and threw herself on the bed as though she were plunging into water. No one pulled her away. She stayed there until her nose and lips were deep into the mattress, her muffled groans of anger a reflection of how all seven disciples were feeling. She left her tears there the way an angry animal leaves piss, marking its territory, telling whoever is around to stay the fuck away. Then she walked to the windowsill, plugged the cord into the socket, and fumbled with the knob on the radio. The occasional sound of static was a reminder of the current disturbance in their lives. She finally found a channel that had no interruptions from ads or a radio jockey—the music just leaked into the room from the radio, as though a gas was stealthily entering in the night, and made everyone's eyes go red.

After a song ended, Madhu went to the floor above, to the room where the pojeetive lay. The pojeetive was in her last stages. If there had been a bet on who was going to go first, gurumai or the pojeetive, Madhu would have put all her money on the pojeetive. She returned downstairs to rejoin her sisters, but the more she tried not to think of the pojeetive, the more the poor soul's dry lips appeared in front of Madhu's eyes and prevented her from sleeping. Here was a human being who had spent her life battling one illness—her hijra-ness—and as though that was not enough, now she had to contend with another, deadlier foe. The very things that made one human— love, hope, health—had been ripped from her calmly and precisely, the way a syringe extracted blood. The parcel would find herself in the same state, thought Madhu. The girl had been betrayed by all, her faith in human beings was gone, and once the pojeetive worm entered her, ruptured its way into her being, her weight would drop and drop, and she would be abandoned, left to rot and dry under a bridge somewhere, or in an alley soaked in garbage. Even rain would hurt her skin.

Madhu wanted to take a pill, to induce a coma for at least an hour or two, but it would be insensitive of her to switch on the light and rummage through her drawer for medicine. Besides, this wakefulness was part of the mourning, a musical lamentation far more truthful than what the hijra elders had offered gurumai the night before. That had simply been a ritual. This was something else, a stirring so deep that nothing needed to be said.

No sooner had Madhu drifted into sleep, than a jerky buzz made her eyes open. It was her mobile phone, a number she did not recognize.

"Madhu," said the voice. "This is Bindu nayak."

"Yes, nayakji," said Madhu.

"I can't get in touch with Bulbul. Where is she?"

"She's asleep," whispered Madhu.

"I need Bulbul to come meet me first thing in the morning."

"Is there a problem?"

The radio was still on. Madhu got up and switched it off. All the sisters were asleep. She went outside to the balcony.

"Our landlord has asked us to vacate Lucky Compound," said Bindu nayak.

"I'm sorry," said Madhu. "I . . . but what do you need Bulbul for?"

"If Bulbul agrees to sell Hijra House to the builder, our landlord will reconsider."

"But . . ."

"The builder and landlord are in business together. As the new leader, Bulbul can make that happen."

"But what about us?"

"You will be looked after," said Bindu nayak.

"What guarantee do you have that we will not be on the road?"

"You have the word of all seven nayaks. Do you understand?"

Yes, Madhu understood. It was so convenient for Bulbul to be the new leader. It was in accordance with hijra law, but it was also convenient. Unlike gurumai, Bulbul was meek, born not to lead. Her arm could easily be twisted. In the face of the seven nayaks, Hijra House would wilt.

It was only after Bindu nayak said goodbye and Madhu stared at the mobile phone in her hand, that she realized the extent of Bindu nayak's reach. The phone Bindu nayak had called Madhu on was the one Padma had given Madhu for parcel work. Madhu replayed in her mind how, only hours earlier, Padma had feigned ignorance when Madhu mentioned Bindu nayak's name. When Bulbul hadn't answered her phone, Bindu nayak must have asked Padma for Madhu's number, and Padma had forwarded the wrong number—the one that was only to be used to discuss the parcel.

———

The early morning temple bells rang in Madhu's ears like warning bells. In a few hours, Bulbul would be forced to sell Hijra House, with the promise that the hijras would receive fair accommodation in the new building. It was a joke.

But what was even funnier was how easily gurumai had fallen for the trap laid by Bindu nayak. Madhu could understand Bindu nayak's motivations. There was no love lost between her and gurumai anyway, and if it was a question of protecting Lucky Compound, then Hijra House could easily be pawned off. The old reptile had played gurumai and Madhu like dholaks, drumming them the way she wanted. That was why the hijra elders had agreed to come to Kamathipura: to get rid of gurumai. As she thought of gurumai's death and the possibility of foul play, she felt sicker and sicker.

There was one person she could unburden her heart to. Would he meet her in the canteen of the Alexandra Cinema?

Madhu was soon at their meeting place. The chaiwala had barely woken up, but his hot brew was steaming in a large vat in the corner.

"They could have put poison on the hookah," said Gajja. "That's the only way."

"How could I have been so stupid?"

"It's not your fault."

"They gave gurumai her own special hookah that night. Bindu nayak kept wiping it with a handkerchief. And gurumai was proud of that. Proud to suck on her death."

Padma must have been in on it too. She had called Madhu to the brothel to tend to the parcel at the precise time when gurumai was smoking opium. It was hard to tell who had led this, Padma or Bindu nayak.

"Don't you see?" said Gajja. "Nothing can stop this place from being destroyed. One day it will all go. With or without us."

Madhu knew he was right. Opposite them, Maharashtra College, the place where her father had taught for years, still stood tall. It would remain untouched, but beside it, the towers kept rising. The college was allowed to stay because it made the area more respectable. It gave a sheen of dignity to the obese buildings surrounding it and made their price per square foot rise. For all this prosperity to happen, feet had to be cut off—the human feet of those who could barely walk to begin with. But a greater purpose had arrived: to provide housing for people who didn't need it.

Madhu had no choice. She had to stop fighting.

"I will come with you," she said. "I will come with you, Gajja, if you will still have me."

Gajja's smile said it all. It was a small one, hardly creating a dent on his rough face, but it made Madhu feel safe.

"But will I be accepted in your village?" she asked. "They are not used to my kind."

"Once they know you, they will."

"And if they don't?"

"Then we can both stay at home and close our doors to the world. Madhu, all I want is a friend. Someone's hand to hold, someone to drink with, to cry with, someone who will scold me when I'm doing wrong. You scold me a lot."

"I'll scold you more as I get older."

"Then I will only care for you more."

"I have one request," she said.

"Anything."

"Two," she said.

"Okay." Gajja smiled.

"We don't take anything with us. No extra clothes, nothing. I want nothing to remind me of this place."

"Done," said Gajja. "And the second?"

"I want us to leave on your motorcycle."

"But you hate that thing."

"I need to wrap my arms around you so tight that I will never have second thoughts about leaving."

"We go tomorrow morning."

"No," said Madhu. "We leave tonight. Meet me here at eight."

By eight, Madhu's work would be done. With the last parcel of her life opened, she would walk away from this place once and for all. If she ever came back, it would be as an old person, a tired hijra staring at the fourteen lanes from a distance, just to see what had become of them.

She had two hours to go. So did the parcel.

The parcel would have to be calmed down with opium. That was the most important part. There could not be any resistance from her. After all, it was to be a ritual, a ceremonial offering made in the presence of a pundit, a poor joke that made temple bells ring on their own and the statue of Jesus burn bright with fever and look the other way.

Madhu needed some time on her own, to ease her nerves.

On Lane Fourteen, there were more lights than usual, or maybe street lamps that had not been working had suddenly come on, giving a golden glow to everything. The brothels were drying out their laundry. Purple nightgowns and yellow sheets hung on nylon strings, giving the old wooden railings a happy lift. The giant wheel was almost full. The operator scratched his belly as he waited for the last seat to be taken.

Madhu slumped into that seat. She needed to be off the ground. If her feet were planted on the earth, she would continue to feel its shocks and vibrations. In the air, her brain would find the peace it needed to execute her final act. The wheel turned slowly, its achy, wobbly machinery grinding away, barely able to support the collection of people it carried: old men, former pimps now hardly able to see, their glassy eyes nearing blindness; and retired prostitutes who cleaned brothels, their hurting backs resting against the seats. These were heavy souls, dense with memories. They reminded Madhu that she was sharing space with a boatful of losers going round and round in circles. Just like her and the parcel.

From her place in the sky, she saw how the environment around Padma's brothel had changed. So many small factories and workshops had sprung up, units that manufactured umbrellas and mobile phones and garments. Even Padma's building was a factory of little hands and feet. It was an underground city in the sky, where children were kept in lofts, fed and drained, then fed again, while somewhere outside the walls of Kamathipura, clean hands were counting money.

Bindu nayak's and Padma's hands were dirty. Madhu had caught their handshake. That she could do nothing about it made her feel a wrath so real that she was totally serene. She now saw the true purpose behind the transformation occurring on the streets. Perhaps the disappearance of Kamathipura was a good thing. With very few brothels remaining in operation, the prostitutes were turning into freelancers. They were being forced to use their mobile phones to take appointments to service men on railway tracks, in cars, and in alleys outside Kamathipura. It was not an act of defeat. It was fantastic. Especially for those women who were pojeetives.

For the pojeetives, it was the ultimate revenge. Shunned by society, relegated to a minuscule plot of land for a lifetime, the pojeetives, before dying, were now reaching out to the rest of the city, spreading their tentacles in a last cry. But it was not help they were asking for; they were offering a parting gift to the rest of the city, while the city was too busy building buildings to notice. The pojeetives would have the last laugh.

And what about Madhu? What was her contribution to Kamathipura's future? The pojeetives were succeeding, but she had failed at everything.

She saw so clearly now that her work with the parcels had not brought them any relief. The plan to go back to her parents had backfired, and she had been unable to protect gurumai. Everything she did, everyone she touched, ended in dust. She was a master at one thing: failure.

If everything was in a state of disintegration—the pojeetive in Hijra House, the parcel's faith in human beings, Madhu's own dream of returning to her family—then why fight it? Why not accept it, celebrate it even? Perhaps her solution lay in failure. Kamathipura's destruction was inevitable, but Madhu could speed things up. Yes, that was the only way forward.

All her life she had run. From herself, her school, her parents, and her own body. But no matter how much she ran, nothing she did had an effect on anyone outside these fourteen lanes. She had led an insignificant life, just like Bulbul, just like all her sisters. They were breaths in the middle of a storm; no one could feel them. When they tremored with loneliness, no one cared.

She could not make anyone care, but she could make people take notice. Through the din of the evening traffic, she could hear her father's words: "For someone with a pointless life, you have a great desire to live."

She had wanted to live because she knew she had something to offer. She realized now that that something had not been her body. Her body had been her failing all along. Her parents had rejected her body. They had not bothered to find out who she truly was. If she had been born a girl, they might not have loved her as much as they loved her brother, but at least they would have accepted her.

When she *was* accepted—by gurumai, by Gajja, by the men who paid for her—it was for her body. All her life she had lived in that body; she had worshipped it, served it, used it to serve others, and so was trapped by it. But now, just like Kamathipura and its tenants, she too was dissolving, like the hot vapour of chai, except that she did not taste like chai. She was not delectable; she had been born and brewed to mortify. But what if that wasn't the case? What if she didn't have a body? Her soul was kind, it was just, and it longed for love—isn't that what we all want in the end? All she had ever wanted was a hand to hold and to feel someone's breath on her shoulder when she was pretending to be asleep. When Gajja lay next to her after their lovemaking, Madhu never slept. She fought sleep no matter how much she needed it, no matter how restful it promised to be, because staying awake with Gajja and feeling his breath on her skin was even more restful, more delicious. At least Madhu had experienced that long ago. It was only fair that the parcel feel it too. That is what she would offer the parcel. And in doing so, she could still make her life count.

As she made her way to the loft, she saw Salma and Padma cooking together. The aroma was inviting; she wanted to bite into the oily potatoes they were making. A feast was being prepared, perhaps for the parcel's client. The hot fires of the stove gave Madhu the idea she was looking for.

"It's time," said Madhu, slowly bringing the parcel out of her hole.

The parcel had the same look on her face that every single parcel had. Whether they knew what was going to happen or not, an unmistakable shadow loomed over them, causing a quiver in their organs that Madhu could feel. The parcels were no different from the goats of Kamathipura. As the day of their sacrifice approached, the goats became more and more silent, and even the little boys who talked to them, fed them, and played with them started retreating. But that was not what gave it away.

The goats knew. They just knew.

It was time for Madhu to make her mark with one last stroke. She wanted to pray for strength but did not know whom to pray to. So she touched the handle of the knife that lay hidden in her sari. She gripped that handle with probably the same commitment gurumai had had when she freed Madhu from her male form all those years ago.

If gurumai's knife gave her strength, Padma gave her inspiration. When Padma, in full view of everyone, had tortured the man who had sold her, she had made herself a household name. Similarly, with one single act, Madhu too would make herself a household name. She would spread her name like butter on these battered streets.

But hers would not be an act of vengeance. It would be an act of love.

She took the five-rupee coin that had been placed in her palm by her mother—all her mother had thought she was worth when she had mistaken her own child for a beggar—and flicked the coin away. She did not care where it landed. Madhu's parting gift to the parcel would be nothing like it. It would be something a real mother would do for her child.

"Do you remember the water tank?" she asked the parcel.

"Yes," said the parcel.

"I want you to hide there. No matter what you hear, no matter what you think is going on outside, you stay in that tank. Stay there until the screaming stops."

"What screaming?" asked the parcel.

Madhu bent down and placed her hands on the parcel's shoulders. Then she went closer to her and whispered something in her ear.

"Remember that name," she said.

The parcel nodded. When Madhu looked at her face, she could tell that the girl was joyous. There was such a surge of emotion inside her, as though a new colour was being born. She knew that anything was better than the fate that awaited her, no risk too large.

"Why are you helping me?" she asked.

"I'm not helping you. No one can help you." But even as she said these words, Madhu wanted to believe they weren't true. She wanted to believe that luck would favour her this one time because she was asking for something that was not for herself. For the first time, Madhu allowed herself to hold a child—not as a parcel, but as a true child. Madhu embraced her with all the love she had failed to receive. She showered the girl with it, and it came in torrents, a gale so strong that if Madhu hadn't held the girl tight, she would have been swept away. Madhu let the girl sink into her breast, her dripping nose pressing hard against Madhu's white sari. Madhu wanted the girl to take in centuries of affection. And it was too much for the parcel; she was trying to tell Madhu that it was overwhelming, that she must let go, but Madhu kept pressing harder and harder, and she sobbed as she did, and apologized, and begged for mercy, until finally a strange elation came over her. She circled her arms around the parcel in one final gush of love. When there was nothing left to give, she released her and watched her run to the water tank.

Epilogue

Hello, my name is Kinjal. I am preparing to tell the story of my life. I will start by saying my name. Then I will show people my arm, on which I have another name: Jhanvi.

It is unusual for a person my age to tell my story, because I am only sixteen years old. Mine is a hard story to tell, and I do not know if people want to hear it. But I have been invited to speak about it on a TV show. I am not comfortable appearing on television. I would prefer to hide somewhere, but I know that would be wrong. People need to know what happened to me.

Even though it is my story, it is not just about me. It is joined with someone else's, someone I knew for a few days, when I was ten years old. It was only after her death that I knew her name: Madhu. Maybe I will start with her.

The producers of the show are telling me not to think about things too much. They don't want me to sound as though I have been trained. They say they will ask me questions and all

I have to do is answer. But I am still nervous. The truth might be easy to remember, but it is the hardest thing to say.

I am told that there will be people in the room while the camera is recording me. I am not sure how I feel about that: so many strangers in the same room, staring at me.

Perhaps I will begin by explaining why the name Jhanvi was pierced into my skin.

No. That is not the correct place to start. It's not the beginning, even though names are important in my story. Apart from Kinjal and Jhanvi, I was called by another name: the parcel. I did not know about that name then, but I do now. That name is what the show is about. There have been many parcels like me, but I am here because I was saved. I am told I can give people hope. I don't know if I can do that. I have a hard time accepting my current situation. The crowd will see that. They will notice how I look down when I talk, how I shift in my chair and cannot stay still for too long. After a few seconds, my body wants to move, from here to there, but it does not know where to go. That is the story of all parcels.

All parcels have the same beginning. All of us were betrayed by the ones we loved. But I am not here because of where I began. I am here because of where I ended up: in a water tank. The tank was supposed to hide me from the police, but it saved me from a huge fire. When I entered the tank, I submerged myself in the water, I kept only my head out, and I told myself over and over not to forget the name that Madhu had whispered in my ear: Gajja.

She had told me to go to the canteen of the old cinema and ask for a man with that name. That was all she said before she let me go.

After entering the tank, I shut the lid and stayed there.
After some time, I heard a blast. It shook the water in the tank.
It shook me up too, so badly that I urinated in the water. I don't
want people to know that. I will just tell them I was really scared.
I was up on the roof, hiding in a tank, hearing the screams
below. Maybe some of them were my own.

I cannot tell you how long I was in there. There were
moments when I could actually feel my mind leaving me. I
thought I was in that water tank for about three hours. I was
wrong. When I climbed out, the sun was up.

There was smoke all around me, but I told myself that
all I needed to do was get to the old cinema, just around the
corner. Luckily, my dress was wet, so I held it against my nose
and ran down. The first floor had a few bodies. I gave them
no importance. I could not. All I wanted was to get out of
that building.

When I came out, there was a crowd, and a fire engine also,
but it was just parked there. It had done its work. Some women
were crying, some were just sitting there, staring at the ground.
There was blood and glass, and everything was dark grey, and
between the tears and tiredness, I just slid out and stood near
the old cinema. I was wet and shivering. I thought about asking
the chaiwala if he knew a man called Gajja. What if he took
me back to the building? It was a chance I had to take. If I had
stood there any longer, someone would have taken me.

My gamble paid off.

When I came face to face with Gajja, I saw that he was
frantic. At first he did not recognize me. But when I said that
Madhu had told me to ask for him, his face broke. I did not
understand what was going on, but I knew we had to get out

of there. He put me on his motorcycle and we rode non-stop for two hours. I held him tight as we went in the wind because I was so cold. I was also terrified of falling off.

I did not feel safe with Gajja. I did not feel I was in danger either. I could see in his eyes that he did not have a bad hunger. His eyes were clean. He told me he would make sure that I got back home. When I told him that my home was in Nepal, he said that was far away but he would get it done because it was Madhu's last wish.

"For someone whose every wish was denied by life, this I have to do," he said.

Strangely, getting back to my country was not as hard as I thought it would be. But Gajja still had to pay a bribe at a border crossing that seemed like a jungle. As we approached my village, so many thoughts were running in my mind. I wanted to see the look on my aunt's face. Her eyes would melt out of shame. But more than anything, I wanted to feel my mother again. I wanted my mother.

I will not get into the reunion with my family because that feeling is not something I can express right now. Maybe on the day of the show I will be able to do so. But I doubt it. At first, what I felt was beyond happiness, a relief so large . . . but my happiness was short-lived. It lasted the duration of a single meal. I had not expected my aunt to bring the entire village to gather outside my house. She had told them where I had been. They objected to my coming back.

Even though Gajja explained that I had not been touched, I was told to leave and never return. My parents and family just stood there. The whole village was against me. If my body had been made out of earth, it would have dried and crumbled there and then. I was told that I was dirty. I would infect everyone. Fear made them take me by the hair and kick me out. Even Gajja was beaten up. I had just come out of a cage and my own people threw me back in. Yes, I *will* talk about this on TV. It hurt me more than anything in the world.

I had no choice but to come back.

Whatever money Gajja had was spent on getting me back into the country. Isn't life strange? We had both wanted to leave Bombay, and now we were both forced to go back. Of course, we stayed far away from Kamathipura. Gajja put me in the care of an NGO that took me to a home for parcels like me, far away from the city. Out of the thirty girls in that place, I was the only one who had not been opened.

Everyone told me I was lucky. But I did not feel lucky. I did feel spared. But for what?

It has taken me a few years to find out. But now I know. This is something I will share on the TV show. It is what I will end with. But first, I will give people a look at my daily routine. The routine is the hardest thing for all of us girls. Seconds and minutes have the weight of steel columns.

When Gajja first left me at this home in a small village, I did not speak for a month. When I did speak, my words could not be understood by anyone. I was told I was in shock. Each morning, all of us were made to sit in a circle and hold hands. This was so we would feel togetherness, that we were unburdening a shared experience, that we were not alone. But no one would speak. I could not, either. Sometimes I could feel a slight tremble in my hand because a girl two bodies away from me was crying. Then one day—I don't know why—I thought of my father. I used to have cold milk with him on winter mornings. My father would leave it outside at 4:00 a.m., and in two hours, it was chilled. I had cold milk that morning, just before I got into the circle. It did not taste the same. It came from a fridge. That day, I burst the silence of the circle with a howl.

I was ashamed of myself. I had been defiled, labelled dirty by the people of my village—and I felt dirty. My aunt was right: I did not belong in the village. That was what I said in between my howls. This was nothing new. All the girls have said the same thing. We feel it is our fault. There is something very wrong with us.

The home is run by the Marys. They are kind women who call us "child." The Marys have a mantra here. "Step by step," they say. "Go one step at a time." That is all we do here. Take one baby step toward hating ourselves a little less.

I am less full of shame now. But all of us still question ourselves, wonder if it was our fault. We could have been more lovable or more useful to our parents. We don't know how to be more lovable, so we are becoming useful by learning how to sew and make embroidered bags. We also make very fine prayer beads. We get paid for our work, too. I have learned how to read and write English, which is an accomplishment. Tomorrow, on the show, they will make me speak in Hindi, English, and Nepali. When I talk about the most painful parts of my story, I use all three languages. I keep jumping from one language to the next as though I am walking on hot coals. The relief comes in between, mid-air.

I should get some rest. I have to wake up early tomorrow. I want to look nice on TV. I still want to look nice, unlike my friend Vaneeta, who hurts her face on purpose. She'll be on the show too, with all her cuts and marks. I pray for her every night before I sleep. The Marys have taught us to pray, especially for others. We have been told it helps us forget our own pain.

They tell us to forget the old life. If we want to move ahead, we must forget the old life. Now, all of a sudden, because of this show, we are being asked to remember. To bring it all back. It is okay. None of us can ever forget. To forget is an act of cowardice, and I am not a coward. All that pain, I have to give it meaning. This is why I have been spared.

After tomorrow, my pain will be public. A few days ago, I went back to Kamathipura for the first time. The TV crew was with me and I pointed to where my prison was. It is still charred and grey and abandoned, much like the old cinema. Around it, towers continue to rise, but not at the rate everyone expected. I am told that many of the flats remain empty. I know why. You can still smell the girls who continue to pine for freedom. Some of the brothels are still there. At this very moment, there are some girls who can barely breathe while I taste clean air.

It is this thought that keeps me going.

In our compound, we have a large garden with all sorts of trees and flowers. I like the bougainvillea. It is my favourite because it is wild and it grows on its own and doesn't need pity from anyone. It is so full, so red and pink and purple, it could be a movie star. On some days, I want to be just like it. But when I think of how girls are still caged, I want to stare the flowers down into being less full. It seems rude for them to be so alive.

Maybe that is just my view. Once you are imprisoned, things take on a different meaning. My friend Vaneeta told the TV people that she cannot listen to any kind of music. "For you, when you hear a song you want to dance," she said. "But each time men raped me, they played music so that my screams could not reach anywhere."

It takes a lot of strength to say this on TV. I pray that Vaneeta can say it. She doesn't pray at all. She thinks it is a waste of time. But I don't. We have all been told to pick someone to pray to at night. Like Jesus, for example. As the Marys have told us, he listens to everyone. I talk to Jesus, but he is not the last person I call out to before I sleep.

In the dark, I seek Madhu. I talk to her and bless her. She caused me a lot of pain, but she gave up her life for me. And when I sleep, her face is next to mine, and the crinkle of her sari, I can hear it. Her face is burned, but she is smiling. Some of the girls here have clean faces, but their insides are burned. Our lives have exploded like the gas cylinders that flew out of the brothel and landed on a taxi when Madhu lit the match. I want to do something like that: light a gas cylinder and make it fly.

No, that is too much to say on TV. Who knows what I will say tomorrow? It might not even matter in the end. Nobody will listen. Still, I will speak. I will look straight into that camera, even though they have told me not to.

I will speak to the one who set me free.

Acknowledgements

I grew up opposite Kamathipura. From the time I was born until I was seven years old, I lived in a compound called "The Retreat," a stone's throw away from the red light district. Even when my family moved, the area was only ten minutes away, and the red light district continued to haunt and inspire me; it does so to this very day. Normally, when an author writes a book, there are specific people he can thank; however, in this case, I am unable to individually list the transgendered people, sex workers, and residents of Kamathipura who opened up their hearts and minds to me over the years. The one person I feel I must specifically thank for her generosity and insight is Simran Shaikh. I am truly indebted to everyone I met and salute their honesty and bravery.

I am grateful to the Canada Council for the Arts and the BC Arts Council for their support. The World Literature Program at Simon Fraser University, The Mordecai Richler Writer-in-Residence Program at McGill University, and the Writer-in-Residence Program at the University of the Fraser Valley provided me with precious time and resources during the writing of this novel. I am especially grateful to my colleagues in the World Literature Program at Simon Fraser University for their help and support.

My deepest gratitude to Lynn Henry for her vision and guidance; to Kristin Cochrane, Brad Martin and Anne Collins for their faith in this book and for welcoming me to Knopf; and to Suzanne Brandreth and colleagues at The Cooke Agency International. I also thank Denise Bukowski for suggesting the title, and for her support over the years.

The work of many scholars, writers, and journalists has been invaluable in the writing of this book. For a complete list of acknowledgements, please visit www.anoshirani.com.